Second Chances in Chianti

T.A. Williams lives in Devon with his Italian wife. He was born in England of a Scottish mother and Welsh father. After a degree in modern languages at Nottingham University, he lived and worked in Switzerland, France and Italy, before returning to run one of the best-known language schools in the UK. He's taught Arab princes, Brazilian beauty queens and Italian billionaires. He speaks a number of languages and has travelled extensively. He has eaten snake, still-alive fish, and alligator. A Spanish dog, a Russian bug and a Korean parasite have done their best to eat him in return. His hobby is long-distance cycling, but his passion is writing.

Also by T.A. Williams

T.A. WILLIAMS

Second Chances in Chianti

CANELO

First published in the United Kingdom in 2021 by

Canelo
31 Helen Road
Oxford OX2 0DF
United Kingdom

A CIP catalogue record for this book is available from the British Library.

Print ISBN 978 1 80032 294 3
Ebook ISBN 978 1 80032 083 3

This book is a work of fiction. Names, characters, businesses, organizations, places and events are either the product of the author's imagination or are used fictitiously. Any resemblance to actual persons, living or dead, events or locales is entirely coincidental.

Look for more great books at www.canelo.co

Printed and bound in Great Britain by Clays Ltd, Elcograf S.p.A.

To Mariangela and Christina with love as always

Prologue

'And this year's Emmy for Outstanding Comedy Series goes to...'

Up on the stage, the presenter in the white tuxedo took his time opening the envelope, deliberately heightening the tension. Alice glanced around her companions on the *Pals Across the Pond* table and read some anticipation, some excitement even, but the air of gloom that had been hanging over most of them all evening was still clear to see on their faces. It was the end of an era, after all.

'...*Pals Across the Pond.*'

The presenter looked up and beamed, as the room erupted into an outburst of applause. The cameras, which had been trained on their table throughout the announcement, relayed their reactions onto the big screen. Alice and her fellow actors bolted on broad smiles at their success – with just an appropriate hint of modesty, as convention demanded. But the smiles belied their inner upset. Richie, her love interest in the series, who was sitting to her right, even caught her by the arm and kissed her cheek ostentatiously for the sake of the watching fans back home. She did her best not to grimace.

Their on-off real-life relationship had stuttered to an unhappy conclusion three months ago and his touch made her feel uncomfortable. She hadn't had any contact with him since then and she had been dreading what she would see tonight. To her surprise, he was looking unexpectedly smart and had even had a haircut. Somebody had smeared make-up over the dark rings under his eyes, but that same haunted look was still all too visible, at least to her. After he had kissed her, she heard him whisper in her ear.

'I really miss you, Al.'

Still beaming for the cameras, she caught his eye for a second. 'You're a nice guy, Richie, but let it go. We both know it wasn't working out.' She deliberately kept her lips towards him and away from the cameras. Slo-mo replays and skilled lip-readers could make a lot of capital out of a momentary indiscretion. Then she turned her face back to the table and the cameras, and did her best to keep looking happy.

Zoë, the director, gave a grunt of satisfaction, rose to her feet and went up to collect the award. She was squeezed into a dress that was far too small for her and Alice found herself making a mental note to be sure to avoid sparkly gold outfits, especially when being filmed from the rear. She felt Millie catch her arm and giggle mischievously in her other ear, as the director climbed the stairs to the stage.

'Looks like a golden sunrise, does she not?' Her soft Irish accent was as charming as ever.

Alice gave her an answering wink out of sight of the cameras, but maintained the elated expression on her face. That was what good actors did, after all. She cast another quick glance at the man Millie had brought with her and nodded to herself. With his gleaming teeth, stylish hair, perfect tan and discreet diamond stud in one ear, he was straight out of the same mould as most of Millie's conquests, and Alice felt sure this fledgling relationship would end the same way as all her friend's other attempts to find love – in tears. Mind you, she reminded herself, she was in no position to talk. After all, she was here on her own tonight.

When Zoë reached the stage, she proceeded to smother the presenter in a bear hug that almost lifted the poor man off his feet, before graciously accepting the golden award from him. She clutched it to her abundant bosom as she turned towards the audience.

'Thank you so much. Thank you all.'

The noise in the room dropped a few notches in anticipation of her speech. Alice felt pretty sure that the content was going to come as a big surprise to most of those listening.

'This is the third time *Pals Across the Pond* has been chosen for this award, and we are so very grateful to the Academy and to all the viewers out there for supporting us.'

Zoë went on to thank the actors, including Alice, as well as a string of producers, editors and, most importantly, her boss, but pointedly not the writers. Alice exchanged the briefest of glances with Benny, and received a wink and a shrug of the shoulders from him in return. Meanwhile, Zoë was still in full flow.

'Alas, ladies and gentlemen, I'm afraid this is going to be the last time you ever see me up here accepting an award for *Pals Across the Pond*.' A distinct hush spread throughout the hall, stilling the background babble. 'As some of you may have already heard on the grapevine, this has been the final series of *Pals*. It's been a wonderful five years and I've been privileged to have worked with such talented actors.' Still no mention of the writers. 'Over the years we've become one happy family and I cherish the fact that we are all such great pals in real life. It's sad to think I won't be seeing them every week from now on, but I know we'll all keep in regular contact.'

As Zoë continued to gush, Alice maintained the same upbeat facial expression, but she couldn't stop her mind from churning at the hypocrisy of it all. The bitter infighting of the past months had been brutal. Agents, studio execs and lawyers, along with all the actors and writers, had found themselves immersed in daily battles over contracts, money, character development, the future direction of the plot lines and, above all, their irascible director, Zoë, who was universally disliked. The studio wanted more sex and more smut, while Benny and his team of writers – and most of the actors, including Alice – had voted to stick with humour and romance. To make matters worse, Harry and Layla, the married couple both in the show and in real life, had been fighting off-set. Alice's own ill-fated attempts at romance with Richie had also been disintegrating and even the normally bubbly Millie had started to see a therapist. As a result, the atmosphere on set had been getting more and more toxic – not what you want when you're supposed to be producing laugh-a-minute comedy.

Zoë was still going. 'But I very much hope to be up on this prestigious stage again this time next year with our brand-new sitcom. It's a big secret so I can't give you any details at present, but I know it's going to be great and I'm sure you'll love it.'

Alice wasn't so sure. The word on the street was that the replacement series was going to be a shameless rip-off of *Pals*, but with different writers and none of the existing actors among the cast. *Pals* had been set in an apartment block in the unglamorous suburbs of LA, where three penniless wannabe actresses – one English, one Irish and one Australian – shared a small apartment. The action revolved around the often strained relations between them and the occupants of the other apartments, in particular the penthouse flat on the top floor inhabited by a pair of tall, handsome law students – played by Harry and Richie – from mega-wealthy East Coast families. From what Alice had heard, the new series was going to be set in Dallas, Texas, and would involve the unlikely juxtaposition of moonshine-drinking rednecks and half-starved fashion models.

What was for sure, of course, was that she and the others from *Pals* were now out of a job, as the negotiations had broken down a couple of months back. The actors and writers had finally called the studio's bluff, refusing to work without a change of director, but Conrad Chesterfield, the big boss, had dug his heels in. He had offered them a substantial increase in pay but had refused to sack Zoë, although he must have realised she was terribly unpopular. In the light of the cast's refusal to work with her any longer, he had pulled the rug out from underneath them. As a result, *Pals*, in spite of being one of the studio's biggest earners, was now history and Alice, probably like the others, was left with mixed feelings. On the one hand there was relief at no longer having to put up with Zoë's never-ending harassment, but on the other was the fact that *Pals* had been a major part of her life, and now it was over. She knew she would miss it, but she also knew this gave her a chance to make a fundamental career change.

Alice's musings were interrupted by more applause, as Zoë made her way slowly and carefully down the stairs towards them again, brandishing the unmistakable golden Emmy award as she did so. When she got back to their table, she set it down with a flourish and then went round embracing each of them – except for Benny. The bad blood between him and the production team was of the indelible variety.

As she reached Alice and air-kissed her theatrically, she lowered her voice and murmured sotto voce, but with her usual acidity, 'Goodbye, Alice. You know you've just made the worst decision of your life, don't you? I bet it won't be long before you come crawling back.'

She accompanied this with a charming and remarkably sincere-looking smile for the cameras. Alice had to admit that, for a director, she wasn't a bad actress. If she had spent more of her working life at least pretending to be a nice human being, instead of a domineering ogre, they probably wouldn't be in this position now.

Alice beamed broadly back at her, conscious of the cameras still on them. 'You say the nicest things, Zoë. But there's no way that's ever going to happen. That's not the plan.' She pointed to the other Emmy on the table in front of her, awarded to her a little earlier in the evening for being the Outstanding Supporting Actress in a Comedy Series. 'I'm taking my little trophy and I'm heading home to the UK.' She saw Zoë hesitate and glance back towards her. Alice blew her a totally insincere kiss. 'I'm out of here. I'm going back to university.'

Zoë's eyes widened in disbelief. 'You – a student? Never! You've got acting in your blood now. You'll never quit.'

Alice shook her head. 'I already have. I'm going back to uni in two weeks' time. It's all arranged. You'll laugh, but I'm really looking forward to getting back into the real world once again.'

Her amazing big break five years earlier had come via a talent contest she had entered as a dare at the end of her second year at Bristol University and the subsequent move to California had stopped her degree course in its tracks. Although the years of success and fame had been fun – up to a point – the more she thought about it, the more the prospect of returning to a 'normal' life now really appealed.

Just for a second, Zoë's amiable smile slipped into her trademark sneer. 'You go back to being a student after living as a star? You'll never stick it out.'

Chapter 1

Five years later

But Alice did. It wasn't always easy, but she did.

Not only did she manage to get herself a first-class honours degree in art history, but she also followed it up with a doctorate specialising in the art of the Renaissance. The transition from famous, fêted actress to academic hadn't been without its difficulties and, in spite of her resolve, she had missed more of her previous life than she had expected, but it had all worked out pretty well in the end.

It was barely a day or two after receiving the news that her thesis had been accepted and that she could now officially call herself *Doctor* Alice Butler that she got a call from the US. She was jogging back to her flat in the rather smart Clifton area of Bristol, when the call came through and she stopped in the shade of an ancient oak tree to answer it. The June temperature was remarkably high for England and she was regretting taking her regular run, up past the observatory overlooking the gorge, in the full heat of the late afternoon sun instead of the early morning. Wiping her sweaty hands on her shorts, she pulled out her phone and saw that the call was from Millie, just about the only one of the *Pals Across the Pond* cast with whom she had stayed in touch over the past five years. In spite of the passing of the years and the thousands of miles between them, they had remained very close friends and Alice had followed the vicissitudes of Millie's subsequent career with interest – and no small amount of sympathy. Things hadn't always worked out too well for her.

'Top of the morning to you, Millie.' She had learnt to do a pretty good impression of Millie's Irish accent over the years they had known each other. In return, she had been on the receiving end of countless attempts by her friend to poke fun at her own 'posh' English accent.

'Good day, your highness. I trust one is in tip-top condition?' Millie giggled. 'You all right to talk, Al? I'm not calling you in the middle of a lecture or anything, am I?'

'No more lectures for me. That's all finished. I'm just out for a run.'

'Great. So, does that mean you've had your results? Are you a doc now?'

Alice assured her that she now had her PhD and, with a certain amount of foreboding, asked for news of her friend's career and love life. But Millie had more pressing matters on her mind.

'Have you seen the email, Al? You must have got it.'

'Email? Who from? I haven't checked my emails since first thing this morning.'

'Then take a look and call me back. I'll be waiting.'

As the line went dead, Alice logged into her mail account, discovering that there were three unread messages in her inbox. She sat down on a wooden bench and took a closer look. One was from Benny, the lead writer responsible for the scintillating scripts of *Pals*. Another was from Layla of all people – just about the first communication from the Australian glamour queen in five years – and the final one, amazingly, was from none other than God himself.

Alice had met Conrad Chesterfield – the owner, CEO and caller of all shots at AAATV Productions – numerous times over her working life but hadn't heard a word from him since the end of *Pals*. He and his company had been the creators of the show and had reputedly made hundreds of millions of dollars out of it but, after the acrimonious end to the series, she had never expected to hear from him again. Intrigued – and, if she were honest, a bit apprehensive as well – she opened the message and found it couched in his usual staccato style. It was almost like hearing his voice.

> Alice, how are you? Good, I hope.
> We have a proposition for you. Take a good, hard look at it. Give it some serious consideration. Please.
> Any queries, just shout.
> Conrad Chesterfield

Attached to the email was a document that made fascinating reading. Although no doubt drafted by his legal team and filled to capacity with disclaimers, provisos and let-outs, it emerged that the studio wanted to revive *Pals Across the Pond*, changing the name of the new series to *Pals Forever*. She and the other cast members were being offered the opportunity of getting back on board. There was no mention of money, but she knew that would all be hammered out by the agents and the money men before anybody signed on the dotted line. The offer ended with a tantalising: *We are confident this new venture will prove to be mutually beneficial and rewarding for all parties, both professionally and financially.*

She took a few deep breaths and sat back. The email had brought a host of memories flooding into her head, some of the later ones bitter and unpleasant, but many of the earlier ones genuinely good. She thought back to the fun they had all had on set, at least in the first two or three years. She remembered moments like the time Millie had got locked in the toilet or when the pair of them had walked in on Layla and Harry in flagrante in the props closet. And, of course, the unforgettable moment when Zoë, the all-powerful director, had fallen off her chair and ripped her dress right down the back as she scrambled back to her feet, revealing some most unexpected leopard-skin pattern underwear.

She remembered evenings in the bar with the writers, led by Benny, with everybody around the table crying with laughter as they were bombarded with one-liners. She remembered the time a pigeon got onto the set and crapped all over Layla's ballgown, and she still shivered as she recalled her chronic embarrassment the day she had had to reveal her bare back to the camera for the first time. In so doing, Alice had exposed the rest of her naked body to no fewer than sixteen – she had counted them – mostly male spectators, including the camera crew, lighting and sound engineers, scenery shifters and, worst of all, Richie. Above all, she remembered the hours of anticipation she had endured leading up to her very first on-screen kiss with Richie. The fact that the reality of the kiss, and the man himself, had not lived up to expectations was even now a source of regret. She had really been drawn to him for a while way back then.

There was no doubt the proposal was an interesting one, so she sat there and gave it serious consideration for a good long while. Her incredible good fortune ten years ago in being catapulted from humble student to internationally recognised actress still continued to amaze her to this day, and she looked back on her time in Hollywood with mixed emotions. Although since returning to her studies she had been focusing on a career in art history, the idea of going back in front of the cameras still had its fascination.

Of course, she didn't need to do it. Her savings, coupled with the syndication royalties her agent had fought tooth and nail to obtain for her – and which she was still receiving – for repeats of the series in no fewer than forty-five countries around the world were more than enough to live on. Now that she was away from Hollywood, she no longer needed expensive designer clothes, a PA, security or a housekeeper. She could live much more modestly and had been able to buy her own rather nice apartment on the top floor of an old Georgian townhouse, where she had been living while studying here in Bristol. And she still had money left over in the bank.

Although there were no immediate openings for her in the art history department in Bristol, she had already applied to half a dozen other universities, where she hoped to find a lecturing position. She had also sent CVs to a number of museums and two big auction houses, in the hope that they might be looking for a medieval art expert, and she had an interview scheduled for the following week in London, which sounded promising. So, all in all, why get involved in the Hollywood madhouse again?

As Zoë had predicted, the change from internationally recognised star to ordinary student had been a bit of a shock to the system, particularly for the first couple of years as she settled down in Bristol, but she now genuinely thought of her *Pals* years as another life, almost as if belonging to somebody else. Back in the UK, she had found fulfilment in a subject that kept her intellectually satisfied and she had relished the far quieter lifestyle, a world away from the glitzy, frenetic world of showbiz and the even tougher world of social media, which she still avoided at all costs. It hadn't taken too long before her fellow students and tutors had got used to seeing her around and accepted her as one of their own. She had gradually dropped out of the media spotlight and she hadn't been bothered by a paparazzo for several years. She had got used to the freedom, so could she see herself diving back into all that again?

And, of course, there was the matter of David.

She had met him a couple of years ago and they had been living together now for almost a year. He was five years older than her, almost thirty-six, and he was the rising star among the staff of the drama department of the university. She had fallen for his intelligence, his slightly reserved manner, which had come as a welcome change after so many of the conceited men she had met, and his good looks. Things between them had been going... all right, but she knew that now she had finished her studies, crunch time was approaching. Now that she was free to take a job anywhere in the world, was she ready to take that big step and move away? And if she did, how would he react? If this new project of *Pals Forever* were to take off, would she be prepared to leave him and head back to the States? How might he feel about going with her?

And the big unknown was whether she would want him to.

She checked out the other two emails and found them remarkably similar in content. Benny was clearly amazed that he had been asked to participate again after the public falling-out he and Zoë had had on set, which had culminated in a lot of bad language on both sides and his being escorted off the lot by Security. Layla's email was as flowery as ever, laced with 'darlings', 'supers' and 'amazings', and it consisted of two distinct strands. The first concentrated on the same question Benny had asked – was Alice interested in the idea of the new series? The second was the news that her marriage to Harry had ended in divorce three years earlier and she had 'never felt better' as a result.

As far as Layla's failed marriage was concerned, Alice had already heard about it via Millie and hadn't been surprised. She had lost track of the number of times she herself had been propositioned and even groped by Harry during the recording of the final series, so it had been patently clear that his eyes – and his hands – were increasingly wandering and his days alongside Layla numbered.

As for whether Alice felt like getting involved in the new series, the more she thought about it the main sticking point would be working with Zoë, the overbearing director, once more. The idea of going back to all that stress was far from appealing, although she had to admit that a return to the TV screen wasn't without its attraction. Finally, still very much undecided, she called Millie back to get her take on the proposal. It came as no surprise to find her enthusiastic, to the point of ecstatic. The reason for her delight was easy to identify – she was broke again.

Millie, just like the character she played in the sitcom, was a bit scatty. Both in her love life – the list of her failed relationships would cover many pages – and in her career, she had a habit of making shockingly bad decisions.

Full-frontal nudity three years ago in a weird Korean movie loosely based upon *The Sound of Music*, bizarrely set in the slums of Seoul, had been one of her poorer choices, but her decision to marry one of her Korean co-stars who spoke no English – and Millie spoke no Korean – had been even worse. The brief lifespan of the truly awful film before it sank without trace had been little longer than that of the doomed marriage.

Along with these poor decisions was a talent for spending and wasting money, and Millie appeared to be permanently insolvent, even though her share of the repeat royalties should have been more than enough to keep her afloat. Whatever the reason this time, it soon became clear she was desperate for this job or, indeed, any job.

'I think it's a simply wonderful idea, Al. It'll be just like old times.'

'That's what I'm afraid of.'

'What do you mean? We had a lot of fun, didn't we? And it would mean loads of money. We all know that the cast of *Friends* each got a million dollars an episode towards the end. That would be great, wouldn't it?'

A million dollars an episode would indeed be great, although it was a forlorn hope. They had been well paid, but never anything like that amount and this would be a brand-new venture for the studio. But even if they were to be offered a whole heap of money, it couldn't compensate for the sheer awfulness of working with Zoë again. When Alice mentioned this, Millie pointed out something that she had missed.

'What if it isn't Zoë? There's no mention of her in the email. Maybe they've finally worked out she's a witch and they've replaced her.'

Alice mulled it over for a few moments. It was true that a pleasant, sympathetic replacement for the irritable director would create a hell of a lot nicer working environment. Certainly, a twenty-episode series at even a fraction of the sort of money Millie was mentioning would provide a healthy income. And, give or take a few paparazzi and the serious constraints on her private life, she really had had a whale of a time in Hollywood.

'I wonder...' Of course, it would mean putting her art history career on hold, but there was no reason that couldn't wait a year or two. 'I'll be honest with you, Millie: I've been sitting here remembering the stress of those last months on set, with Zoë screaming and shouting at everybody, and I've been dreading finding myself back in that situation again, but maybe it *is* worth a thought. What does your agent say?'

'She's all for it. After all, her cut would add up to a load of money. What about yours?'

'I no longer have an agent. Students don't need them. Apart from exchanging a few holiday greetings, I haven't been in touch with Amos for ages. But I think I'd better give him a ring and see what he says.'

After speaking to Millie, Alice checked her watch to make sure it wasn't too early in Hollywood and called her former agent. When she was put through to him, he greeted her with a cheery laugh.

'Alice, honey, hi! I've been expecting your call. It's great to hear from you after so long. You just beat me to it. I was about to call you. So, what do you intend to say to Conrad Chesterfield?'

So he already knew all about the plan to revive *Pals*. Not that this surprised Alice in the slightest. Amos had always had his finger firmly on the Hollywood pulse and his ear glued to the ground. Alice told him what she had discussed with Millie – in particular whether Zoë would be involved as director or not – and he came up with a sensible suggestion.

'Why don't I go back to them and say you *might* be interested, but you're gonna need a hell of a lot more information first? Apart from anything else, we need to talk money, serious money. It probably needs a meeting – and a long one at that. How're you fixed? Could you come back over here if required?'

Alice told him she had finished her doctorate and was currently free to travel. 'I'm sure you're right about a meeting being a good idea. Apart from anything else, we need to find out if the other cast members are also interested. What about Richie? I haven't heard from him for ages and I haven't heard anything from Harry for years.'

'Harry's still around. Since breaking up with Layla, I hear he's been working his way through most of the pretty girls in Hollywood – and there's a hell of a lot of them. As for Richie, I don't know. He's disappeared off the radar. I'll do a bit of digging.'

Richie, the highbrow one of the group in the sitcom and Alice's will-they-won't-they on-screen – and for a few months off-screen – love interest had turned introspective towards the end, although he had never missed a day on set and had rarely fluffed his lines. The stress had got to him more than the others and, as a result, he had got himself a 'spiritual counsellor' as well as a variety of tattoos and piercings, and a permanent aroma of marijuana hung over him. Even so, he had become ever more morose and taciturn with everybody, including Alice, and his sense of humour had deserted him completely. Being with him had become ever more draining, until Alice had had enough and had finally been forced to call time on the relationship.

Since returning to the UK, she had lost contact with him and had feared the worst. She had enough experience of actors going off the rails under the influence of too much fame and too much money. It would be really interesting to find out how and where he was now. As for Harry, Amos's description of how he was spending his time sounded par for the course. Still, she thought to herself, pretty girls, spiritual guides and illegal substances demand money, so both men might well be up for this new project. It would be interesting to find out.

And, of course, how this might impact her relationship with David was also going to be interesting.

When she got back to the flat, she found David there with five of his acolytes. Young drama students had always clustered around him like bees around a honeypot, and she had grown used to finding her living room taken over by the cast of whatever production he was working on at the time. Today was no exception and she groaned inwardly. Four girls and a boy were sprawled around the room, while David had fun holding court from her favourite armchair. As she came in, dripping with sweat, he glanced up and waved.

'Alice, hi. Good run?'

There was the usual flutter of interest from the students at the sight of her once famous face, but she didn't stop to chat. Instead, she headed straight for the shower to cool off. Refreshed, she changed into shorts and a T-shirt and went back to the living room to find David just ushering the last of his young disciples out of the door. He turned back towards Alice.

'Feel better for your run?'

'Much better, thanks.' She went around, rearranging cushions and picking up the empty cans, wrappers and bottles that his groupies always managed to strew about the place. She almost complained but she knew by now that it would just be a waste of time, so she tried a different topic. 'You should come running with me instead of staying indoors all the time.' She knew this was a forlorn hope and she saw him grimace, as ever. 'Anyway, David, something's come up and I don't know at this stage how it might impact my life… our lives.'

He disappeared into the kitchen to emerge a few seconds later with two cold beers from the fridge. He slumped back down into her favourite armchair and passed her a bottle.

'Tell me all about it.'

Chapter 2

As Amos had indicated, a meeting with the representatives of the studio was arranged for early July. Although this was less than two weeks away, Alice said yes, particularly once she heard where it was to take place. To her surprise, it wasn't to be in Hollywood, but in what looked like a secluded hotel in Tuscany, Italy, and it was to stretch over five days, presumably to test whether the various egos were going to be able to coexist in close proximity once more. As a venue, this suited Alice down to the ground.

For anybody with an interest in art, particularly medieval and Renaissance art, Tuscany was the epicentre. From Leonardo da Vinci to Michelangelo, from Botticelli to Donatello, this historic region in the heart of Italy had spawned some of the greatest names in the history of world art. The more she thought about it, the more appealing the idea of going there became.

She found David eager to join her – no doubt keen to experience a bit of Hollywood for himself – and they decided to stay on for a few weeks' holiday in Tuscany after the meeting ended. This would serve two main purposes, as far as she was concerned: she would have the opportunity to visit the region more fully and seek out as many incomparable works of art as she could. Additionally, she and David would get three or four weeks together, uninterrupted, to see just where their relationship was going. She still liked him a lot and she felt confident she had even loved him at some point, but she sensed they had reached a crossroads, or a point of no return. She had been feeling for quite a few months now that they were just going through the motions and she sometimes felt herself slipping more into the role of housekeeper than lover. If things were on the slide now, what were the chances of them improving as the years went by? Some big decisions needed to be made about the two of them, as well as the direction of her future career. A bit of alone time amid the scenic beauty of Tuscany would give them the chance to talk, to think and to come to a decision — one way or the other.

—

The week after the bombshell email from Conrad Chesterfield, Alice took the train up to London for an interview with a big international auction house who were looking for an expert to work with the valuers in the Medieval and Renaissance art department. This had been arranged before Conrad Chesterfield's email and, although the pay on offer didn't compare with the kind of money she might be able to make with a return to her acting career, the job sounded fascinating and Alice arrived for the interview in good spirits. However, once again, her past threatened to get in the way.

Throughout the early years after her return to university, she had often had to struggle to be taken seriously, whether by fellow students, lecturers or potential boyfriends. The problem was that *Pals* had been a massive hit in the UK, as well as the USA, and she was a very recognisable face, but people often appeared unable to grasp the fact that she and Polly – the character she played – were not one and the same. Polly, her alter ego, had been a flirty and fairly superficial sort of girl, with a penchant for tarty clothing, and whose romantic exploits had occupied much of the five series. As she had lurched in and out of relationships with a never-ending succession of random men, including Richie, Polly had gained a reputation for being a bit loose, a bit of a good-time girl. Slipping out from her shadow had been hard for Alice.

In reality, she was very different from Polly the flirt. Her mother had brought her up to accept that she had had the good fortune to be born with a pretty face but to resist the temptation to believe that her appearance was all that counted. She had had a few relationships while working in the US, culminating in the ill-fated liaison with Richie, but none had lasted. Back in the UK, she had found herself, time and time again, having to come to terms with the fact that potential boyfriends were actually more interested in hooking up with Polly the good-time girl than Alice the postgraduate researcher, and this had destined each of these fledgling relationships to a hasty conclusion. Finally, she had met David and, in him she felt she had found somebody who was prepared to accept her as Alice, not the infamous Polly.

Today at the job interview, she soon realised her face and her fame were going to be working against her yet again.

She was interviewed in the formal boardroom of the long-established auction house, situated above the main salerooms overlooking the Thames. There was a hushed, solemn feel to the place and the oak-panelled walls were hung with oil paintings of austere moustachioed gentlemen – but not a single woman. She found herself sitting in front of a daunting panel of three: two men and a woman. The fact that the latter bore a passing resemblance to Zoë, the short-tempered director, did little to reduce Alice's nerves.

The problems started almost immediately: the silver-haired chairman of the panel, whose surname was the same as the famous auction house, homed in on her lack of previous experience in the field, and she explained that before completing her degree and doctorate she had been an actress. It was quite clear that this imposing elderly gentleman had never even heard of the show, let alone seen her in it, but the same could not be said about the two people flanking him. The woman was the first to pick up on it.

'Just how serious are you about making a career in our company, Dr Butler? We're looking for a professional, not a dilettante.' There was definite disapproval in her voice.

Alice did her best to assure them that she was keen on this as her future profession, but she sensed considerable scepticism. The intense-looking younger man on the left then revealed that he not only knew who she was, but was also familiar with the show and with the vicissitudes of Polly the flirt.

'We have to make it absolutely clear, Dr Butler, that there's no place in this company for a flibbertigibbet.'

Alice stopped and stared. Although she was sitting in such austere and historic surroundings, she hadn't been expecting equally ancient vocabulary. In fact, his choice of such an archaic word actually helped and she found herself smiling back at him.

'I can assure you that I am no such thing. The fact that my previous career was in television doesn't need to concern you, and you certainly shouldn't make the mistake of believing that my on-screen character is who I am. That's all in the past. My academic results and the comments of my referees should make it clear to you that I know how to work hard and I'm good at my subject.' Drawing upon her years in Hollywood, she accompanied this retort with just the right amount of fire in the glare she gave him and was delighted to see his cheeks flush.

'I'm sorry, I'm certainly not trying to downplay what is indeed an excellent academic record, Dr Butler.' He sounded decidedly flustered now. 'And I apologise if my words gave offence. That was not my intention.' He looked positively contrite.

Allowing her glare to soften, Alice transferred her attention to the elderly gentleman in the middle of the panel. 'I really am good at my subject and it would be an honour for me to work for such a household name.'

This appeared to hit the spot and by the end of the first part of the interview she felt pretty confident that she had both men on her side. As for the woman, she wasn't so sure. Alice was probably twenty years younger than her and the thought crossed her mind that she might even be jealous of a younger colleague – especially one whose face was still known the world over.

As they embarked upon the second part of the inter-view – what they referred to as the 'practical' – Alice was given the chance to prove her worth and she took the opportunity with both hands. They led her across the room to where two easels had been set up and shrouded in dark cloths. The covers were removed to reveal two identical oil paintings – at first sight. Both depicted a woman, wearing an intricately woven and embroidered brocade dress. Alice felt a shiver of real excitement. This was what her years of study had been leading up to. She glanced back at her interviewers.

'Here are two versions of the same painting. I assume the idea is that one is authentic and the other a fake.'

Nobody contradicted her so she studied them more closely. She was pleased to see a magnifying glass lying on a side table, so she picked it up and used it to study them both in more detail. She took her time and waited until she felt sure, before giving her verdict. Her three interviewers were standing close by, watching her intently. The woman had a little superior smirk on her face that gave Alice just enough stimulus to subject her to a steely stare as she replied.

'The portrait is fairly typical of Renaissance paintings of the first half of the sixteenth century; Florentine School, pretty obviously, and supposedly the work of Bronzino, I assume.' She turned towards them and took a deep breath. 'The fact is, however, that they're both fakes – the one on the left considerably better than the other, but without question still a fake.' She was delighted to see an expression of surprise replace the smirk on the woman's face, while the two men merely exchanged glances. Taking heart, she carried on. 'Pity, really. This would have been a Bronzino I'd never seen before. I've seen his painting depicting Eleonora de Toledo, the influential wife of Grand Duke Cosimo de' Medici, in the Uffizi Gallery. In that one she has her son alongside her, so I assume the artists who produced these were trying to copy a part of the original and hoped people might think them hitherto unseen versions of the same subject.'

'Very good, Dr Butler, very good.'

The elderly gentleman sounded impressed and even the woman was now looking far less condescending. They returned to the table and the interview continued, but the atmosphere had noticeably changed for the better. The final question from the chairman sounded positive.

'If offered the position, Dr Butler, when would you be available to start?'

'I have a commitment in Tuscany for the month of July, but I could start in August, if that suits you.' This was not the time to mention that by then she might have decided to head back to her former incarnation as a Hollywood actress. All that would be decided – one way or another – in Tuscany next week.

Nods were exchanged around the table and the interview came to an end. As he escorted her out of the building, the younger man, whose name she now knew to be Tobias something double-barrelled, allowed himself a little indiscretion. He glanced over his shoulder to check he wasn't being overheard and lowered his voice.

'I thought you might be interested to hear we have so far interviewed five other candidates for this position and you're the only one to get the practical right. Well done.' He held out his hand towards her. 'And my apologies once again for giving you a hard time at first. It was just weird seeing your face here. My wife's a huge fan of *Pals Across the Pond*.' His cheeks reddened guiltily. 'To be honest, so am I.'

As Alice shook his hand, she smiled at him. 'Thank you, Tobias, and I can assure you I've had worse reactions to my face before this. I've learnt to just roll with the punches.'

'We'll be in touch. Very soon. I look forward to seeing you again.'

That sounded hopeful.

Alice was spending the night with her mum, but she had arranged to meet up for lunch with Millie, who had flown in from LA the previous day for a brief stop-over. Tomorrow Millie would fly to Limerick to see her mum, dad and extended family, before travelling over to Tuscany for the all-important meeting next Monday. Although Millie was by her own admission broke, it came as no surprise to Alice to find her staying at the Inter-Continental at Hyde Park Corner and they met in the restaurant there. Millie was typically ebullient, calling out Alice's name as she spotted her and rushing across the crowded room to throw her arms around Alice's neck and embrace her. Even back in Alice's Hollywood years this sort of ostentation had never suited her and she felt more than a little embarrassed, not least as several of the other guests immediately grabbed their phones and started photographing them. She kissed Millie on the cheek and bustled her back to her table by the window.

'Have a heart, Mil, I'm just a student these days. I'm not used to all this.'

'All this what?' Millie sounded puzzled.

'Riches, luxury, ostentation… you know, the usual.'

Millie gave a dismissive wave of her hand, which only served to call the waiter. He arrived at their table and bowed obsequiously. Millie glanced up, noticing him for the first time, and had no hesitation.

'A bottle of Bollinger.' No please, no thank you. Alice realised she had somehow passed through a time warp and was once again in the world of celebrities for so many of whom politeness and expressions of gratitude were unnecessary. She caught the waiter's eye and gave him a big smile.

'That would be kind, thank you.'

For the second time that day a man before her blushed and this evoked a flashback to the days when Cosmo readers had voted her one of the most desirable women on the planet. Interestingly, this memory, rather than strengthening her confidence, actually brought a flush to her own cheeks. She had got out of the habit of being an object of desire to random men and knew she would find it unsettling to return to that role again.

'You're looking great, Al. So slim, and I love what you've done with your hair.'

Alice grinned. It was typical of Millie to home in on her looks before anything else. For her part, Millie was looking good, if a bit weary – presumably after her transatlantic flight – and her dress revealed quite a lot of her tanned body. Alongside her, Alice felt positively pasty. 'And you look great, too. I haven't done anything to my hair, apart from wash it before my interview this morning. The days of expensive salons are long gone.'

Millie looked suddenly worried. 'Interview? You're not thinking of going for some other part, are you? I heard Paramount are casting for a new romcom. You're not up for that, are you? You can't do that to me. This new *Pals Forever* series without you would be a non-starter.'

'Nobody's indispensable, Millie. They'd find a replacement. After all, Layla and Harry are the main characters, really.'

'I'm not so sure. But please don't go off and get another job. Apart from anything else, I'd miss you.'

'And I'd miss you, too. Don't worry, Mil, it was an interview for a job as an art historian.'

'So not the Paramount movie?'

'No movie, no TV show, no stage show, no travelling circus – nothing, I promise. My acting days are behind me – unless we really do end up doing the new *Pals* series.'

Millie looked reassured. 'If this new series gets off the ground, I know it'll be fun.' But then another look of concern appeared on her face. 'Are you planning on taking David to Italy next week? In the invitation it said we could bring a partner if we wanted. I'll just be on my own. I'd hate to be the odd one out.'

'I bet you won't be. It is a business meeting, after all. I'm bringing David, but I'll spend all my time with you if you're feeling left out.'

'So… you and David? How's that going? Getting serious?'

As they were close friends, Alice had often talked to Millie about her concerns as to where the relationship might be going. Now she decided to tell her the truth. 'I honestly don't know, Mil. We're still together and I still like him a lot, but I really don't know where we go from here. It's all just a bit stale somehow. I know it's inevitable that some of the spark dies out after you've been together for a while, but I'm not convinced I'm going to be happy long-term if that's the way it's going already. And, anyway, there's the question of where I'm going to end up. What if I get the art history job? That would be here in London. And if *Pals Forever* were to go ahead, that would take me back to Hollywood. Would he want to come with me – and would I want him to? It's complicated.'

'But you still love him, don't you?'

'I still like him, Mil. I just can't decide how much.'

Millie must have sensed that Alice needed cheering up, so she gave her one of her trademark cheeky winks. 'Well, if it all goes belly-up, remember there are thousands –

millions! – of men out there who'd give anything to get together with the famous Polly from *Pals*.'

'That's the thing, Millie, I'm not Polly from *Pals*. Apart from on-screen, I never was, and I'm certainly not now.' She caught her friend's eye. 'Don't get me wrong. I'm very grateful to Polly. As well as providing me with more than enough to be able to pay my way through university, she also let me dress up in all sorts of clothes I'd never dream of wearing in real life and she supplied me with a whole host of put-downs for men who annoy me. Before I became Polly, I was far less confident and she did wonders for me, but now I have to shoulder the burden of being forever associated with the flirt. The way I am now, though, if things don't work out with David, the next man I decide to date is going to have to want me for my brain, not my face.'

The look she received in return was a wonderful mixture of disbelief, incomprehension and ridicule. 'Good luck with that, Al. Somehow I don't see that ever happening – unless the man's visually challenged.'

'Then it won't happen at all.' Alice looked defiantly across the table just as the champagne arrived. 'I really mean that.'

Chapter 3

Alice and David flew over to Florence on Monday afternoon and were met at the airport by a smart uniformed driver who took charge of their suitcases and accompanied them out to his slick black Mercedes. He spoke good English, but Alice decided to practise her Italian with him anyway. While doing her PhD, she had spent several months over here in Italy, visiting galleries, churches, castles and libraries as she carried out the research for her thesis on an obscure Italian artist who had allegedly shared a studio in Florence with Michelangelo for several years. She had done Italian A-level at school and her visits to the country had helped to keep her command of the language reasonably up to speed. David didn't speak a word of Italian, but she felt sure he wouldn't mind. As it was, he appeared quite happy to sit back and enjoy the luxurious interior of the limousine.

Alice waited until the driver had navigated his way through the heavy local traffic around the airport and had got onto the *autostrada* before asking him about the hotel where they were going to be staying. A quick check of the address on Google Earth had shown her a charming old villa surrounded by trees some way to the south of Florence, but that was all she knew.

'Do you know the hotel we're going to?' She reckoned that sounded fluent enough, without too many mistakes.

The driver glanced round in surprise. 'Ah, so you speak Italian. *Bravissima!*'

He replied in Italian and she was pleased to understand everything he said. Reassured, she carried on.

'Not very well, I'm afraid. That's why I'm using you to get in a bit of practice. So, is it a nice hotel?'

'It's not a hotel; it's a private house. I'm not sure who Villa delle Vespe belongs to, but it's very beautiful. I've taken people there a few times so I know it quite well.'

This came as a definite surprise to Alice. Somehow she had been expecting a hotel. She relayed the information to David and he suggested that the villa might have been rented for the occasion or might even belong to Conrad Chesterfield. Certainly, her former boss had the money to buy himself a nice villa or two.

'You know what *vespe* are, don't you?' The driver was clearly taking his job as language trainer seriously.

Alice returned her attention to him and nodded. 'In English, it's wasps – Villa of the Wasps. It's a strange choice of name. I hope this doesn't mean the place is infested with them.'

'I doubt it, but I've no idea how the villa got its name. You'll have to ask.'

'I will. When I checked it out on the internet, it looked as if it's in the middle of the countryside.'

'Almost. There's a village a kilometre or so away, but not a big one. The villa's right in the heart of the Chianti region. You know the wine, I'm sure. Even over in America it's famous, isn't it?'

Alice nodded and went on to explain that although her reception and transfer had been booked by an American company, she was in fact English, but he already knew that.

'I recognised you as soon as I saw you. You're Polly, aren't you?' His eyes met hers in the rear-view mirror for a moment and she saw he was grinning. 'I had a poster of you on my wall for years.'

This wasn't the first time Alice had heard this sort of comment and she found herself hoping it wasn't the infamous wet-bikini poster that left very little to the imagination. Snapped by a paparazzo as she emerged from the Pacific in an unguarded moment, an unscrupulous print shop had produced a poster from the picture. Her lawyers had finally managed to get it removed from circulation, but not before tens of thousands had been printed and sold. It had made her feel angry then, and thinking about it still made her feel awkward now. Hastily, she returned the subject to less contentious issues.

'And do you know the Chianti area well?'

'I'm from Florence, but we all know the Chianti region. It's still mostly rural, with lots of vineyards everywhere. It isn't far from Florence and there are some very exclusive, and expensive, villas there. We turn off the *autostrada* in ten or fifteen minutes and that's pretty much the start of Chianti. The villa's near Greve in Chianti, which is no more than another half hour at most. It won't take too long.'

After leaving the busy motorway, the drive into the heart of the Chianti region was a delight. As the much quieter country road weaved its way along the valleys and up the flanks of the steep hills, the views got better and better. The hills, as the driver had said, were clad for the most part with meticulously kept vineyards – their rows of vines laid out with mathematical precision – that were often flanked by olive groves. Clumps of woodland here and there – particularly on the hilltops

– added patches of dark green in contrast to the bright new leaves on the vines and the grey-green of the olive trees. Quaint little villages and lovely old farmhouses and villas dotted the landscape, and everywhere she looked she saw the tall, slim cypress trees so typical of Tuscany. Alice gave up on her Italian lesson, sat back alongside David and soaked up the view.

Altogether, the drive from the airport to the villa took well under an hour and the sun was just beginning to drop towards the horizon as the limousine came to a halt in front of two imposing metal gates set in a formidable high wire fence that stretched off into the distance on either side. The driver leant out of the car window and spoke into an intercom. A few seconds later the gates hummed open and they drove in, flanked by thick clumps of bright yellow broom bushes, some several metres tall, shaded by tall trees. As they did so, Alice spotted two security cameras pointing down at them. Clearly, the owners of Villa delle Vespe valued their privacy – and that of their guests. As the car crunched up the long, winding, white gravel drive, the trees gave way to vines on either side of them and ahead, on a ridge, she could just make out the roof of the villa amongst a cluster of ancient cypress trees.

As they rounded the last bend and crested the ridge, the villa of the wasps came into full view and Alice whistled softly to herself in appreciation. It was a large, wide, two-storey building in traditional Tuscan style, with red roof tiles and a little tower rising up from the centre. The walls were a delightful weathered yellowy ochre colour, with dusty-green louvred shutters at the windows. It was surrounded by charming formal gardens and the whole place looked enchanting. The driver drew up in a fan-shaped parking area, protected from the sun by huge old umbrella pines, and pointed towards the villa.

'If you'd like to make your way up to the front door, I'll bring your suitcases.'

Alice thanked him and they stepped out of the air-conditioned interior of the car into the heat of the late afternoon. It had been a hot day and the air was still warm even now, at six o'clock. Judging by the cloudless sky above, tomorrow was going to be equally fine. She and David set off up a short stretch of stone-paved path, flanked by meticulously trimmed box hedges, punctuated every few metres by enormous old terracotta pots containing lemon trees, oleander bushes and clumps of sweet-scented lavender. The mixture of aromas was intoxicating and she breathed in deeply, savouring the moment. Beside her, she heard an intake of breath from David.

'Wow, how the other half live!' He looked across at her and she could see the wonder on his face. 'I suppose all this opulence takes you back to happier times.'

'Not necessarily happier times, David – different times. I was never really that into the whole glitzy showbiz world. My five years in Bristol have been great and, don't forget, they allowed me to meet you.' She reached over and gave him a little kiss, but his eyes were still trained on the view.

As they approached the steps leading up to the entrance to the villa, a figure appeared at the door and came running down to greet her.

'Alice, hi, it's great to see you again.'

For a moment she almost didn't recognise him. The intervening five years since she had last spoken to him had altered Richie, her on-screen and off-screen boyfriend, so much that he almost looked like a different man. His former shoulder-length brown hair was now barely an inch long and his once clean-shaven chin was dark with stubble. However, compared to a photo of him she had seen in *Hello!* a few years back, when he had looked scruffy, unkempt and sad, this new incarnation of Richie didn't look too bad at all. From the tightness of his T-shirt around his shoulders and biceps, it looked as though he had been working out. She was relieved and delighted for him – and, if she was totally honest, she maybe even began to feel that same original spark of attraction for him resurface. That was something she hadn't been expecting, not least while her live-in boyfriend was at her side.

'Richie, hi, this is David. Hey, you look great, really great.' She really meant it.

He jumped the last few steps and came over to shake David's hand. Then he hugged her tightly to his unexpectedly muscular body, which confirmed her suspicion that he had been hitting the gym. Unlike the last time she had seen him, all of five years ago, his touch no longer made her feel uncomfortable – quite the opposite, in fact. She glanced guiltily across at David, but her boyfriend was still gawping goggle-eyed at the grandeur of their surroundings.

Richie stepped back, still holding her shoulders. 'Don't sound so surprised. I tell you what, Al, you're looking absolutely fantastic, stunning… amazing!'

Alice had to remind herself that she was once more in the world of Hollywood-speak, where nothing was 'nice' or 'good', but had to be 'wonderful' or 'fantastic'. Hyperbole in these circles was the rule, not the exception. She was back in the land of superlatives. She gave him an even bigger smile.

'If I sound surprised, it's because I heard some stuff about you a few years back that had me worried. You can't imagine how happy I am to see you looking so good.'

'Well, if it helps, I was expecting to see you in scruffy jeans and a T-shirt after all these years as a student, and just look at you. You haven't changed a bit. As for me... yeah, I went through a rough patch, and it took me a bit of time to get myself together. My analyst told me it was all down to the way things turned so sour at the end of *Pals*. Anyway, it's all good now.' She saw his eyes flick across to David. 'Are you guys together?'

'That's right. As of a couple of years now.'

Richie gave no response and led them up the steps. 'You and I are the first of the bunch to arrive, but they tell me the others will be here later tonight.'

'Who's "they"? And what is this place?'

'This is *one* of Conrad Chesterfield's holiday homes. The word on the street is that he also owns an island in the Caribbean and half a ski resort in the Rockies.' He lowered his voice, although there was nobody else to be seen. 'I rather think he bought it with the profits we made for him with *Pals*.'

'Wow, it's quite some place.' And it was. As she and David followed Richie inside, Alice found herself in a charming wide entrance hall with marble tiles on the floor, gold-framed mirrors on the walls and a domed ceiling high above. The ceiling was totally covered by a magnificent fresco of nymphs, angels and what were probably saints, all floating around amid the clouds. Alice's art historian instincts were immediately aroused. It looked almost like Michelangelo might have come here for a bit of practice before heading south to the Sistine Chapel. It was stunning. She was still standing there, open-mouthed, when she heard an all-too familiar voice.

'Alice, my dear, you look lovely.'

Her heart sank as she turned and found herself confronted by none other than the formidable figure of Zoë. As she did so, she registered that it looked as though Millie's theory that their unpopular director might not be involved in the new project was going to prove to be wrong. Still, swallowing her disappointment and drawing upon what vestiges of thespian skill she could still master, she treated her former tormentor to a beaming smile.

'Zoë, what a pleasant surprise. I didn't expect to see you here.'

'And why would my presence come as a surprise to you?' The smile of welcome had already slipped, as Zoë reverted to her trademark barbed tones.

But this time Alice had resolved not to be intimidated. The very fact that Zoë was here made her own decision to participate in the new series distinctly less likely, so she stood her ground and fired a shot across the director's bows. After all, she reminded herself, the best form of defence is attack.

'Oh, I don't know, I thought you might have retired by now.'

As Zoë was still in her fifties, this was a low blow, but Alice was determined to fight fire with fire. At her side, she felt Richie's fingers catch hold of and grip her arm in shock. She saw a cloud pass across Zoë's face but then was surprised to see it move on, to be replaced by an attempt at another smile – albeit about as warm as the plates of congealed lasagne they had often had to pick at with their forks for hours on end during filming of meal scenes for *Pals*.

'There's still life in me yet, Alice. And what about you? Failed your exams?' There was a distinct sneer to be heard in her voice. 'I presume the fact that you're here means your academic career hasn't worked out.'

Alice was steeling herself to launch a vituperative counter-attack when the cavalry arrived.

'Alice, sweetie, you look simply wonderful. Many, many congratulations on doing so well at college. Is it true we have to call you Doctor Butler now?'

Emerging from a side corridor came Antonia, the head of light entertainment at AAATV. They had always got on well, and Alice was genuinely happy to be on the receiving end of a warm hug and real kisses to her cheeks, not just the routine air kisses into the middle distance.

'Antonia, hi. It's so good to see you again. I've been hoping I'd see you here. And yes, thanks, I got my doctorate. I'm so pleased to see you looking as wonderful as ever.'

'Just getting older, dear.' Antonia was probably in her early sixties, but she had always been a dynamic, decisive woman – and Alice admired, and liked, her a lot.

'You look great, Antonia. Can I introduce you to David? We met at Bristol University. He's a senior lecturer in drama.'

'Hi, David, it's great to meet you.' Antonia shook his hand warmly and then pointed across towards Zoë. 'Have you met Zoë? She was the director of the old *Pals* series.'

Alice glanced sideways and was amused to see Zoë now wearing a totally unconvincing smile again, as she reached out and shook David's hand. 'Hi, David. Drama, eh? So does that mean you're a wannabe actor?'

As the opening to a polite conversation, it was pretty chilly, but Alice had warned him of the possibility of coming up against Zoë and he didn't bristle – in fact, very much the opposite. The expression on his face was one of almost hero-worship.

'I'm a wannabe *director*, if the truth be told. If I could ever become even half as good a director as you, I'd be immensely proud. Your results speak for themselves.'

Alice saw Zoë's expression warm at the compliment, and she was impressed. David certainly knew how to suck up to Zoë. Of course, he was right – up to a point. Zoë's results as a director over the years had been great. It was the methods she had employed to achieve them that weren't. Alice saw her acknowledge the compliment with a little nod of the head and reply graciously enough.

'Thank you, David. It's a pity more people don't share your opinion.' The sideways glare she shot at Alice said it all.

No doubt sensing the tension in the air, Antonia took Alice's arm, prising her away from Richie's grip, which had remained firmly in place ever since Alice's counter-attack against the bullying director.

'Come and we'll ask Paolo to show you to your room.' She glanced over Alice's shoulder and beckoned to a friendly-looking man in a porter's uniform who had just appeared. 'Paolo, would you mind showing us the way? I believe you said Alice is in the Green Suite, didn't you?'

'I'll see you later, Richie.' Alice gave him a wave, rather regretting leaving him at the mercy of Zoë with nobody to protect him. He had never been able to stand up to her and, in spite of his newfound muscles, it looked as though that might not have changed. She caught hold of David's hand, although he looked as though he would have been happy to stay there with Zoë. She found herself thinking that if this was an act, it was a damn good one. He had really given the impression he meant those things he had said. She resolved to warn him once more of the true toxic nature of the director he was complimenting.

Richie, seeing them leave, waved forlornly back, but as Alice followed Antonia and the porter towards the stairs, she caught a glimpse out of the corner of her eye of him hastily making good his escape, leaving Zoë standing alone in the hallway.

Alice was delighted to have found that Antonia – who was Zoë's boss, after all – was going to be here to act as arbiter. During the worst of the problems with the petulant director in the final years of the series, Antonia had been one of the few senior execs to express sympathy for the actors but, ultimately, the decision to back Zoë – even at the expense of the show – had come from over her head.

Alice's room was on the first floor at the rear of the villa, looking out over delightful formal gardens and, beyond them, across rows of vines to where the sloping hillside rose more steeply into thick woodland. A stone tower emerged from the trees on the distant hilltop and Alice wondered if that also formed part of the estate. Returning her attention to the room, she saw that it was predictably immaculate and spacious, with a high ceiling and an air-conditioning unit situated above the window. The window itself, she noted, had a fine mesh screen across the opening, no doubt designed to keep out mosquitoes and other undesirable insects.

Paolo, the porter, set her suitcase down on what looked like an antique chest and let himself out again without a sound. Antonia stayed there with Alice and David, who was standing by the window, looking around appreciatively.

'What a magnificent house and what a lovely room.' There was wonder in his voice and Alice gave him an encouraging wink. It was clear that he was a bit overawed by it all. She looked back at Antonia and added her own appreciative noises.

'You've got to hand it to Mr Chesterfield – he's got good taste. I love the space and I love the views. I'd almost forgotten just how gorgeous Tuscany is.'

'So how was it being a student, Alice?' Antonia perched on a corner of a fine old ottoman. 'Didn't you miss the bright lights?'

While David continued to direct his attention out of the window, Alice sat down opposite Antonia and nodded slowly. 'Yes, of course, to some extent, but mainly just in the first year or two. I've always been hooked on art and art history, and it soon took over my life as completely as *Pals* used to do.'

'And now? Are you seriously considering coming back to us to do this new series?'

Alice knew her well enough to be frank. 'I honestly don't know. I'm quite settled back in the real world now and I'm aiming at a career in art history, but I'd be lying if I said the idea of a second chance at Hollywood – even if it was only for a year or two – didn't appeal in many ways. I suppose it'll depend on all sorts of things.' Her eyes flicked across to David, who was staring out into the garden while doing his best to look detached. As she looked back again, she read comprehension in Antonia's eyes.

'Of course. And there's the question of money, I imagine.'

'No… well, yes, to an extent, of course. But it's more a question of who I'd be working with.' She caught Antonia's eye. 'I'm not talking about the other *actors*.'

'I know who you're talking about.' Antonia nodded slowly. 'And you're not the only one who's been wondering how things are going to pan out on that front. Conrad's playing his cards very close to his chest on this one.' She straightened up, glanced at her watch and headed for the door. 'Anyway, let's see what this week brings.'

Alice knew enough not to press her on what was no doubt a tricky subject, seeing as Zoë and Conrad Chesterfield went way back and he had always stood resolutely behind the grouchy director up till now. She got up and followed Antonia to the door. 'Yes, of course. By the way, are we going to get a visit from Mr Chesterfield himself, do you think?'

'That's anybody's guess. I suppose, seeing as we're in his house, he might put in an appearance, but I haven't heard. Now, why don't you two freshen up and come back down when you feel like it? I believe the others should be here before too long.'

Chapter 4

When Alice and David came back downstairs, there was
no trace of Antonia or Richie so, rather than risk finding
herself caught in a potentially toxic conversation with
Zoë, Alice suggested going for a walk and David was all for
it. They went back up to their room, changed into shorts
and trainers, and headed out. Alice took her sketchbook,
just in case something caught her eye.

The sun hadn't yet reached the horizon, but it was
already casting long shadows. They started out by touring
the formal gardens, mainly consisting of rose beds whose
perfume filled the air. As they walked along the gravel
paths, the constant background soundtrack was the hum
of bees labouring industriously in among the multi-
coloured blooms. For now, at least, there was no sign of
the wasps that had given their name to the villa. There
was little other extraneous noise, apart from the twittering
of little birds and the hammering of a distant woodpecker
in the trees on the hilltop.

They headed roughly in that direction, passing out
of the formal gardens into the vineyards, following a
path around the side of the vines as the ground started
to tilt gradually upwards. Lizards ran for cover as their
shadows fell on them, and a handsome male pheasant
suddenly erupted into a fit of what sounded like coughing
as it flung itself into the air and flew off into the trees.

Although the *vendemmia*, the grape harvest, wouldn't be until September, the grapes were already the size of large peas and beginning to turn darker. Before long they would develop a deep blue-black sheen, as they grew and swelled. It was a charming walk, and Alice caught hold of David's hand and gave it a little squeeze.

'What do you think?'

'It's another world. Not just the scenery and the plants and the sunshine, but the luxury of the place. The villa's stunning and our room is about the same size as my whole flat before I moved in with you.'

Alice could hear the awe in his voice and she remembered her first exposure to the sort of luxury that millions of dollars could buy. Her first year in Hollywood had been a succession of assaults upon the senses as she was invited to parties at the spectacular – and often spectacularly tasteless – homes of the rich and famous.

'It's not always like this. Don't forget, we're pretty much at the top of the pile here. Not all of Hollywood's as opulent as this place.' He nodded but she could see that underneath his façade of maturity and sophistication he was beginning to feel just a bit overwhelmed. She remembered she had a warning for him. 'By the way, don't get too cosy with Zoë. She'll eat you for breakfast and spit out the pieces if you aren't careful. But you did a good job of inflating her ego back there – not that she needs much encouragement.'

'I meant it. I've been dying to meet her. She's a legend to anybody thinking of becoming a director.'

So he hadn't been putting on an act. 'Results aren't the only thing that count. It's how you get them. Surely you wouldn't want to be as unpopular as her?'

He shook his head. 'It wouldn't bother me. They say the best generals were universally feared and hated by their men, but they won the battles.'

This didn't match Alice's recollection of history at all, but she made no comment, feeling more than a little surprised at his attitude. Clearly David had found himself a role model and she didn't like the sound of that one bit. Still, a bit of brown-nosing by him might help to keep Zoë sweet – or at least a bit less acid than normal – which had to be no bad thing.

Everywhere they walked, the earth underfoot was tinder-dry, but deep ruts in the baked soil showed where tractors had previously sunk down into soft mud. It seemed almost incredible that the now rock-hard ground could once have been so soft. The weeds and grasses around the edges of the field had been burnt yellow by the sun, and the dry leaves under their feet rustled and crackled as they walked over them. It was still hot and it came as a pleasant relief when they reached the relative cool of the shade cast by the trees that clothed the hillside further up, not least as the ground sloped more steeply now and the going started to get a bit tougher.

Not long after reaching the shade of the trees, they came upon what looked like the same sturdy wire-mesh fence they had seen by the main entrance and realised that this probably marked the end of Conrad Chesterfield's territory. On the other side of the fence, the thick undergrowth and dense forest looked untouched by human hand, and the shadows under the trees were so deep that it was almost like looking into the mouth of a wide cave.

They carried on up the hill, shaded from the direct sunlight by the trees on the other side of the fence, following the line of the wire until they reached a little promontory. Here somebody had positioned a wooden bench with its back to the fence, in just the right position for them to be able to look back down across the parallel lines of the vines to the villa and then on past it to the tree-covered hills beyond. An acacia tree, festooned with sweet-scented bunches of white blooms, provided welcome shade. It was a charming place and a charming view, and Alice stopped.

'Would you mind if I did a bit of sketching?'

David shook his head. 'Of course not. Why don't you stay here and I'll walk on a bit further? I'll come back in… what, a quarter of an hour or so?'

'Or a bit longer if you see something that interests you. You know me when I start sketching.' She pecked him on the cheek, released his hand and sat down on the bench, pulling out her pencil and opening her pad. She normally worked in oils, and she felt sure a good sketch of this view could form the basis for a full painting when she got back to Bristol. In all likelihood, given that she had just seen Zoë, it would become a permanent memory of the charming location of her last-ever dealings with AAATV.

However, before she could start drawing, her phone bleeped and she saw that she had an email. Her excitement grew as she discovered it was from the auction house in London. She opened it and, to her delight, she saw that she had been shortlisted for the position. While she started to read it through, she found herself giving a little squeak of pleasure. As she did so, she heard an answering squeak from behind her – well, not so much a squeak as a brief high-pitched yelp – and she turned round to see what sort of animal might be on the other side of the fence. At first she could detect nothing in the dark shadows cast by the thick canopy of trees, but then she noticed some movement. From the depths of the forest, a far from wild animal emerged and trotted across towards her.

The dark shape emerging from the undergrowth was a dog, a handsome big black Labrador. He was wagging his tail and continuing to make little whining noises of canine pleasure as he came towards her. There was absolutely nothing of the aggressive guard dog about him and Alice felt confident he had identified her as a friend.

She had always loved dogs, but had never been able to have one. Her mother was allergic to animal hair and since Alice had left home for university – and then the USA and then university again – it just hadn't been feasible for her to keep one. Although she hadn't finished with the auction house email, she set down her phone on the bench, got up and went over to say hello. The fence was taller than she was, so the only way she and the dog could get acquainted was by him sticking the tip of his nose through the wire. She rubbed it with her fingers and he emitted a series of happy grunts.

'Hello, dog.' It occurred to her he would probably respond better to Italian, so she tried again. '*Ciao, cane.*'

In response, her fingers received a lick from the tip of his tongue. She wondered where his owner might be. His leather collar was a bit scruffy but his coat was glossy and he certainly didn't look underfed, so it seemed unlikely he was a stray. She had just spotted a silver medallion attached to his collar when she heard a piercing whistle from somewhere in the woods. The dog immediately spun round and charged off, crashing through the dry undergrowth as he obeyed the command to return to his master.

Alice went back to her bench and sat down again, returning her attention to the email from the auction house and reading it through carefully to the end. It contained more details of the conditions of employment and the salary on offer which, as expected, wasn't great by comparison with Hollywood. However, she knew she had more than enough extra money coming in from her royalties to enable her to live comfortably, even in an expensive city like London, if she got the job. The email informed her that she was invited to a second interview in ten days' time and, as they knew she was in Italy, they offered to pay her airfare.

She picked up her sketch pad, settled back and let her eyes run over the lovely, relaxing Tuscan scenery before her. The email had come at exactly the right time. Of course, there was no guarantee they would offer her the job but, if they did – and hopefully she would know by the end of next week – this would give her an attractive alternative to making a return to Hollywood. If, as looked likely, Zoë was indeed to be the director in charge of the new series, Alice felt pretty sure she would decide to walk away. Millie wouldn't be too happy, but she would survive – as would the others.

Alice had come here with serious doubts about picking up her acting career again, and now she was reasonably hopeful that she might get the offer of an excellent alternative job. It could prove to be the way into a fascinating and fulfilling future, relying upon her brain, rather than her appearance, and drawing upon the expertise she had studied so hard to develop. Of course, she knew she would feel some regret at not being able to work with her friends again and drop back into the glitzy showbiz world once more, but if Zoë was going to be involved, she would certainly be better off out of it.

Whatever she decided, the unresolved dilemma remained David. Taking the job in London would mean either an exhausting and expensive commute every day from Bristol for her, or a change of university for him. If she accepted the Hollywood job, it would mean even more upheaval. Either way, it would be complicated – assuming they stayed together. Hopefully, the next few weeks here in Tuscany would provide an answer to the viability or otherwise of their relationship and that, in turn, would help with all the other decisions.

David returned from his walk half an hour later, still enthusing about the villa, the grounds and the stunning panorama all around. He sat down beside her and she told him about the email from the auction house. He sounded happy for her, but surprised.

'Are you really sure that's what you want? After all, ninety-nine per cent of the world's population would give their eyeteeth for the chance to star in a high-profile series like *Pals Forever*. You'd be famous – even more famous than you already are – and I'm sure you'd be very well paid. Take a look around you. This sort of place could be yours.'

Alice checked him out. That same dreamy expression was back on his face again as he stared down at the villa, but she did her best to explain. 'Don't think I haven't considered it, but it wouldn't all be glamour and riches. First and foremost, it looks as though it would mean working under Zoë and I'm not sure I want that stress all over again, but it's more than that. When you're a celebrity, your whole life changes. You have no privacy – unless you spend a fortune on security, private jets and all the rest. For a woman, it means never eating a square meal again. Appearance is everything – well, almost everything

– in that world and it demands sacrifices. Yes, you can get rich, but I know from experience that it isn't all a bed of roses.'

He nodded, but she could see he didn't get it. To him – as to so many people – it must seem like Willy Wonka's golden ticket to a happy life. She reached across and caught hold of his arm, hugging herself against him. 'Anyway, I haven't decided anything yet. Let's see how the next few days and weeks pan out.'

She closed her sketch pad on her drawing and they made their way back down the hill to the villa. Two people were sitting under a parasol on the terrace and, as she drew nearer, she saw that Layla had now arrived – and so had Benny, the writer. There was no sign of Richie and she wondered where he had gone – hiding from Zoë, most probably. The good news was that, at least for now, there was no sign of her either.

She knew that Millie was definitely coming, although Harry remained an unknown quantity. Maybe the idea of meeting up with Layla, his ex-wife, had put him off, and Alice wondered for a moment what difference to the dynamic of the show his absence might make, if he decided not to join in. Together with Layla, Harry was one of the lead characters, and if he deserted the new show, there was a real risk of his absence damaging its chances of success. And, Alice realised, if she too were to turn her back on the offer, *Pals Forever* might never even get off the ground. She went across to greet them, genuinely pleased to see Benny and Layla again after so long.

'Hi guys. It's great to catch up with you again.'

'Alice, darling, how absolutely wonderful to see you.' Layla's language was as extravagant as ever. Alice vaguely noticed that the five years since they had last met up had removed almost all trace of her Australian twang and replaced it with a pretty convincing California accent, but the passage of time certainly hadn't removed any adjectives from her vocabulary. 'You look simply gorgeous, stunning, even more beautiful than before.'

Alice slipped seamlessly into Hollywood-speak in return. 'And you just keep on getting more and more beautiful, Layla.' Suspiciously so. Were her boobs bigger now? She glanced across at David's face and almost burst out laughing. His eyes were bulging out of his head as he came to terms with being in the presence of such a world-famous actress, and the extravagant language from both of them probably reinforced his sense of having set foot in an alien world. Alice caught hold of his hand and introduced him to them.

'Layla, Benny – this is David. David, I'm sure you recognise Layla, but you also need to meet Benny. Without him, *Pals* would never have had the success it did. His comic scripts are second to none.'

Layla extended a languid hand in David's direction and gave him her most alluring smile. 'So pleased to meet you, David. Have you and Alice been together long?'

'Almost two years now.' His voice sounded hoarse and he actually had to clear it as the emotion of finding himself in such illustrious company sank in. 'It's amazing to meet you in person. I'm honoured.' After reverently accepting and shaking Layla's hand, David greeted Benny.

Alice grinned to herself. She had never seen him as tongue-tied as this before. Somehow, she got the feeling that this week was going to be a real shock to the system for a simple university lecturer.

Alice gave Layla a big hug, before going over to do the same to Benny. She had always got on very well with him – maybe even better than with her fellow cast-members, except for Millie. Apart from being hilarious, he was one of the most genuine, natural people she had ever met in Hollywood. It was this same directness and honesty that had inevitably brought him into conflict with Zoë. If he didn't like something, he told it like it was. The inevitable showdown had been explosive and Alice wished she could remember more of the absolutely stunning stream of invective that Benny had unleashed upon the director shortly before being hauled away by Security. One line that still stuck in her memory was, 'You have the charm of a blocked toilet and the moral fibre of a rabid raccoon!' The upcoming confrontation between them was something Alice was awaiting eagerly, but with considerable apprehension.

'Hi, Benny. How's it going?'

'Hi, Alice. I'm good, thanks. It's great to see you again. It's been too long.'

After they all sat down, Paolo appeared and asked if he could get them a drink. Layla already had a glass of champagne and a bottle in an ice bucket in front of her, while Benny had opted for a cold beer. David pointed wordlessly towards the champagne, while Alice just asked for a cold mineral water. She was determined to keep a clear head this week.

They sat and chatted for half an hour or so, without any of the others appearing, and Alice sensed that David was gradually settling down. A couple of glasses of champagne probably also helped steady his nerves. Layla went into considerable detail about her career post-*Pals* and Alice was delighted to hear it was going well. She knew that

Layla had made the transition to movies, as she and David had been to see her in a recent thriller – in which she had been remarkably good in a serious role. This, too, was interesting. As Layla already had a good career, it could well be that she might decide not to do *Pals Forever*, so if Conrad Chesterfield chose to dig his heels in once more, the project could well be destined never to get off the ground. Alice nodded approvingly to herself. If this were the case, it added considerable strength to their collective bargaining power to get shot of their nemesis.

In return, she told them about her years as a student, although she didn't mention the possibility of the auction house job for now. When quizzed about her feelings with regard to *Pals Forever*, Alice made her position quite clear.

'It's such a pity, really. Zoë's a good director – no, a great director – but her people skills are non-existent. For the first couple of years of *Pals*, I managed to put up with it, and there's no question she deserves a lot of credit for the success of the series, but as the years went by, I found her harder and harder to bear. I felt dehumanised, like a puppet, with Zoë pulling the strings. Life's too short for that. If Zoë's going to be out of the equation or if she's miraculously morphed into a completely different personality – and that doesn't look too likely – then I think I'm in. Otherwise, almost certainly no.'

Both Layla and Benny nodded in agreement, while David still looked disbelieving that anybody should even consider turning down such a golden opportunity.

'What about Millie?' Layla knew that she and Alice had remained close friends. 'What's her view?'

'You'd better ask her yourself, but I get the impression she might be forced into it for financial reasons.'

She saw the other two exchange looks. They both knew Millie of old. Alice told them that Millie was on her way, but neither had any idea whether Harry was coming or not. When Paolo reappeared, he confirmed that Harry and Millie were both expected but had not yet arrived. Alice asked him where Zoë, Antonia and Richie might be and received a slightly puzzling answer.

'I believe they're at the pool. It's round at the rear of the villa.' He glanced at his watch. 'But I expect they'll be in soon, as dinner's scheduled for eight o'clock.'

Alice thanked him, wondering just who was at the pool. Surely not all three together? The idea of those three relaxing in each other's company seemed highly improbable. In the end she decided there was only one thing to do. She stood up, followed by David who looked reluctant to leave Layla, told the others they would see them at dinner and headed round to the rear of the villa, in the direction that Paolo had indicated. By this time the sun had disappeared behind the hills and the light was fading fast. As they approached the pool enclosure, screened by a mass of pink and red oleanders in full bloom, she heard splashing and wondered idly what Richie looked like with his shirt off after his new health kick.

When she reached the pool, she found that Richie had already changed into shorts and a T-shirt but, considering she was here with David, that was probably for the best. Beside him, an attractive blonde in a bikini had clearly just emerged from the water and was patting herself dry. In the half-light it was hard to tell whether the hair colour was natural, but Alice had to admit that she looked good. Two things were immediately clear – Richie had also exercised his right to bring a companion, and from the affectionate way the woman was looking at him, they were more than casual friends. Alice was happy for him. Clearly, his therapist had done a good job.

'Hi, Richie. I thought I'd just come and check that you weren't being held against your will by our director friend.'

'Oh hi, Alice, that was a nice thought but no, I haven't seen Zoë since she spoke to you. Maybe she's sulking... or sticking pins in wax figures of us. This is Carrie. She's a good friend.'

A good friend? As a description, this was open to numerous interpretations but, for now, Alice just held out her hand.

'Hi, Carrie. I'm pleased to meet you, and this is my boyfriend, David.'

'Gosh, I'm just so thrilled to meet you, too, Alice. You're my hero. I often dreamt of being like you when I was growing up.' It would appear that Carrie was a good bit younger than Alice had first thought – maybe mid-twenties or even less, which would make her a good bit younger than she was – or Richie. 'I even used to try to dress like you, but my mum kept forbidding me from buying the stuff I wanted. She said it was too provocative.'

'I take it you mean you tried to dress like Polly in *Pals*, not me.'

'Yes, sorry, I meant Polly.' Her eyes strayed to Alice's T-shirt, shorts and dusty trainers. 'So you don't dress like her normally?' She sounded quite disappointed.

Alice shook her head. 'It's taken five years, but I'm gradually getting the message across that Polly and I are two very different animals.'

'Oh...' Carrie looked even more disappointed now, but she soon snapped out of it. 'Well, I'm still really pleased to have met you, Alice.'

56

'Me too.' Alice returned her attention to Richie. 'We're waiting for Millie, and I'm surprised to hear that Harry's also coming – is that definitely true?'

'He's coming. He called me a week or so ago to see if I was up for it. When I told him I was coming, he said he would, too. I think he mentioned that he was flying over to Switzerland first to stop over with a friend, but he'll be here, I'm sure.'

No prizes for guessing the gender of the friend with whom he would be breaking his journey. So, Alice thought to herself, all five of the cast – plus Benny – had elected to come to this meeting, which meant all of them, to a greater or lesser extent, were at least considering getting involved with *Pals Forever*. No doubt Conrad Chesterfield would be well pleased, although it seemed clear from talking to Benny and Layla that the show would only go ahead if Zoë were no longer at the helm. Alice wondered how that little conundrum was going to work itself out.

Together, they walked back to the villa and, just as the other two disappeared up the stairs, the front door opened. Paolo appeared, pushing a trolley holding two big suitcases, and was followed, just a few paces behind, by Millie.

'Hi, Al. What a gorgeous place.' She gave Alice an enthusiastic hug, kissed David's cheeks and then turned back to the door, glancing out into the twilight. 'Harry, Alice is here. Come and say hi.'

So they were all here. The *pals* were reunited.

Chapter 5

Millie appeared at Alice's door just before eight, all dolled-up in a dress that must have cost a fortune – which she most probably didn't have – and refused to let Alice go down to dinner in her dusty T-shirt and shorts. Under pressure, Alice reluctantly changed into a relic of her former life, a light summer dress by Stella McCartney which had been hanging at the back of her wardrobe for over five years. It felt really strange to be wearing something so pricey and, for that matter, revealing. She had completely got out of the habit of wearing the sort of clothes that young Carrie would no doubt have identified as 'Polly' clothes, and she found herself apprehensively checking her appearance in the mirrors in the hallway before walking through to the dining room. French windows at the end of this fine room opened onto the terrace, where a dinner table had been prepared outside, illuminated by a line of imposing silver candlesticks running all the way down the centre of the table.

The atmosphere on the terrace when they got there was uncomfortable. Zoë was standing by the door, clutching a glass of champagne and greeting each of them as they emerged into the warm evening air. As Millie, Alice and David walked past, she raised her glass in a little toast, even summoning a smile.

'Thank you for coming. Millie, you look charming. And you, David.' Zoë's smile even warmed a little at the sight of him, but she pointedly ignored Alice.

Millie gave her a kiss on the cheek. As Alice had already been through these formalities, she just carried on out of the door and into the open air. The first person she saw was Layla, who had also changed and looked stunning – and knew it. She was wearing a silk dress that reassured Alice she wasn't going to be the one with the most skin on display tonight. Yes, she reflected as she walked over towards Layla, those boobs were definitely bigger now. At her side, she caught an intake of breath from David and she almost giggled. If he had been feeling star-struck before, he was no doubt feeling blown away now.

Next to Layla was Antonia, and Alice settled at her side. Benny and Harry were standing a bit further up the terrace, drinking bottled beer and, from the expression on Harry's face, feeling no less uncomfortable than Alice herself. Benny had made an effort with his appearance, although Harry hadn't changed and was still wearing the same jeans and polo shirt he had been wearing upon his arrival. Nevertheless, he was still the same handsome heart-throb he had always been in the *Pals* group. He wasn't looking at Layla and she was studiously avoiding looking at him. Alice wondered if they had at least shaken hands.

'Alice, what a delightful dress.' Antonia sounded as if she meant it. Beside her, Layla proved that she had a good memory.

'I know that dress. You wore it to the last of the end-of-series parties, didn't you?'

Alice accepted a glass of champagne from Paolo, thanked him and then nodded towards Layla. 'And this is its first outing since.'

By this time Millie had joined them. 'Are you telling me you never wear smart clothes these days, Al?'

'Smart, sometimes, but not this kind of thing. You don't find many university students wearing designer clothes, at least not in Britain.' She gave Millie a grin. 'I'd have stuck out like a sore thumb. In fact, wearing something as open as this tonight feels positively weird. I keep looking down to check I'm not going to fall out.'

She caught David's eyes looking down her cleavage as she spoke and she choked back an attack of the giggles. Although he had seen her naked countless times, this was the first time he had ever seen her in such an expensive and revealing dress, and it was probably making him feel even more disoriented. She caught hold of his free hand and gave it a reassuring squeeze, as she saw him swig down the champagne he was holding in his other hand in one go.

At that moment Carrie wafted along, clad in a diaphanous little number that could have come straight out of a production of *A Midsummer Night's Dream*. Alice had to admit she looked lovely. As Carrie walked past Harry, Alice couldn't miss the look he gave her as he caught sight of her. It was not dissimilar to the look on a python's face at the sight of an unfortunate little white mouse being dropped into its cage. Luckily, Richie was chatting to Benny and didn't notice. Alice didn't have time to dwell upon the possible ramifications of this, as the unmistakable sound of a knife tapping a glass attracted her attention and that of the whole gathering. Antonia was holding up a hand for silence.

'Welcome everybody and thanks for coming. On behalf of Conrad and all our colleagues at AAATV, I hope you have an enjoyable, restful and productive few days here. Tomorrow morning I'd like us all to sit down together so Zoë and I can run through what we have planned for *Pals Forever*. We're all very excited about it and we hope you will be, too. We're going to leave the afternoons free for you all to relax or maybe visit some of the lovely places around this part of Tuscany. But, for tonight, just take it easy and catch up with each other. I'm looking forward to hearing what you've all been doing since I last saw you.' Antonia glanced across at Paolo, who had changed out of his porter's waistcoat and was now wearing a plain white shirt with a black bow tie, a spotless white napkin folded across his forearm. Clearly, he was a man of many talents. 'Paolo, would you be so kind as to tell the cook we're ready to eat?'

As he bowed and disappeared back through the French windows, Antonia directed them all to their seats. Little handwritten cards indicated where they were all expected to sit and Alice breathed a sigh of relief as she realised that she and David were going to be at the opposite end of the table from Zoë, although she had a feeling he might have preferred to be closer to the director he idolised. The not-so-lucky candidates for that honour turned out to be Layla on one side and Millie on the other, while Alice and David were next to Antonia who was at the other end of the table.

The meal was excellent. Paolo was assisted by a young waitress in a white blouse and short black skirt who blushed every time she came near Harry. He gave no sign of noticing her, but clearly his presence alone was enough to keep her cheeks permanently glowing. Alice concentrated on chatting to Antonia and Benny, and tried to involve a visibly shell-shocked David.

They were served a sumptuous selection of antipasti, ranging from freshly carved Tuscan ham with fresh figs to a cold seafood salad of mussels, prawns and baby octopus – all accompanied by typical Tuscan bruschetta made with wonderful crunchy unsalted Tuscan bread loaded with chopped tomatoes and dripping with thick green olive oil. To drink there was excellent local Chianti Classico or white wine from a producer only a few kilometres down the road.

The antipasti were followed by another traditional Tuscan dish – *pappardelle al cinghiale*. These broad strips of pasta in a rich wild boar sauce were delicious, but Alice did her best to resist temptation when Paolo came round with seconds. Five days of eating like this could seriously affect her ability to fit into her clothes, if she wasn't careful. She was quite proud of the fact that, as a result of eating sensibly and taking a decent amount of exercise while at university, she was still able to fit into her old clothes, like the dress she was wearing, and she didn't want to have to invest in a whole new wardrobe.

After the pasta came some of the biggest steaks Alice had ever seen – and when living in the USA, she had seen some pretty massive slabs of beef. Fortunately, they were not expected to attempt to eat a whole one each. Paolo cut the meat vertically into strips, sprinkled the slices with scales of Parmesan and rocket leaves, drizzled olive oil over them and gave the guests as many pieces as they felt they could manage. The result was delicious. Alice was mildly surprised to see Layla eating meat again. The last time they had dined together, Layla had been on a celery-and-carrot diet and had wrinkled up her nose as the others ordered real food. Tonight, at least, it looked as though she had let herself off the leash a bit. Thoughts of leashes reminded Alice of the black dog she had seen earlier, and she queried this with Paolo.

'He belongs to our neighbour. He's often out working on his estate and the dog's always with him. The place was really run-down before he took it over, but it's coming on well now.'

'And does he live in the woods?'

'He lives in the old tower. He bought it a couple of years ago and he's been working hard since then. He's a nice guy but we don't see a lot of him.'

'Well, at least he's got a nice friendly dog for company.'

At the end of the meal Paolo brought in a fine porcelain dish laden with profiteroles covered with warm melted chocolate, while the waitress – whose name was Rosanna – added scoops of smooth vanilla ice cream for those who could find space. David had by this time consumed a considerable number of glasses of red wine, as he sought to come to terms with the luxurious surroundings and being in the company of so many celebrities. After what she had already eaten, Alice felt full, but the profiteroles and what tasted like home-made ice cream were so good, she couldn't resist. As she finally set down her spoon, she sat back with a contented sigh.

'That was wonderful, but tomorrow morning I'm going for a run.'

She was surprised to hear Harry respond, 'I'll come with you. I need the exercise.'

Alice had been studying him surreptitiously during the meal and it looked as though he, too, had been working out. He was still undeniably an extremely handsome man, but his predatory eyes were as scary as ever. From time to time throughout the evening she felt his gaze on her and struggled not to shiver. Still, it was unlikely he would try anything during an early-morning run, so she gave him a little smile and they arranged to meet up at eight.

Layla's voice came from the other end of the table. 'David, do you run?'

He shook his head. 'No, I'm more of a lounge lizard. Alice is always trying to get me to come out with her, but I'm happy as I am.'

'And you look just fine.' At receiving a compliment from the actress once voted one of the five most beautiful women in the world, David's already ruddy cheeks started positively glowing and Alice found herself fighting back the giggles once again.

It had been a pleasant evening and a very good dinner. Nobody at her end of the table talked about work, but she knew that would all change the following day. For now, at least, the atmosphere was remarkably relaxed and, as she sat back with a little cup of coffee at the end of the meal, she reflected that there were worse places to be than in a gorgeous old villa in Tuscany.

Chapter 6

The following day, she woke up early and lay there for a while, enjoying the relative cool of the morning. They had gone to bed with the window open – but with the mosquito screen closed – and she had slept pretty well, in spite of the snores from her inebriated boyfriend beside her. She didn't blame him for overdoing it last night. Suddenly finding himself effectively catapulted onto the set of a world-famous romcom must have been a real shock to the system.

Just about the last thing she had found herself thinking about before drifting off to sleep had been a handsome big black Labrador with a scruffy leather collar. Clearly, he had made a considerable impression on her.

As it happened, she was soon to be reunited with her four-legged friend.

She got up just before eight and, leaving David still dead to the world, she changed into her running clothes and let herself out as quietly as she could. She was mildly surprised to find Harry already in the hall, waiting for her. Together, they went out through the gardens and jogged up past the vineyard until they came to the line of the fence. As they ran up the hill alongside the wire, there was suddenly a joyful woof from the woods, as the big black Labrador reappeared and came running along with them on the other side of the wire, barking excitedly. But this morning, the Labrador wasn't alone. As they reached the top of the ridge near where she had sat and sketched the previous evening, she spotted two figures ahead.

An elderly man leaning on a walking stick was chatting to another man who was on his knees, hard at work. The older one had a friendly, weather-beaten face, while his companion was a lot younger, with broad shoulders and fair hair. This man looked a few years older than Alice – maybe in his mid-thirties – and was wearing shorts and trainers, but no top. He had been sweating and the early morning sunshine glistened on his well-honed body. Once she and Harry reached him, Alice slowed, got a closer look and was mildly surprised to find she liked what she saw.

Surprised because – with the exception of that little frisson of attraction she had felt for Richie last night, before discovering he was with Carrie – she couldn't remember the last time she had felt any particular interest in any man apart, she reminded herself, from David. This realisation was immediately followed by a stab of guilt at the thought of her boyfriend of two years lying in her bed while she was eyeing up some random man, and she did her best to nip any feeling of attraction in the bud. But it wasn't easy. The man on his knees looked fit and he was undeniably good-looking – not in an airbrushed front-page-of-*Cosmo* way, like Harry, but in a rugged outdoorsy sort of way.

As she approached the two men, she realised what they were doing. Something big had ripped a piece of the fence out of the ground and the wire mesh had been torn wildly out of shape, creating an opening. As the Labrador reached the gap in the wire, he didn't hesitate. Seeing his new friend so close by on the other side, he dived through and came charging up to Alice, tail wagging. She slowed to a halt and looked down at him affectionately, confident his intentions were not belligerent.

'*Ciao, cane.*'

He reared up on his hind legs and stretched his front paws up to her waist, poking her with his nose and making contented little whining noises as he did so. Alice was vaguely aware that Harry had suddenly accelerated away and disappeared down into the vineyard, and she remembered he had always been afraid of dogs. In one of the episodes he had had to handle a toy poodle and he had been petrified throughout. Ruffling the Labrador's ears with both her hands, she glanced across at the older man, who was smiling affably at her, while his younger companion wrestled with the wire mesh. She gave them both a little wave of the hand.

'*Buongiorno, signori.*'

'*Buongiorno a lei.*' The elderly man's accent was unmistakably local. 'Are you staying at the villa?'

'Yes, just for a few days.' Alice read comprehension on his face, so she assumed her Italian wasn't too bad. 'What's this lovely dog's name?'

'Guinness, but he answers to food like all Labradors.'

As the man on his knees looked up and gave her a wave of the hand, she noticed, for the first time, how light blue his eyes were – and how strangely appealing. No sooner did the thought occur to her than she hastily reminded herself she was here with David, so she would do well not to start checking out other men. She transferred her attention to the dog, who was happily nibbling at her fingers. 'Well, hello, Guinness, my friend. I'm pleased to meet you.' He also appeared to understand her Italian and she took that as a little triumph.

'What happened to the…?' She didn't know the word for 'fence', so she pointed.

The fair-haired man carried on working and left it to the elderly gentleman to reply. He leant on his stick and sucked his teeth in annoyance. 'Wild boar. They're a real pest. They do so much damage every year. Ripping a hole in a fence is the least of it. They can destroy a whole vineyard by uprooting the vines with their tusks. We're going to have to organise a hunt to get rid of at least some of them.' His face cracked into a grin. 'Besides, they taste so good.'

'They certainly do. I had *pappardelle al cinghiale* last night. They must be very strong to tear a hole as big as this. Were they coming into or out of your property?'

'In from your side, we think, judging from the direction of the footprints – although, God knows how they got into your property in the first place. And they're strong, all right, however many of them there were.' He pointed vaguely towards the ground at his feet with his free hand and Alice could clearly make out the faint impression of trotters in the dry soil. 'We're closing the gap so that the dog doesn't get out. He's still young and he's always keen to explore.'

'I'd better tell the people at the villa about this. There has to be some way the animals got in. I wonder if they did any damage over this side.'

Alice remembered the surveillance cameras by the main gate. Wild boars were unlikely to have got in that way, so presumably there had to be another hole in the fence somewhere. She stood there for a few more seconds, finding that she was enjoying watching the fair-haired man at work, in spite of her scruples. He pulled the bent wire back into shape and began to crimp it together again.

She could see the muscles of his chest flexing along with his arm muscles as he worked and it was a most appealing view, but then she told herself to snap out of it. She decided she had better return the dog to his own side of the wire and leave the men to their work.

'Off you go, Guinness. Back into your territory.' She gave his head a final pat and he dropped back onto all four paws and obligingly squeezed through the gap in the fence to the other side. 'Well, I'd better carry on with my run.'

The elderly man gave her a knowing look. 'You don't want to keep your boyfriend waiting! Goodbye.' He gave her a half-wave of the hand, before returning to supervising the repairs once again.

'*Arrivederci.*'

As she jogged away, she wished she had specified that Harry was nothing to her and then spent the rest of the run wondering why she should have felt it mattered to either man that she and Harry weren't an item. After all, Harry or no Harry, she was here with her boyfriend and she reminded herself sternly that she shouldn't be thinking about strange men with their shirts off – and she would do well to remember that.

Back at the villa, she found David nursing a headache and with the sort of morning-after breath that could probably kill at ten feet. Even so, she went over and gave him a kiss, reminding herself that he was her boyfriend and that she loved him... or at least liked him a lot. They both showered and changed, and came down to a sumptuous breakfast. This was again served outside on the terrace and it was pleasant to sit there, looking out over the rose beds, the wonderful scent filling their nostrils, while colourful butterflies flitted about their heads. Beyond the gardens the ground sloped upwards towards the old stone tower.

She wondered how long it would take the two men to fix the hole in the fence and she found herself revisiting the view she had had of the fair-haired man with the bare torso. She hastily dismissed him from her mind but, interestingly, she omitted to mention him to David.

As Paolo appeared and took their orders, she told him about the wild boars and he sounded unexpectedly pleased.

'That's good to know. Presumably that means they must have got out again. This morning Pierangelo, who looks after the grounds, discovered a load of plants in our kitchen garden uprooted and chewed, and the unmistakable tracks of at least one wild boar. He then found a gap in the fence, not far from the main entrance, where the things must have got in. He was worried they might still be here on the estate – they can do an awful lot of damage and can even be dangerous. Since there's another gap, hopefully they came and went. I'll tell him to go up and check if he needs to do any mending from our side.'

'Your neighbour seemed to be doing a pretty good job of fixing it.'

'He works hard, I have to say, but I'll ask Pierangelo to pop up there anyway in case he needs some help.'

At that moment Harry and Millie appeared at the French windows. Millie looked more relaxed than last night but, in fairness, she had had to put up with sitting next to Zoë for the whole dinner. Alice waved to them to come over to their table.

'Hi, you two. The breakfast's amazing.'

Millie took a seat alongside her. 'Hi, Al.' She subjected her to a mock-searching stare. 'So, what's all this I hear? Harry tells me you've found yourself a new man.'

Even through his hangover, David must have registered the remark, as his head came up and his eyes focused. 'What's all this? Just because I drank a bit much last night, she's leaving me...?' He even managed a weary smile.

Alice leant over and kissed him on the cheek – not least with a little twinge of guilt. 'Don't worry, David. No, it wasn't so much a man as a handsome big dog.'

'Handsome?' Harry sat down on the opposite side of the table and shuddered. 'Huge great thing with teeth. Frightened the crap out of me.' He asked Paolo for an Americano and sat back. 'No sign of Richie and his lady?'

Alice shook her head, glanced around and lowered her voice. 'By the way, I saw you looking at Carrie last night. She's here with Richie, so you make sure you back off.'

'Good to see you've still got his back.' Harry laughed. 'But you don't need to worry. She's too old for me. I prefer younger women these days.' Seeing the look on their faces, he added, 'So you're safe too, girls.'

Alice considered throwing her toast at him but decided to let it go. Guys like Harry never changed. Instead, she decided to transfer her attention to Millie. There was still no sign of either Zoë or Antonia, but she lowered her voice anyway.

'How did it go with Zoë last night?'

Millie rolled her eyes. 'She's still the same tough cookie, but it could have been worse. She didn't say anything too outrageous and, to be honest, she was almost pleasant at times.' She caught Alice's eye. 'Really, I mean it. She was hitting the vino a bit hard and, maybe because of that, there was one thing she said towards the end that was interesting. She let it slip that the series with the rednecks and fashion models bombed, big time, and the studio lost a lot of money. She didn't exactly say they're desperate now, but I got the impression they're really keen to sign us all up for this new series.'

Alice glanced across at Harry. He might have the morals of a tomcat but he had a pretty sound business head on his shoulders. 'Is that right, Harry? Since I've been in the UK, I've been avoiding social media and I'm out of the loop. I know next to nothing about that show… I can't even remember the name.'

'It was called *Beauties and Beasts*, and I heard it sank like a stone. Yeah, Millie's right, I reckon they'll do almost anything to get us on board for this new series.'

At that moment Antonia appeared and the conversation changed to less contentious matters. One thing was for sure – the meeting this morning was going to be interesting.

Chapter 7

The meeting was indeed interesting, and far less confront-ational than Alice had been expecting. Antonia did most of the talking and Zoë was quite clearly on her best behaviour. The irritable director was unusually quiet and subdued and in light of what Millie had said, Alice wondered if she was maybe hung-over, just like David. Certainly, it was impressive – and pretty much a first – that Zoë managed to get right through the two-hour session without insulting anybody.

The basic premise of the new show was to be the same group of five people, five years on and now nudging thirty, all still living in LA. Layla and Harry would now be divorced – as in real life – but, through force of circum-stance, living within a few doors of each other. Millie, still single, would become the main love interest as she strove to find a suitable mate for life. As for Alice, she would now find herself married to Richie and trying for a baby. As this was announced, Alice glanced across the table at him and saw what might have been satisfaction on his face. She hastily dropped her eyes once more. There had been no sign of Carrie at breakfast and she, along with David, had been excluded from this meeting. Alice wondered what Carrie would think of this new twist to the old plot when she saw Richie and her sharing a bed – albeit just in the show.

The only awkward moment came when Antonia asked Benny how he would feel about taking over the scriptwriting. He, like the five actors, had been excluded from the studio after the end of *Pals*. Since then, he had carved out a successful career for himself, writing sitcoms for ABC and a couple of screenplays for movies. His reply was predictably honest and direct.

'It would all depend on two things, Antonia: I would expect to be paid a good deal more than I got for *Pals* and I would only do it if you could promise me no outside interference.' His eyes locked onto Zoë's. 'From anybody.'

Antonia answered quickly, no doubt to avoid any possible outburst from the director. 'As far as money's concerned, that can all be sorted, I'm sure. Conrad has authorised me to tell you that he envisages it being generous – that's the word he used. Your agents will be able to handle that for you, okay?' She glanced round the table and received nods in response. 'As for outside interference, I can promise you that any major changes in the direction of the script will have to be approved by me and me alone. Does that satisfy you? You know you can trust me.'

'I trust *you*, Antonia, you know that, but I would need it written into my contract.' Again, he stared hard at Zoë and, again, she didn't rise to the bait. Could it be that the bullying director had been tamed? Alice caught Millie's eye across the table and they exchanged looks – from Millie, hopeful, but from Alice still sceptical.

When they emerged from the meeting at lunchtime, Millie wasted no time in grabbing Alice and taking her for a walk in the garden, far from curious ears.

'What do you think, Al?' She sounded animated.

'What do *you* think, Millie?'

As Alice stopped by a little fountain, her eyes followed a succession of bright green and blue dragonflies as they swooped and hovered over the lilies in the water. It was another hot day and she resolved to go for a swim this afternoon, maybe followed by a walk down to the village that was barely a kilometre away.

'I love it, Al. And did you see Zoë? She was as good as gold and hardly said a word. I really think it could work out well for us all.'

There was excitement and real optimism in Millie's voice, but Alice knew her of old. Whether it was a new job opportunity, a different man or a ridiculously expensive dress, Millie had this habit of psyching herself up to a point when she just had to have it – even though her track record revealed that her poor choices far outweighed the good decisions. Alice sat down on the low stone wall at the side of the fountain and did some serious thinking.

'I wonder...'

After this reunion with everybody, part of her wanted to believe that Millie's optimism was justified; after all, she felt sure it would be fun to join up with them again for this new series. A couple of years of earning a good salary should allow her to build up enough to buy herself a nice house in London for when she decided to give up acting and take up her chosen career in Renaissance art. Her more cautious, pragmatic side told her to keep her options open and wait until she could be sure that Zoë was either right out of the equation or at least firmly muzzled, before committing herself. On this morning's showing, she had to admit that it was looking more hopeful that Zoë had indeed calmed down – at least to some extent. And if it turned out she wasn't going to be a problem, the idea of signing up for *Pals Forever* did have considerable appeal.

At that point, of course, the next question to be answered would be the fate of her relationship with David. Although determined not to think of the fair-haired man again, she had to acknowledge that lusting – if that was what she had been doing – over a man working in a field was hardly the sign of a woman in a settled, long-term relationship. Setting aside any more thoughts of this for now, she did her best to respond to Millie.

'It's certainly sounding more positive than I expected. Antonia said we've got a meeting tomorrow when Zoë's going to go deeper into the nuts and bolts of the new series. That'll be the crunch. Let's see what emerges from that before getting our hopes up too much.'

That afternoon, after a light lunch, David retired to the bedroom to have a much-needed siesta, while Alice sat on the terrace for an hour or two, reading a book she had bought in London about Leonardo da Vinci. This informed her that there was a villa not far from where they were staying which had, allegedly, been the home of the Mona Lisa herself. Lisa Gherardini, a Florentine girl, had been married at just fifteen to a wealthy silk merchant called Francesco del Giocondo and moved to this part of Chianti. As the wife of del Giocondo, she became known as La Gioconda, which is the name the Italians have given to the painting known to much of the rest of the world as the Mona Lisa.

Alice knew that a growing number of other academics felt that a major question mark remained over the painting, as recent studies had revealed the striking like-ness in terms of facial structure with the few known self-portraits of Leonardo himself. Could it be that one of the most famous female faces of all time might, in fact, be that of its narcissistic creator – a man? Nevertheless, the idea of taking a trip to see this villa was fascinating, not least as Michelangelo had also allegedly owned a house not far from there. The villa in question was now an upmarket hotel and Alice reflected that she and David might go and stay there for a night or two when this meeting ended on Friday.

Around mid-afternoon she went up to their room and found her boyfriend wide awake, looking and sounding more like his old self again.

'If I so much as pick up a glass of wine tonight, Alice, just slap me, will you?' He gave her an apologetic look. 'Hope I didn't make a fool of myself – or you.'

She sat down on the bed alongside him and gave him a kiss. 'Of course not. I'm sure it must have come as a shock to the system to find yourself surrounded by a number of household names, but you'll get used to it.' She grinned back at him. 'And I promise I'll slap you as often as you want. Now, how do you feel about walking down to the village and then coming back for a swim before dinner?'

The others had disappeared to the pool or to their rooms, so she and David set off by themselves. Paolo gave them the combination which would open any of a handful of locked pedestrian gates set in the perimeter fence and pointed them in the direction of one a few hundred metres along from the main entrance. He told them that beyond that they would find a track between a vineyard and an olive grove that led down the hill. They found the gate easily and it only took twenty minutes or so to stroll down from there to the village. It was a charming walk: they saw nobody, and the only signs of life were a few lizards and a pair of magpies that flew off as they approached. The village was a pretty little place, predominantly composed of red-brick or stone houses, many of them clearly ancient. There was a quaint square in the centre, with a fine old church at one end and a bar at the other. They decided to get themselves ice creams and eat them at one of the tables on the piazza.

Leaving David at a table outside, she went in to see what the cafe had to offer. Inside, the first thing she saw was a familiar face. It was none other than the fair-haired fence-mender from this morning and she felt an immediate shiver of what could only be attraction. She was still giving herself a mental kicking as he collected his change, thanked the lady behind the bar and turned for the door. As he passed Alice, she saw recognition dawn on his face and he gave her a friendly wave but, before she could think of anything meaningful to say, he had left. As for her, she knew it would take more than ice cream to calm the confusion this brief encounter had set swirling inside her.

When they got back to the villa, she was ready for a swim, but David decided to stay in the room and check his emails. She felt pretty sure this was just him being unwilling to expose his pale English body to the eyes of honed Hollywood stars used to perfection. She did her best to persuade him to come, but he just shook his head so, in the end, she changed into a bikini, picked up a towel and left him to it. As she got to the bottom of the stairs, she ran into Richie, who was standing in the hall. She had hardly spoken to him since yesterday afternoon, but now that she knew he had brought Carrie and was no longer pining for her, she went over to say hi. He looked happy to see her.

'Hi, Al, you're looking gorgeous.' She felt his eyes run across her body and rather wished she had stopped to wrap the towel around her before coming downstairs. She almost did it now but then discarded the idea as being too obvious and too lame. After all, he had seen her in a whole lot less than a bikini, even if it had been five years ago, so she did her best to tough it out.

'Compliments are always welcome, thank you, and I told you yesterday you're looking good, didn't I? So, how's life? We haven't had time to talk. What are you doing these days?'

He shrugged his shoulders. 'A bit of this and a bit of that. If you're heading for the pool, I'll walk with you. Carrie's down there.'

As they stepped out into the sunshine, she threw him a question. 'Talking of Carrie, how long's that been going on? Are your intentions honourable towards the poor girl?'

'My intentions are always honourable, Al – at least nowadays.' He stopped and turned towards her, his expression serious. 'Listen, I've never had a chance to apologise properly, to tell you how sorry I am for treating you so poorly. All the bad blood on set really got to me and that was a tough time in my life. I was in a really dark place.' He looked directly into her eyes. 'Seriously, Al, I'm really sorry.'

She felt remarkably touched. 'Thanks for the apology, but you didn't really treat me badly. You were never nasty to me, nor were you rude or, God help us, violent. No, you were just distant, and so unbelievably grumpy and uncommunicative. I tried and tried to get you to open up to me. I would have done my best to help you, but you just clammed up. In the end, it was the silence that did it for me. I just couldn't handle it.' She reached over and gave his arm a little squeeze. 'But thanks for the apology. It's all in the past now and I'm happy to see you've moved on as well. So, tell me about Carrie. Is this serious?'

To her surprise, he shook his head. 'Not really. I like her a lot but, to be perfectly honest, I only met her a few weeks ago. I felt sure you would all turn up with companions and I didn't want everybody – you in particular, Al – to think I was a loser, so I asked her if she'd like to come with me and she said yes.'

Alice shook her head incredulously. 'You idiot, Richie! Of course you're not a loser. But Carrie seems like a nice girl. Maybe this could be the start of something good for you both.'

'Maybe... Anyway, what about you and David? Is that serious?'

'Um... yes.'

He must have noticed her hesitation. 'So yes and no?'

'No, I mean yes of course it's serious, Richie.' She ensured there was a stronger note in her voice, even though it maybe belied the way she really felt. Hopefully, the next three or four weeks would sort that out once and for all. 'We've been together for a couple of years and we get on well together.'

'You get on well together? And who says there's no romance left in the world?' He caught her eye and gave her another of his cheeky grins. 'So, does this mean there's still hope for me?'

She could feel her cheeks glowing in spite of her best efforts, but she did her best to sound resolute, as she replied. 'Richie, you're here with Carrie, and I'm with David. Just forget me, would you?'

He didn't say any more and she was glad when they reached the pool.

Layla was stretched out on a sunbed under a parasol, her bikini positively microscopic. Beside her was Millie, reading a book, also in the shade. Carrie, wearing a different bikini from yesterday, was taking photos of the wonderful flowers all around the edge of the pool, which effectively sheltered it from any wind and any prying eyes. As she spotted Richie, she came running.

'Hi, Richie, finished your homework?' She caught hold of him and kissed him warmly.

Alice waited until Carrie had released him, before satisfying her curiosity.

'So what's this about homework, Richie? Have you gone back to school?' She asked it in jest, but was surprised to see him nod shyly.

'Yes, but nothing on your level. I'm trying to get myself a degree. I never had a chance to get all the way through college.'

Alice was mightily impressed. 'That's amazing, Richie. Good for you. What're you studying? Drama?'

'I didn't dare – everybody would realise what an awful actor I am. Don't laugh! I'm doing climatology. It seemed like a useful thing to learn about, seeing as the Earth is busy burning itself up.'

'Terrific, Richie, really. Well done, and you're a great actor.' Although terribly low on self-esteem. 'I'm so impressed.' She saw him smile shyly again and was reminded of the insecure little boy she had once thought she loved, lurking beneath his handsome grown-up exterior. 'Have you got long to go?'

'September's the start of my final year, but I've got a whole bunch of reading to get through over the summer.'

'And if *Pals Forever* goes ahead, what happens then?'

'I've already talked to them and they say they'll let me take a couple of years out before picking up the course again if necessary. So it's all good.'

Alice dropped her towel on a sunbed alongside Millie and walked down the steps into the water, relishing the refreshing feel after her walk in the hot sunshine. As she swam up and down the pool, she wondered if the Labrador next door had somewhere to swim – she knew that an obsession with water was typical of the breed. She stubbornly refused all attempts by her brain to think about the dog's master. She was in a relationship with David and that was that.

At least for now.

Finally, she climbed back out of the pool and dabbed herself dry, before stretching out on her sunbed. She closed her eyes and started thinking about yet another man who wasn't her boyfriend: Richie. She was really pleased that he appeared to have successfully turned his life around and she applauded his decision to go back to college. If the new series took off, she would find herself in very close contact with him – probably fairly intimate contact, if they were indeed trying for a baby in the show. How did she feel about that? Was there any lingering attraction?

As soon as that thought came to her, she shook her head angrily, doing her best to dislodge it. She was here with David. Why had she suddenly started having these kinds of thoughts about two other men, while she was still in a good, solid relationship? And it was a good, solid relationship, wasn't it? Had all her common sense started to desert her because she was back in the Hollywood bubble? She growled to herself in frustration.

'Something wrong, Al?' Her train of thought was interrupted by Millie's voice alongside her. 'What's all the growling about?'

'Nothing, Mil. Just thinking about Zoë, I'm afraid.' The little white lie was definitely preferable to admitting that she had been hallucinating about two men, neither of whom was the one waiting upstairs in her bedroom. What on earth was going on inside her head? She did her best to sound normal as she hastily changed the subject. 'What are you reading?'

Millie held up the paperback and Alice recognised the cover immediately. *The Playboy and His Women* had been an international bestseller for some years now, allegedly turning its author into a multi-millionaire. She hadn't read it and had no desire to do so. From what she had heard, it was a bitterly depressing attack upon the concept of love, romance and relationships – at least from a male perspective. Whatever women told themselves, the book made it brutally clear that all most men wanted was sex. Although this pretty much matched up with a lot of her experiences of men over the years, until she had met David, she saw no reason to read anything so cynical.

'Why on earth are you reading that crap, Mil?'

'I bought it at LAX before I left. I needed something to read on the plane. And it's not crap. It's pretty bleak, but he's not that far off the mark.' She caught Alice's eye. 'His main character, Justin, reminds me of a lot of the men I've dated.' She gave a little sigh. 'I've almost finished it. I'll let you have it when I get to the end. Really, it's a good read and they say there's going to be a movie next year.' She dropped the book onto her lap and looked across at

Alice. 'Anyway, what do you think Zoë's going to tell us tomorrow?'

'Hopefully, that she's decided to give up and pass the new series over to another director, but don't hold your breath.' She caught Millie's eye and winked. 'Tomorrow morning's going to be an interesting meeting.'

'It certainly will be. By the way, Paolo said that tonight we're having a barbecue. Maybe Zoë will get plastered and tell us all about it over dinner.'

–

The barbecue was amazing.

The chef had prepared a variety of kebabs – some laden with beef and others alternating chunks of chicken with vegetables from the villa garden. Some were made up of baby octopus, squid and prawns, along with cherry tomatoes and green peppers. To be on the safe side, some were straight vegetarian. There was grilled pecorino cheese, little wild boar sausages and, for any homesick Americans, home-made burgers complete with bacon and cheese. Tonight, as well as wine, there was ice-cold German beer in huge glass mugs for those who wanted it, and the whole thing was accompanied by a selection of salads and a mountain of fries.

Alice helped herself to a couple of the kebabs and half a slice of hot cheese and sipped her beer, which was excellent. She grabbed a beer for David and pressed it into his hand.

'It's beer, not wine, so I won't be slapping you, unless you're into that sort of thing.' She was feeling really guilty after all her thoughts about other men, so she reached up and gave him a smacking kiss that clearly surprised him.

He glanced back at her. 'What was that for?'

'No reason. Enjoy your beer.'

Tonight there were several little tables strewn around the terrace and they took their seats with Millie. Seconds later, Richie appeared with Carrie and politely asked if they could sit down with them. Carrie had more salad than meat on her plate, while his was piled high with fries and the biggest burger Alice had seen since her days in the USA. The thing was almost as big as the litre of beer alongside it.

'Blimey, Richie, are you going to be able to manage all that?'

Carrie answered for him. 'He'll manage. I've never seen somebody so slim eat so much and not get fat.' She caught Alice's eye and grinned. 'It's not fair.'

Alice's attention was then gripped by a little cameo playing out at the table opposite them. Layla, resplendent in yet another designer dress, had taken a seat there and was looking at something on her phone. As she did so, Harry appeared on the terrace and helped himself to a big mug of beer from Paolo. He stood there for a moment, checking Layla out, before taking a few big mouthfuls for Dutch courage and heading across to her table.

'Um, Layla, do you mind if I sit with you?' He sounded unusually hesitant. Layla's head jerked up and Alice caught her breath, waiting for the explosion. The divorce had been caused by his multiple infidelities, after all. Time stood still for what seemed like an age, before Layla's face cleared and she waved dismissively towards the seats opposite her.

'Sit where you like, Harry.' And she returned to her phone.

Harry swallowed another huge draught of beer and sat down. As he did so, Zoë came out onto the terrace, accepted a glass of red wine from Rosanna and went across to Layla's table.

'You two not eating?' She sounded amiable enough. 'Something smells good.'

As if only just realising there was food on offer, Harry jumped to his feet and nodded. 'Good idea. Can I bring you anything?' Layla ignored the question and Zoë shook her head, so he went over to the table alongside the barbecue, where Paolo was serving the food. Zoë sat down opposite Layla and swallowed half her wine in one go. She either really liked wine or was nervous – either way, it looked promising. Maybe Millie's prediction that she might drink too much and spill the beans was going to come true.

Alice felt a touch on her arm. It was Millie. 'I think that's the first thing Layla and Harry have said to each other since we got here.' She was whispering, but Richie must have heard and he leant across the table towards the two of them.

Keeping his voice equally low, he added. 'That's progress. He rolled up at a party she was at a couple of years ago and she threw an ice bucket at him… and it was full.'

A minute or two later Antonia and Benny arrived, and Alice took the fact that they were together and talking as a good sign. She knew full well that his scripts would be every bit as important to the success of the new show as any one of the actors. The two of them collected plates of food and drinks, and sat down together on another table. As Antonia passed the other two tables, she raised her wine glass in a little salute. So far so good, Alice told herself. For now, at least, peace would appear to have broken out and she settled down to eat her meal.

Chapter 8

When Alice left David in bed next morning at eight o'clock and went downstairs, there was no sign of Harry, so she went for a run by herself. Although she rather liked the idea of seeing the Labrador again, she deliberately decided not to run up towards the neighbour's estate, just in case the fair-haired man might be there. She felt strongly that the unexpected frisson of attraction she had felt for him was just plain wrong for somebody in a relationship as she was, so she set off in the opposite direction. Using the key code, she let herself out of the same side gate she had used on her way to the village but, this time, instead of heading downhill, she turned left and started jogging uphill along the track. Everything she passed was bone dry and she wondered when it had last rained here. Although there were no clouds in the sky, it was a bit hazier this morning, and the air felt clammy and humid. Maybe there was a storm on the way. Of course, she reminded herself, at ten o'clock they were scheduled to have the big meeting chaired by Zoë and there was the very real likelihood that a storm would erupt in there, irrespective of what the weather outside was doing.

She climbed steadily, speeding up as she fell into her regular cadence, and breathed deeply, savouring the aroma of wild rosemary in the air. After a little while, the track joined the road that passed the main entrance to the villa and carried on upwards. She stayed on the narrow road and didn't see a single vehicle. It took another ten minutes or so to reach the top of the hill and she allowed herself a short breather at the point where the road curved sharply to the right and began to drop steeply away into the next valley, while a gravel track led off to the left. This track, she told herself, headed roughly in the direction of the villa, and it was also pointing directly at the old tower, which she now realised wasn't really at the top of a hill, but on a spur sticking out from the hillside. Either way, it occupied an exceptional defensive position and no doubt this had been the reason its original builders had chosen the spot.

The view from up here was spectacular. Although Villa delle Vespe, directly below her, was concealed by the curve of the hillside and the dense woods that covered this part of the slope, the view into the distance was superb. To the east, rank upon rank of green hills finally melded into a darker mass that she felt pretty sure had to be the Apennines. On the other three sides it was all remarkably empty and altogether very rural: trees, fields, hills and woods were interspersed with a scattering of red-brick farmhouses and occasional small villages. For somebody who had spent most of her life in big cities, this land-scape was completely different, alluring and maybe just a tiny bit intimidating. There was no noise apart from the omnipresent bees and invisible little birds twittering from the bushes – no rumble of traffic, no aircraft overhead, no human voices. She could have been the last person on Earth, and for a second or two she felt really alone, but then, just to prove her wrong, she heard the unmistakable sound of a vehicle approaching.

A cloud of dust rising up through the trees along the line of the track to her left indicated where the car was coming from and she stepped off the road onto the dry grass verge to let it pass. When it came into view, she saw at once that it was a battered old Land Rover – no doubt a sensible vehicle in this sort of terrain once the rains came. There was no roof on the vehicle and, as it drew closer, she saw a movement inside: a black shadow reared up on the front passenger seat, put his big paws on the dashboard and his head popped up above the screen. There could be no doubt who this was, and she felt her heart give an involuntary – and most unwelcome – leap when her eyes landed on the driver. As he drew up alongside her, she saw recognition on his face.

'Good morning – out for a run before the rain comes?'

It took her a moment to realise that he had addressed her in English – fluent UK English, without any particular regional inflection. While she was still trying to get her head around this, Guinness the dog started barking happily and bouncing up and down on the passenger seat, his tail wagging furiously. She leant over the side of the vehicle and made a fuss of him. As she did so, she became acutely conscious that she was streaming with sweat and not exactly at her most appealing. Still, she told herself, the dog didn't mind and what this man thought was unimportant. Guinness by now was balancing his forepaws on the top of the door and doing his best to reach out and kiss her, fortunately his master showed no such signs of open affection. He did, however, allow himself a smile at the antics of the dog. Alice smiled back.

'Good morning, Guinness, and good morning to you.' Since she didn't know his name, she made an attempt to rectify that. 'By the way, my name's Alice.' She wondered if he had maybe already recognised her face, but she decided to tell him anyway. From his reaction, her name meant nothing to him.

'Hi, Alice, I'm Matt – short for Matthew.'

'I'm pleased to meet you, Matt, short for Matthew. So, what's a Brit doing in the wilds of Tuscany?'

'It's a long story. I'll bore you with it some other time.'

She noted his reluctance to talk about himself, so she didn't press him. 'Is Guinness your dog? I wasn't sure if he belonged to you or the other gentleman.'

He nodded. 'Yes, he's my dog and my best buddy. And what about you? Where are you going on your run?'

'I've just come up the road and I was wondering if there's any way this track you've just come along might lead me back towards the villa.'

She saw him nod. 'The gates to your place all have combination locks. Do you have the code? I imagine they'll all be the same. Well, there's a path leading off left, just as you reach the drive leading up to my house. Go down there for a hundred yards or so and you'll come to the gate.'

'Thank you.' She hesitated, not really knowing why she still hadn't moved – except for the dog, of course. By this time Guinness was scrabbling, trying to get his hind legs on the top of the door as well as his front paws and it looked as though he was preparing to launch himself bodily into her arms, so she leant forward and gently returned him to a safer position on the front seat. She glanced across at his master. 'I'd hate to see Guinness fall out onto the road.'

'It hasn't happened yet, but I've never seen him up on top of the door like that. He must really have taken a liking to you.'

'Well, I love him, too – he's a sweetie.' Keen not to spend too much time with this unknown man, however sweet his dog might be, she decided to make a move. 'Anyway, I'd better be off. Have a good day.' She gave the dog a final cuddle and turned away.

As she set off down the track, she heard the engine rev as the vehicle pulled out onto the road and the noise gradually diminished, until silence returned. She jogged along the track, her head filled with mixed emotions. The overriding feeling was one of mystification. For whatever reason, this man had managed to get under her skin and risked stirring feelings in her that she hadn't felt for ages... not since first meeting David – or maybe not ever, if she were honest. How this could happen after barely a few minutes' exposure to him remained a mystery but, she told herself firmly, she was here with another man, so she would do well just to dismiss Matt from her mind.

Easier said than done.

After a couple of hundred yards of rough track, tall wooden gates set in hefty stone walls announced the entrance to his home. She saw a metal postbox bolted to one of the gateposts and, out of curiosity, she slowed down and went over to check the name on it. There was no name: just one word written on it – *Torre*, the Italian word for tower. Clearly, he valued his privacy.

She peered through the narrow gap between the gate and the post and saw a gravelled drive leading up through the trees to the base of the tower. Even from a distance, viewed through a two-inch aperture, the place looked amazing. For somebody with an interest in history, it was fascinating. Entirely built of stone, it was higher than she had imagined, probably as tall as a three- or even four-storey building. The windows at the lower levels were little wider than arrow slits, while the upper floors had larger openings and the views from up there must have been spectacular. It would have been wonderful to get the chance to see for herself but that, she knew full well, wasn't going to happen. She gave a little sigh and headed down the path he had indicated, back in the direction of the villa.

—

That morning's meeting turned out to be not so much a storm as an unstoppable tsunami. Antonia was nowhere to be seen and from the very first minute Zoë took charge. She talked – or, more precisely, preached – for two hours almost without a break, laying down how she saw the series developing, refusing questions and silencing any opposition. Any lingering hopes they might have been nursing that she had mellowed over the past five years or that she might be handing the directorial reins over to somebody else were soon dashed. As the morning's sermon progressed, the others exchanged ever gloomier looks and a mood of grim depression settled upon them all.

As the church bell in the village chimed midday, Zoë finally swept out of the room, leaving them in stunned silence that lasted for several minutes, before Benny put everybody's thoughts into words. First, predictably, there was an outburst of heartfelt and inventive expletives, and then he gradually settled down.

'Well, that's that, then. And to think I travelled six thousand miles for this. Thank God the food's good.' He pushed back his chair, stood up and stretched, before looking around at the others. 'Well, I suppose the good news is that we now know exactly where we stand.'

Alice looked across at the others and read frustration, resentment and disappointment on the faces around her. She also felt betrayed and, although she had thought she didn't really care about a return to Hollywood, she now realised that she had been kidding herself. A second chance at the bright lights could have been a lot of fun and would have cemented her financial security. Now that it was clear it was to be Zoë or nothing, she knew that her answer would almost certainly have to be nothing. Life was too short for getting back into all that stress. She took a deep breath and headed for the door. What she did know was that she needed some fresh air.

'I don't know about you guys, but I need to get out of this room. I think I'm going for a swim to clear my head.'

Outside, the sky was no longer clear blue, as clouds had bubbled up over the course of the morning and her predicted storm looked to be on its way. As well as humid, it was also very warm; she went up to her room but found no sign of David. She changed into her bikini – remembering to wrap the towel around herself this time – and went out. When she got to the pool, she was surprised to find Antonia there, sitting fully clothed under a parasol and holding her iPad in her hands. She looked up as she heard footsteps and, from the expression on her face, Alice could immediately see that she was fully aware of what had just happened.

'Hi, Alice. There was an email from Conrad overnight.' Antonia sounded weary. 'I imagine Zoë's told you what it said. Zoë's in charge of *Pals Forever* and that's that.'

Alice went across and perched on the edge of a sunbed alongside her. 'She didn't mention an email, but the message came through loud and clear.' She hesitated.

'How does this make you feel, Antonia? You're Zoë's superior, after all.'

A shadow passed over Antonia's face, but she made no comment other than to say, 'I think it's a big mistake and I've told Conrad that, but I'm not holding my breath for a change of heart from him.' She pushed up her sunglasses and caught Alice's eye. 'What about you?'

'I'm going to think it over, but I'm afraid I'll end up saying no.' The more she thought about it, the more likely this became. 'It would have been really great to work with you and the gang again – and with a lot of the production crew back in Hollywood that I haven't seen for years – but it's the prospect of being treated like dirt by Zoë all over again. I'll give it some more thought before making a final decision.' She glanced around but nobody else had come to the pool. 'Just between the two of us, I've got a second interview next Thursday for a job in London that really appeals to me. It's nothing to do with showbiz. It's an art history thing.'

'That sounds wonderful.' Antonia reached out and tapped her briefly on the arm. 'You've invested so much time and effort in getting to this point with your studies, I'm sure you're anxious to put what you've learnt into practice. I would love to work with you again, too, but I must confess, I wouldn't be surprised if you decide you aren't interested. What about the others? Do they feel the same way?'

'You'd better ask them. I really don't know. I get the impression both Layla and Benny have got successful careers without getting involved with *Pals Forever*, so maybe they'll duck out. As for the others, who knows?'

'So it looks as though it's either going to die a death or be very different. It's such a pity...' Antonia's voice tailed off and she sounded so dispirited that Alice decided to try to cheer her up by changing the subject.

'Are you interested in art, by any chance?'

'I don't know much about it, but yes, I like art.'

'How about the art of the Renaissance?'

'Again, I know precious little about it. Why do you ask?'

'I was just thinking... I know a girl who works in the Uffizi – you know, in Florence. Getting tickets to visit the gallery in mid-summer is terribly difficult but if I give her a call, I'm pretty sure she could get us in. How about taking a trip up there some time and I'll give you a tour of the gallery?'

'That would be amazing. And having my own expert guide would be terrific. Shall we make it tomorrow after-noon, if you're free, seeing as we're all supposed to be leaving the day after? I can give the limo people a call, and get them to take us to Florence and drop us back again.'

'Sounds perfect. I'll call Teresa now. I'll check with David to see if he's interested in coming, but I doubt it. Art isn't really his thing.' As she mentioned his name, she thought guiltily that she should really talk the whole *Pals Forever* thing over with him before giving her final decision. After all, it could affect him deeply. She wondered what he would say. 'If you arrange the car for just after lunch tomorrow, I'll ask her to book us in around mid-afternoon. Okay?'

Chapter 9

Lunch was a sober affair – well, not so much from an alcohol point of view but as far as the atmosphere on the terrace was concerned. In fact, the bottles of wine emptied a lot faster than they had done the previous day, as most of those around the table sought solace in drink. Even Alice, who had vowed to herself to stay off the booze – or at least to limit her intake – allowed herself a couple of glasses of red wine and was therefore feeling quite sleepy by the time the coffees were served at the end. The only people who looked cheerful were Carrie and David, who hadn't been subjected to the morning's haranguing. During the meal, he spent a good deal of time talking to Layla, and Alice was pleased they were getting along.

Neither Zoë nor Antonia appeared for lunch and Alice wondered whether they were eating together or if they had both decided to go their separate ways. Alice told the others what Antonia had said about the email from the big boss, and shoulders slumped all round. Some had been hoping that a direct appeal to Conrad Chesterfield might have had some success, but it was now pretty obvious this wasn't going to work. As Alice had expected, Benny and Layla sounded as though they had decided to vote with their feet, while Millie was still keen – or rather, desperate.

As for Richie and Harry, it was hard to tell. Harry, in particular, couldn't get his head round it.

'Conrad's no fool. Surely he can see that this series could become a real money-spinner – and by the sound of it, the studio needs a success badly. So why stick by Zoë if it means torpedoing the whole thing?'

'Well, of course, he doesn't know what our response is going to be yet.' Richie had always been the pragmatic one. 'None of us has given a definite reply so far, have we? Maybe it's all just a double bluff by him. He thinks we'll cave and go for it, but if we all turn round and say no, maybe he'll have to give in.'

Layla looked up. 'So, are you saying you'd go for it if Zoë was out of the equation?' Seeing him nod, she threw the question open and everybody nodded in agreement.

Alice joined in. 'So, it looks as though we're all prepared to go for it without Zoë – and that includes me – but what if she remains in charge? You all know what I think about that. I don't know if I can stand the thought of working with her again. From what we saw of her this morning, this particular leopard hasn't changed its spots. If anything, she sounded even more obstinate than before. What about all you guys?' Seeing uncertainty on some of the faces, she decided to delay putting them on the spot. 'Why don't we all take a bit of time and think it over? How about meeting up again this evening before dinner and taking a vote, or at least saying whether we're each in or out?'

This was greeted by general agreement and the group broke up. Alice found herself yawning after her lunchtime wine, and she told David she was going upstairs for a snooze. To her surprise, he decided to go for a walk, so she climbed back up the stairs to the room alone. Outside, the sky was getting ever darker and the atmosphere was growing increasingly clammy, so she slipped out of her T-shirt and shorts, and stretched out on the bed, covered only by a sheet. She fell asleep straightaway, but was woken barely half an hour later by a knock at her door. Yawning, she climbed out of bed and stepped into her shorts. Slipping on her T-shirt, she went over to the door and opened it to see Richie standing there.

'Sorry, Al, were you sleeping?'

'Like a baby. What's the problem?' She brushed the hair out of her eyes and blinked a few times.

'Not really a problem... I just need to talk to you. I saw David out on the terrace with Layla, so I knew you'd be on your own. Can I come in?'

Alice hesitated. Although she had been getting along fine with him since arriving here, letting him into her room – particularly when she had just tumbled out of bed – was another matter. Still, she felt sure she had nothing to fear from him – even if he now had a few more muscles – so she stepped back and beckoned him in.

'But if David comes along and objects to you being in my bedroom, it's down to you to do the explaining. Understood?'

'Sure.' He went across to the bed and perched on the side of it. She thought about joining him there but then decided against it. Instead, she took a seat on the old wooden chest against the wall and rested her back against the cool plaster. 'So, have you decided what you're going to do about *Pals Forever*?'

'Not really. I'm going to wait and see what the others say this evening.'

'So what's so important you had to wake me up in the middle of a lovely dream?'

'Yeah, I'm sorry about that.' He hesitated. 'It's about you and me, Al.'

Suddenly she was wide awake. 'There is no you and me anymore, Richie. We both know that.'

'But I'm not that guy anymore. I've changed.' He sounded quite plaintive. 'You can see that, can't you?'

'You're looking and sounding a lot better. Yes, of course I've noticed that – I even told you so. But, apart from anything else, I'm with David and you're with Carrie now.'

He gave a dismissive shrug. 'I'm not really with her. Like I told you, there's nothing serious there.'

'In that case you just dragged the poor girl halfway across the world for what? So you wouldn't feel left out? That's no way to treat anybody, Richie.'

'Yeah, I know, but she's having a great time, mixing with all her heroes – especially you, Al.'

'Her hero wasn't me, it was Polly the flirt and those days have gone. Richie, five years have passed. You're not the only one to have changed. So have I.'

'In the way you feel about me? I haven't changed the way I feel about you. Won't you give me a second chance?'

Alice hesitated. She could see he had convinced himself that he meant what he said. She studied him in the gathering gloom of the cloudy afternoon. He was still a good-looking guy and now, with his apparent return to being the nice, open man with whom she had first fallen in love – or had thought she had – could she develop feelings for him again? The answer, she told herself firmly, was no. She was with David and, unless the next couple of weeks' holiday with him resulted in a break-up, that wasn't going to change.

However, before she could say anything, there was a blinding flash, accompanied almost instantaneously by an ear-shattering thunderclap, and both of them shrank back. Her window was open and the shockwave set the toothglasses in the bathroom rattling. Two seconds later, torrential rain came cascading down, as suddenly as if a dam had collapsed. The noise of the falling water almost drowned out her voice as she did the only thing she could do – prevaricate until she could clear her head.

'Now's not the moment to talk about this stuff, Richie, but like I told you, time has moved on and so have I. Okay?'

For a moment it looked as though he was about to object, but the deafening crashes of the thunderstorm directly overhead convinced him that it was pointless. He allowed her to usher him out of her room and into the corridor. At the door she repeated her message to him.

'We both know that time has passed. Find yourself a nice girl and get on with your life.'

He left without another word.

–

It poured with rain all afternoon and Alice spent it in her room, dozing, reading and chatting to her friend Teresa at the Uffizi. David must have taken refuge from the rain somewhere else, as there was no sign of him. As she had hoped, Teresa arranged entry to the world-famous gallery the following afternoon, and Alice texted the good news to Antonia. David had opted not to join them, saying he would be quite happy just relaxing at the villa, and Alice wasn't surprised. Getting him to visit art galleries had always been an uphill struggle.

As she lay there, listening to the rain, she let her mind roam. Here she was, in the enviable position of having been offered a job that most people would kill for and, at the same time, she also had a second interview for a different job which was ideally suited to her training and interests. Which had more appeal? The answer, when it came to her, almost took her by surprise. In spite of everything she had been telling herself and others over the last five years, the lure of Hollywood was still there, lurking in the background, and these few days here at the villa had brought it back to the forefront of her mind. The sixty-four thousand dollar question was whether she was prepared to endure another spell of tongue-lashing from Zoë, which was looking inevitable. Maybe the sensible choice would be to stick to art history but, deep down, she had a feeling she might end up regretting that decision. What to do? Maybe David would be able to help her make up her mind.

Finally, around six o'clock, the rain stopped and, minutes later, David reappeared, looking sheepish.

'Hi, Alice, I got marooned in the summer house. I went for a walk and then the heavens opened.' He pointed across the room to the bedside table. 'Stupidly, I left my phone here so I just had to sit it out.'

She held out her arms and gave him a hug. Now that she had successfully banished the man with the fair hair from her mind and Richie from her life, she was feeling more secure of her feelings for David – at least for now. She kissed his lips and clung to his arm.

'What would you do if you were in my position?'

'As far as *Pals Forever* is concerned?'

'Yes, considering that it now looks definite that Zoë's going to be calling the shots.'

He didn't hesitate. 'If I were in your shoes, I'd jump at it. How many people get a second chance to do something as amazing as starring in a show that'll be seen by half the population of the world?'

Although this was a glaring exaggeration, she let it go. 'But it would mean working with Zoë... You don't know what it was like towards the end. She was unbearable.'

He gave a dismissive snort. 'So what? You're a strong woman. You could cope. And remember, Zoë's a star in her own right. So much of the success of *Pals* is down to her. She's entitled to be a bit awkward.'

'A *bit* awkward? She was a right cow!' Alice shook her head slowly. 'I can be strong if I need to, but I'm not so sure I could put up with it.'

'Of course you could. Besides, I'd be there to support you.'

Alice looked up in surprise. They hadn't discussed this eventuality yet and she hadn't really expected him to offer to give up his job in Bristol so readily to accompany her to the other side of the world.

'You'd come to Hollywood with me?'

'Of course. I'd love it.'

'And your job?'

'I'd find something. Don't worry about me.'

Well, Alice told herself, that answered one fundamental question. He was prepared to follow her to LA. This immediately raised an even more vital question – for her. Did she want him to come with her? Was he The One? Hopefully, she would be able to decide that one way or another before they left Chianti. She glanced at her watch and then stretched up to kiss him.

'We've got a bit of time before we need to go down for dinner. I can think of a few ways we could occupy ourselves.'

To her surprise, he shrank back. 'Sorry, Alice, but I need to have a hot bath. I got really cold in the summer house. No, let's save it for later.' He pecked her on the cheek and headed for the bathroom.

What had Richie said about romance being dead? Alice decided to leave him to his bath and went outside for some fresh air, her head still churning with all the different ramifications of the decisions she had to make. The buzzing of the bees had now been replaced by a symphony of drips, accompanied by the gurgling of little streams that had spontaneously appeared among the flower beds. The plants were all bowed down as a result of the battering by the rain, with petals strewn all around, but she could almost feel the collective sigh of relief from all the vegetation after the arrival of the long-awaited water. The tracks and paths were sodden and muddy, but she went for a short stroll along the drive to the main gate and then decided to continue down the hill towards the village.

All the way down the road she turned over and over in her head what Richie and David had said. As far as Richie was concerned – yes, he was a nice guy. Yes, she still liked him, but could she ever see it going any further? The fact that he had opted to do a degree course was interesting, as maybe this meant there could be a 'normal' life for the two of them, far from Hollywood, if she and David were ever to split up. But nevertheless, her conviction grew that any relationship with Richie was long dead in the water.

She then spent a lot of time thinking about David's advice to take the acting job and his offer to accompany her. Maybe having him in Hollywood alongside her would provide the support she would need to weather the Zoë storm, but she had her doubts. She also had her doubts as to the viability of her relationship with David going forward. Might she end up unhappy at work and unhappy at home? It could be the sort of double whammy that would ruin her life. Besides, was he offering to come with her out of love or out of a desire to experience the glamour of Hollywood for himself? After all, there had been his rather offhand response to her suggestion of a bit of intimacy. She hoped this wasn't because he was feeling ignored while she was renewing old friendships and going through all the negotiations about the new show. Mind you, she told herself, what better way of showing him she cared than by leaping into bed with him? Men could be strange animals sometimes.

The tarmac was awash with water and her trainers and socks were damp by the time she got to the village, but it had been a pleasure to walk in the fresh country air. When she got to the bar in the square she went inside and asked for a cup of tea, specifying that she would like it English-style, with a drop of cold milk, and Rita, the lady behind the bar, set about preparing it. As Alice waited for the tea, they chatted and, quite by chance – or so she told herself – the subject of Matt came up. She discovered that his full name was Matthew Livingstone, but the lady referred to him by the Italian equivalent of his first name, Matteo. It transpired that he came in most mornings just before nine for a coffee and he brought his big black dog with him. She also confirmed what Paolo had said: he had been here for a couple of years, spoke pretty good Italian and was generally liked by everybody who knew him. Alice thanked her for the information but immediately did her best to relegate it to the back of her mind, as she already had enough to think about with the uncertainty about her current boyfriend, the amorous propositions of her former boyfriend and the discussions about the new show.

She told the lady that she and David were thinking about staying on in Tuscany for a bit longer and asked if she maybe knew of any apartments or houses available to let from the end of the week. Seeing as they were now in the busy holiday month of July, this was almost certainly a forlorn hope, but she thought she would ask anyway. As expected, the answer was an apologetic shake of the head, but the lady said she would ask around, just in case.

As Alice walked back up the hill to the villa, she tried and failed to stop her brain from debating just why she had thought it a good idea to look for a place in this area, so close to the tower, Matt and his dog. In spite of Richie's declaration of enduring love and David's offer to accompany her to the US, she had to accept that this other man who had barely spoken to her for more than a couple of minutes in total was stubbornly lodged inside her head, if not her heart, and refusing to budge. To say she was feeling confused was an understatement.

She did her best to banish all of these thoughts and concentrated on the lovely views as well as the mixed aromas of wild thyme, rosemary and the almost sickly sweet scent emanating from the vivid yellow flowers on the broom bushes. She heard distant whistling sounds and looked up to see two big birds of prey circling high above, no doubt scanning the fields for their dinner. It was a delightful walk and, once again, she didn't see a single vehicle – although her brain unhelpfully pointed out that the appearance of a battered old Land Rover would not have been unwelcome.

They all met up on the terrace at seven thirty, as planned. By this time David had warmed up and changed, and was looking unusually smart. Although the rain had stopped less than two hours before, the stone paving slabs were already dry and the sound of dripping water had been replaced by the high-pitched cries of swallows swooping and darting around the villa, catching insects on the wing. The sunset was a glorious rich red tonight, and Alice felt sure tomorrow would once more be dry and sunny.

Yet again, Antonia and Zoë kept their distance, and the members of the group were able to talk freely. It emerged that Harry and Richie had decided they were prepared to join Millie in accepting Zoë as director, if there was no alternative, but Layla and Benny were still steadfast in their refusal to work with her again. Alice would dearly have liked to sleep on it before making her final decision but in the end she came down on the side of Layla and Benny, and she sensed David's shock and disapproval, although he didn't comment. Layla volunteered to compose an email to Conrad Chesterfield, explaining their position. It was agreed that they would sleep on it and if they all approved the email next morning, she would send it. As Benny said, 'Light the blue touch paper and stand well clear.' No doubt the reaction to their email would be explosive.

After dinner, Alice took David by the arm and walked him around the gardens in the moonlight. The aroma of roses in the air was almost overpowering, and the only sounds were their feet crunching on the gravel and an occasional owl hoot from the woods around Matt's tower. It was a charming and romantic setting, and it would have been idyllic if she had been able to shake thoughts of the owner of the tower from her head. Beside her, David also seemed preoccupied and they barely spoke a word. Neither of them brought up the subject of *Pals Forever* and she actually felt relieved. She had done enough soul-searching for today.

They took their time and made a slow circuit of the villa, before ending up back on the terrace once more, where the others were lounging, chatting and sipping cold drinks. Having already drunk some wine at lunch, she didn't feel like any alcohol and, in fact, realised she was quite tired. To her surprise, when she suggested going up to bed, David told her he would stay for a drink, so she went back upstairs on her own.

Chapter 10

Next morning dawned fine and clear. Alice woke to find David fast asleep alongside her in the bed, but she had no recollection of hearing him come in last night. She must have gone out like a light. Very quietly, she slipped away and went downstairs for her morning run. Today she found not only Harry, but also Richie and Carrie ready to join her. As the ground underfoot was still soaked, she led them along the drive, out of the gate and up the road, just as she had done the previous day. It was a quarter past eight and there was, of course, the possibility she might once again see the old Land Rover and its driver but, seeing as she was surrounded by the others, she knew all she would be able to do would be to wave. Still, that was probably for the best.

As they jogged up the hill, Alice deliberately hung back alongside Carrie, so as not to end up being monopolised by Richie, and the two men gradually opened up a lead. Carrie was evidently fit and they were able to carry on a conversation as they climbed. Although it started off harmlessly enough, as they were nearing the top it became a bit awkward.

'Alice, you and Richie used to date, didn't you?'

'On-screen I've forgotten how many times – ever since series two, but each time the writers fixed it so one of the characters – usually Polly – screwed it up. Off-screen we were together on and off for three months or so and then we managed to screw that up, too – all by ourselves.'

'Why did you and Richie break up?'

Alice knew very little about Carrie, except that she apparently worked in public relations, and there was no way she was going to reveal the struggle Richie had had with his demons back then, so she took refuge in a cliché. 'Fundamental incompatibility, I'm afraid.'

'You didn't get on?'

'Maybe we were overexposed to each other – you know, what with working together as well.'

'And would you think about taking him back?'

Alice glanced across at her. 'What makes you ask that? We broke up five years ago. This week's the first time I've seen him since then.'

'It's just that he's pretty clearly still in love with you.'

'He's what?' Alice had to stop and take a couple of deep breaths. 'What on earth gave you that idea?'

'He did. He almost said as much. He's always talking about you.'

'Well, I can assure you that nothing's ever going to happen between us, and that's that.'

As she spoke, she realised she really meant it. With the arrival of a new day had come the conviction that she needed to get Richie on his own and spell out to him in words of one syllable that they were definitively not getting back together again. She would not, however, tell him that the reason for her refusal wasn't necessarily her current boyfriend, but the way she had been affected by a different man she had only just met.

'You mean that?' Carrie didn't sound convinced.

Alice nodded, as the certainty that she was doing the right thing crystallised inside her. 'Totally. Yes, I went out with him for a few months a long time ago but that's as far as it went – and as far as it'll ever go.' She caught Carrie's eye. 'Whatever he might say or think, it's all over between us.'

'Because of David?'

'Yes, of course, because of David.' She was conscious she had maybe answered a bit too hastily.

'And if David wasn't in the equation?'

'Why shouldn't he be?' Alice shot her a sharp look. 'Has he said something?'

'No, nothing. I was just wondering, that's all.'

At that moment they heard the sound of a vehicle coming down the road towards them and Alice glanced up the hill. Sure enough, it was the Land Rover and, once again, there was a big black shape in the passenger seat. As it came closer, her heart gave another involuntary leap and, as she saw the vehicle slow and then stop alongside her, she was powerless to prevent a beaming smile from spreading across her face. Today she found herself standing beside the driver's door, rather than on the dog's side of the car. She was looking directly down at Matt, who was wearing shorts, and she couldn't miss the fact that she liked what she saw. Restraining a feeling of impropriety, she stepped forward.

'Good morning, Matt.'

As the dog recognised who it was, he leapt across from the passenger seat to give her an enthusiastic greeting. Unfortunately, this resulted in fifty or sixty pounds of canine bone and muscle landing in his master's lap, and this must have been in a particularly sensitive spot. The Englishman gave a cry of agony and doubled up, banging his forehead against the steering wheel as he did so. The dog, bewildered by this unusual reaction from his master, set about licking his face to soothe the pain and it was all the two girls could do not to burst out laughing. It took almost a minute before Matt recovered the power of speech.

'Guinness, you little...!' Benny would no doubt have been able to help him with a few choice expletives, but Matt controlled himself and gingerly persuaded the dog to return to the passenger seat. As he did so, he looked up at Alice and made a plea. 'Do you think you could maybe move round to the other side of the car before my dog makes another attempt to emasculate me?'

Alice and Carrie did as instructed and were duly given a warm welcome by Guinness while his master surreptitiously massaged himself. As he did so, Alice caught his eye and did her best to keep her composure for a few moments but, finally, the floodgates burst and she exploded into fits of laughter. She saw him blush and then he, too, started laughing. Beside her, Carrie was in hysterics, while Guinness, seriously concerned at this extraordinary behaviour by these three humans, started whining uncertainly. He nudged his master with his nose while his big brown eyes gazed up with deep concern. Alice could see that with a smile on his face – even though his eyes were still watering – Matt looked even more handsome and, in spite of her best intentions, her heart fluttered yet again.

'I can imagine how much that hurts.'

Matt caught her eye and shook his head ruefully. 'I really don't think you do, Alice.' He straightened his back and took a few deep breaths.

'Maybe you're right. Anyway, I can assure you I don't want to find out. It's good to see you again, Matt. This is Carrie, from the US.'

'I'm pleased to meet you, Carrie. Are you both staying at the villa?'

Alice nodded and he then added a less comfortable question.

'And you're here with the two guys I saw a bit further up the road?'

Carrie answered for both of them. 'I'm with one of them.'

'I see.'

Alice felt a bit more explanation might be in order. 'We're a bunch of old friends.' This would have been the moment to mention David, but she didn't, and subsequently spent much of the rest of the morning asking herself why not. 'We leave tomorrow.' Was that a flash of regret she spotted on his face? But, even as she was still debating what she had seen, he put the car into gear and gave them both a little wave of the hand.

'Well, goodbye. It's been good meeting you. Safe journey home.' And with that, he drove off.

'That's one hell of a good-looking guy.' Clearly, Carrie had been impressed but Alice knew where her own priorities lay — at least for now.

'I've already got one of those, and so have you. But, I have to say, that's one hell of a good-looking dog he's got.'

—

Over breakfast, they got together and read the email that Layla had composed for Conrad Chesterfield. It was well-written and surprisingly diplomatic, and Alice reckoned she had probably run it by her agent, or even her lawyer, for approval before showing it to them. The message, although couched in tactful, respectful terms, was unequivocal. The email recognised Zoë's unquestionable contribution to the success of *Pals*, but it spelt out that her attitude and overbearing behaviour had become unbearable as time went by. As a result, if Zoë were not involved, all of them would be happy to sign up for *Pals Forever* – subject to successful financial negotiations – but if the director retained her position, then Layla, Alice and Benny were out. Although she hadn't had the chance to speak to David any more about this, Alice knew it was the right decision to make. If Zoë was in the mix, the best thing to do was to turn her back on this second chance of Hollywood glory. Life was too short.

They all agreed that the text looked fine and Layla pressed Send. Back in LA, the time was around midnight, so there was no guarantee Conrad Chesterfield would see the email for another eight hours, but none of them felt particularly hopeful. His reaction would probably be incandescent, but would he blink? Would he be prepared to sacrifice Zoë for the greater good of the new series?

As she sipped her cappuccino, with David sitting quietly at her side, Alice told Millie what she would do if Conrad didn't agree to their terms. As far as she was concerned, that would be the end of the matter. This afternoon she and Antonia were going to Florence, but there would be no point staying any longer than that and in consequence she knew she would head off next morning.

'Didn't you say you were going to stay on in Tuscany?' There was nothing wrong with Millie's memory. 'Have you found a place yet?'

Alice shook her head. 'No. I've been asking around, but I must get onto sorting something out. I know I'd like to go and stay at least a night at a villa not that far from here, where the Mona Lisa had once lived. I know it's silly, but I'd just like to breathe in the atmosphere of the place – you know, imagine myself maybe even in the same room where Leonardo da Vinci painted what is arguably the most famous painting in the world.'

Millie caught her eye. 'You're really deeply into the whole Renaissance art thing, aren't you?'

'Body and soul. That's why, if I'm being totally honest, Mil, it won't bother me too much if Conrad says he won't replace Zoë. I know it would be tough on you, but the more I think about it, the more I reckon I'd be quite happy doing my own thing in a "normal" life.'

Just how true this was remained to be seen.

'If the show does go ahead without you, we'd all miss you terribly. I'd miss you terribly.'

Alice patted Millie's hand on the tabletop. 'I'd miss you too, Mil. But don't worry, we can still meet up. We'll always be friends.'

Millie glanced across at David, who was following their conversation but so far without contributing. 'I bet you'll be glad if Alice doesn't have to shoot off to Hollywood after all. Long-distance relationships are always difficult.'

Alice saw him nod slowly as he answered. 'I'd have gone with her, but if she decides not to go to Hollywood, it's her decision.' He didn't sound totally convinced.

'So you'd give up your job in the UK?'

'I'll be quite honest, Millie, I've been dreaming of Hollywood most of my life.' He sounded unexpectedly serious. 'I enjoy my job at the university but my first love is, and always has been, the stage and the screen. I'd love to direct a real movie.'

'So the idea of a move to Hollywood wouldn't scare you?' Millie shot Alice a sideways look. 'This means if

Conrad says Zoë's out of it, there's nothing to stop you signing up for the new show, Al. That's great news.'

'Let's not get ahead of ourselves, Millie. Wait and see what Conrad says.' Millie was right, however. This fairly unexpected decision by David would indeed simplify things – assuming the two of them were still a couple. Whether or not they were was what these next few weeks here in Tuscany, just the two of them together, were designed to resolve.

One way or another.

At ten o'clock Antonia and Zoë had offered to host a Q&A session, but when they assembled in the dining room – minus David and Carrie – it was to see no sign of Antonia and to hear from Zoë that not only had Conrad received Layla's email, but he had already read it and replied. Not without a great deal of satisfaction in her tone, Zoë read the answer aloud to them. It was not long and the gist of it was that the new series of *Pals Forever* would go ahead with Zoë at the helm, and if that didn't suit Layla, Benny or Alice, then that would be their own hard luck. As Zoë reached the end, Alice stood up.

'Thank you, Zoë. I see no point in staying on for your Q&A session, so I'm going for a walk.' She waved to the others and left, closely followed by Benny and Layla. Outside, on the terrace, the three of them paused for breath.

'I'm taking bets it doesn't last more than one season.' Benny was shaking his head sadly.

'I think that's a pretty safe bet, although I hope it does better, just for Millie's sake.' Alice glanced across at Layla. 'Any regrets, Layla?'

'Some… I've enjoyed these past few days, all of us together again, but I just can't stand that woman. Why on earth is Conrad being so hard-nosed and stubborn? Surely there must be other good directors out there who could step in and, that way, the cast would stay on board. It makes no sense.' She took a couple of deep breaths. 'Still, my agent tells me he's got me a leading role in a new romcom to be filmed in Scotland next winter. I'll try to call in and say hi, if you're still in the UK.'

'I hope so.' Alice had always liked Layla.

Alice went on to tell her and Benny about next week's interview for the auction house job, and they wished her well. Layla then announced that she was catching a flight home that same evening and Benny decided he would accompany her. As the two of them went off to pack, Alice went upstairs to look for David, but the room was empty. Typically, his phone was still on the bedside table, so she had no way of contacting him. Presumably, he had gone out for a walk, so she slipped on her trainers and went out to look for him. As there was no sign of him at the pool or in the gardens, she set off down the road to see if he had gone to the village for a coffee and a change of scene.

When she got to the bar, she found he wasn't there either, so she ordered an espresso and took a seat outside in the shade. When Rita brought her coffee, she had some promising news. She told Alice that she had been asking around for a rental property and she had found one. The builders had literally just finished modernising a little house in the village, and furniture was being moved in today or tomorrow.

'It's number 5, Vicolo del Centro, and it's just across the piazza from here. Why don't you go and take a look. The owner, Signor Innocenti, told me he'd be there most of the day today.'

Alice thanked her profusely and reached for her coffee. It was boiling hot so she had to wait, impatiently, for it to cool before heading over to Vicolo del Centro. While waiting, she suddenly discovered she had company. A cold, wet nose thudded against her thigh as Guinness the Labrador skidded to a halt beside her and did his best to climb onto her lap.

'Ciao, Guinness. How're you today?' As she did her best to dissuade him from climbing all over her, she looked up and saw his master coming across the piazza towards her. Trying to ignore the involuntary hiccup from her heart, she gave him a little wave. 'Hi, Matt.'

'Hi, Alice. I'm sorry about Guinness. He has absolutely no manners at all.'

She grinned at the dog who, having accepted that he wasn't going to be allowed onto her lap, was now sprawled at her feet, all four paws in the air, grunting happily as his wagging tail raised a little cloud of dust. 'He's fine. It's lovely to see him.' She decided she had better make it clear that she had better manners than the dog and added, 'And it's lovely to see you.'

He was wearing sunglasses so she couldn't see his eyes, but she distinctly saw a smile cross his face and linger for a moment. 'It's great to see you, too.' He hesitated for a few seconds before carrying on. 'And you're looking terrific. No wonder Guinness is in love with you.' As he spoke, it looked almost as though his cheeks flushed, but she barely caught a glimpse before he turned towards the cafe door. 'Can I get you anything?'

'I'm fine, thanks. Do come and join me if you have time.'

He disappeared inside, leaving her to reflect that she had just asked a strange man to sit down and chat to her while her long-term boyfriend was waiting for her back at the villa. Common sense kicked in. She picked up her espresso, managed to swallow it without burning her throat, and stood up, determined to get back to David as soon as possible. What had she been thinking?

She went inside to pay and found Matt about to come out of the door, holding a crate of mineral water in his arms. She stood aside to let him pass and, as he did so, he gave her a little smile.

'I'm afraid Guinness and I have to get back. Have a good day. Come on, Guinness, we're off.'

Alice wasn't sure whether to be relieved or disappointed.

When she arrived at the charming old red-brick cottage situated in a narrow side street just off the square, she found the front door wide open so she knocked and called out in her best Italian, 'Hello, anybody there?'

A few seconds later, an elderly man appeared at the door. '*Buongiorno, Signora.*'

She introduced herself. 'Good morning. Signor Innocenti? Rita at the bar sent me over. My name's Alice Butler.'

His face split into a smile. 'Of course. Rita told me you were interested in the house. You're the English lady, aren't you?'

He invited her in and showed her around. It was small, with just one good-sized room downstairs, a little kitchen area at the rear, and two bedrooms and a bathroom upstairs, but as far as Alice was concerned, it was more than enough for David and her for a few weeks' holiday. There were two women already in there, giving the place a good clean, although the little patch of garden at the rear was still piled high with builders' rubbish. Signor

Innocenti assured her that this would all be removed the next day, and the place would be furnished and ready for her to move in as early as Saturday if she was interested.

Alice was definitely interested. Signor Innocenti reeled off a list of furnishings, cutlery, linen and utensils that would be provided, and named a weekly rental figure that was remarkably reasonable. Alice hesitated for a moment, wishing she could run it by David first, but then decided to go for it and told Signor Innocenti she would take it for four weeks, right up to the end of the first week of August. She gave him a couple of hundred euros from her purse as a deposit, and he scrupulously wrote out a receipt and gave it to her. She told him she would get the rest of the money while she was in Florence in the afternoon.

As she walked back to the villa, she savoured the thought that she would be staying here in Tuscany, with ample time to do some exploring. The fact that she might meet Matt and his lovely dog again, she assured herself, was totally coincidental and she reminded herself that she intended to dedicate herself to David and the state of their relationship while they were here.

When she got back to the villa, there was still no sign of David so she went up to her room, contacted a car rental company in Florence and booked a little Fiat 500 for the month, arranging to pick it up from the town centre at the end of the afternoon. Then, as she had told Millie, she booked a double room for the following night at the expensive luxury hotel in the villa where the Mona Lisa had once lived. She felt pretty sure David would approve – not least as she was determined to pay as her treat.

Finally, she phoned her mum to give her the news that she was staying on in Italy for the month and to tell her there was a spare room if she wanted to come over. Since her dad had died, she had been keeping a close eye on her so she was delighted – and secretly quite relieved – when her mother turned down the offer, telling her that she had already arranged to go to Cornwall with a friend. Alice promised to take lots of photos to show her the following week, when she came over to London for the second interview at the auction house.

Well pleased with all the arrangements she had made, she went downstairs again. Out on the terrace she found Millie all alone, picking at a salad. As she spotted Alice, her face lit up.

'Al, you're still here. I was afraid you'd gone off as well. The others are all leaving this afternoon, but I'm staying until tomorrow.'

'Same as me. I was looking for David and I ended up down in the village. I don't suppose you've seen him, have you?'

Millie shook her head. 'No sign, I'm afraid. But I'm glad you're here for a bit longer.'

Alice went over to give her a reassuring kiss on the cheek. 'I wouldn't go off without saying goodbye to you, Mil.' She sat down, glanced around to see if the coast was still clear, and leant forward. 'So, how did the meeting go?'

Millie grimaced. 'Zoë had obviously been told to be on her best behaviour, so it went okay. With you out of the equation, they're now talking about making me and Richie hook up, while Harry gets to charm the pants off no fewer than two new girls.' She caught Alice's eye and nodded grimly. 'It looks like it's all going to get a bit more raunchy – although it'll still be for a general audience, so they can't make it too explicit.'

Alice did her best to sound supportive. 'So no full-frontal nudity?'

'No way, but I'm just a bit worried that the two new girls will be younger and better looking than me...'

'You'll be fine, Mil. You're a brilliant actor, and you're gorgeous and you know it.'

At that moment Harry and Richie came out and joined them. There was still no sign of Carrie or David, so Alice asked them.

'You guys haven't seen David, have you? We're renting a little house in the village and I wanted him to see it.'

'He might have gone to Siena with Carrie. She took a taxi and said she'd be back mid-afternoon.' Richie caught her eye. 'Didn't he tell you?'

'The idiot's left his phone in the room so he couldn't. Yes, I imagine that's what he's done. Anyway, I'll catch up with him this afternoon...' She stopped to correct herself. 'Or, rather, this evening, as I'm off to the Uffizi this afternoon.'

Harry grinned at her across the table. 'So, *Pals* without Polly... That's going to be interesting.'

She smiled back. 'It'll be fine, and I won't miss being Polly the flirt. All right, it was fun while it lasted but it's taken me five years to get out from under her shadow. I suppose it'll be a bit strange for you without Layla, but Millie tells me you're getting two new girls to keep you occupied.'

His grin widened. 'And Millie gets to fill your shoes – or rather, I should say your bed, alongside Richie.'

Alice wagged an admonitory finger across the table at Richie. 'Make sure you treat her well, Richie, or you'll have me to deal with.'

He looked back across at her with big hangdog eyes and she sighed inwardly. She knew she had to speak to him before leaving, to reinforce the message that he and she were history.

Chapter 11

The limo that collected Antonia and Alice to take them to Florence was driven by the same man who had met her at the airport. Although only four days earlier, so much seemed to have happened since then. Alice chatted to him in Italian, but she and Antonia, by tacit consent, made a point of not discussing the events of the past few days while they were in the car. He dropped them on the Lungarno and they strolled the short distance to the Uffizi through the crowded streets of the pedestrian zone that makes up almost all of Florence's *centro storico*.

Alice had spent quite a few weeks in Florence in the course of her studies and she loved the city. The last time she had been here had been out of season and she had avoided the worst of the crowds, but even on a busy July day like today, the mass of humanity in the streets couldn't conceal the sheer beauty of the place. As they crossed the Ponte Vecchio, they paused and looked down: even after yesterday's rain, the level of the sluggish brown water of the river was still low. It was hard to imagine how it had risen so drastically back in 1966 and had submerged the very heart of the city, destroying thousands of irreplaceable treasures. On a hot, dry day like today, it seemed impossible.

Alice's friend, Teresa, was waiting for them at a table outside a cafe in a little piazza just past the Uffizi Gallery, and Alice greeted her warmly. Teresa had been invaluable when Alice had been researching her doctoral thesis and it was wonderful to be able to give her the good news that she now had her PhD. Alice introduced Antonia and they chatted in English – which Teresa spoke fluently – for half an hour or so, before she led them over to the gallery, where they entered by a side door. Teresa excused herself, as she had an important meeting, and Alice took over guiding duties for Antonia.

Altogether they were in there for almost two hours and they still hadn't covered half of all there was to see. They did, at least, see the most famous artworks, like Botticelli's *Birth of Venus* and many more by a glittering pantheon of artists from Leonardo to Michelangelo, Bellini to Bronzino. Alice took particular pleasure in showing Antonia the real portrait of Eleanor of Toledo, telling her the story of the 'practical' test she had passed with flying colours at the auction house interview the previous week. By the time they emerged, they were both in a cultural and historical daze. Outside, in the late afternoon sunlight, Alice still felt as though she was in the Middle Ages – she almost expected to see the streets filled with gentlemen on horses and ladies wearing sweeping robes trimmed with intricate lace, instead of the innumerable tourists with their phones, taking selfie after selfie.

They went back to the same cafe and ordered long, cold drinks. Antonia stretched back in her seat and looked across at Alice, raising her glass in a little toast.

'Thank you, Alice, from the bottom of my heart. Having my own personal guide to such a treasure house of masterpieces has been amazing. I would never have known the history behind these wonderful paintings and I have you to thank for making me understand what's going on beneath the surface of the canvas, which is often almost as amazing as the artwork itself. I can understand now just why Renaissance art has got you under its spell. Compared to what we've just seen, a few romcoms seem so trivial somehow.' She clinked her glass against Alice's. 'I wish you all the very best with your future career and – if you want my opinion – although you've always been an outstanding actress, you've chosen such a worthwhile subject to devote your life to. I just know you've made the right decision.'

Alice took a refreshing mouthful. 'Thanks, Antonia, and I've enjoyed this afternoon every bit as much as you have. I'm sure you're right: my heart's firmly in the Renaissance and that's just the way it is.' In spite of her words, Alice couldn't help feeling a tiny little shiver of regret at her rejection of a Hollywood career. The thought of a second chance had been tempting for a while, but art history really was the sensible option – and wouldn't involve Zoë.

She went on to tell Antonia about the little house she had rented for the rest of July and her plan to take David to the Mona Lisa villa the next day. Antonia told her that she was leaving early next morning for a series of meetings in London, before flying back to the USA in a few days' time. Inevitably, the subject then came round to *Pals Forever* and she told Alice how sorry she was that Conrad had not decided to have a change of heart.

'It won't be the same without you and Layla.' Antonia shook her head ruefully. 'And I'm not sure they'll ever be able to find another writer with Benny's talent. It's such a shame.'

'Why doesn't Mr Chesterfield see that, Antonia? He's a clever man and a smart businessman. Surely he can see he stands to lose an awful lot. And all for the sake of – please excuse me – a cow like Zoë. Yes, she's a good director, probably a great director, but there have to be others.'

'I've been asking myself the same question for years, but it's inexplicable. He must have his reasons, but they're beyond me.'

After their drinks, they set off to pick up the rental car. On the way, Alice stopped at a bank and took out the money to pay Signor Innocenti the balance of the rent on the little house. The car rental office was in a narrow street near the station and from there, not without difficulty, Alice threaded the little Fiat through the heavy traffic until they were out of town and onto the *autostrada*, following the signs pointing south.

As they drove down to the Chianti turn-off, Antonia made a suggestion. 'How desperate are you to get back to the villa? I must admit I'm reluctant to sit down to a meal with Zoë tonight – and I daresay you feel the same way – so how about I buy you dinner to say thank you for today? I noticed a nice-looking little restaurant at the side of the road as we drove past Strada in Chianti. How does that sound? I can contact Paolo and tell him not to worry about preparing dinner for us tonight.'

Alice nodded approvingly. 'That sounds perfect, thank you. It's still early, so I'll be back at the villa in good time to see David and tell him about the little house I've rented. I'll text him to let him know, so he doesn't worry.' Although, it occurred to her, he hadn't taken the trouble to tell her about his excursion to Siena. Men!

The restaurant turned out to be fancy and expensive, but Antonia's gold card didn't bat an eyelid. They had an excellent meal although to Alice, after five years as a student, it was all a bit over the top. They opted for a self-indulgent starter of scallops served with Jerusalem artichokes and foie gras, which was exquisite. They decided not to have a pasta course after this and chose grilled venison with roast fennel as their main. For dessert they shared a chocolate soufflé with spicy chilli pepper ice cream which was... interesting. As she was driving, Alice only allowed herself one glass of a good Chianti Classico, but Antonia drank much of the rest of the bottle, and by the end of the meal she was looking and sounding very relaxed. So relaxed, in fact, that she took Alice into her confidence.

'There's something I want to tell you, Alice.' Antonia was suddenly sounding serious. 'Do you know what I did this lunchtime, before coming to Florence with you? I quit.'

Alice looked back at her in considerable surprise. 'You're leaving the company? But you've been there for ages, haven't you?'

Antonia nodded. 'Twenty-seven years, but I've had enough. I'm off – with immediate effect.'

'And what are you going to do?'

'That's what I'm going to be talking about in London this weekend. The time's come to think about working for myself, or at least in a company where I'm calling the shots. This whole Zoë business has brought home to me how powerless I really am here.'

Alice reached out and grasped her hand for a few seconds. 'Well, I think you're doing the right thing. Life's too short for accepting second best and for working alongside people like Zoë. I wish you the best of luck. Do, please, let me know how it all pans out.'

Antonia squeezed her fingers. 'Of course I will, and you must promise to do the same for me.'

When they got back to the villa, Antonia went up to bed, while Alice looked for David. Although she had sent him a text to let him know where she'd been, she had received no reply, and she was beginning to get a bit worried. Finding no trace of him downstairs, she went up to their room and it was then that it all suddenly became surreal.

There was no sign of David, and the first thing she noticed was that his bag and all his clothes had gone. The second thing she saw was a note lying on the bed.

> Dear Alice,
> Sorry to do this by letter, but maybe it's for the best. Now that I know you've decided not to take the job in Hollywood, I assume you'll be staying in the UK. The problem is that I've decided I want to go to Hollywood and I'm on my way there now.
> Layla's been giving me the names of some of her contacts in LA and I really think I might be able to find myself a job over there in the movie business, doing what I've always wanted to do. I've got almost two months' vacation, so I've decided to fly over and see what emerges.
> Not sure what this means as far as you and I are concerned. If I decide not to stay in the States, maybe we can pick up again from where we left off.
> Sorry again for making this so impersonal.
> Love,
> David.

Alice just stood and stared blankly at the sheet of paper in her hand. How on earth could he write her a message like this, effectively telling her he was dumping her in favour of some vague possibility of a job in the US, and still have the gall to insert the word *love* before his signature? And as for picking up again where they had left off! Suddenly, his detached air and his absences made sense. Presumably, when he had gone missing, he had been talking to Layla… or maybe doing more than talking? Yesterday afternoon he had claimed to have been stuck in the summer house because of the rain, but had he been alone? Might he and Layla have hooked up? And, of course, that would explain his unwillingness to take advantage of Alice's offer of a bit of physical comforting when he returned.

Whether anything had happened between Layla and him or not, one thing was now crystal clear – this letter had effectively answered the question she had been hoping to resolve over the coming weeks alone with him here in Tuscany. She felt an upsurge of anger, coupled with the bleak realisation that, after two years, it was all over between them. Her eyes started stinging, but she stubbornly refused to let the tears flow. She reminded herself that she had been having her doubts already before leaving Bristol. And, ever since setting eyes on Matt, the realisation had been taking shape in her head that what she had with David maybe wasn't the real thing after all. The letter proved that point beyond doubt.

At that moment her phone bleeped and she saw she had a message from none other than Layla.

> Hi Alice. I'm just getting on the flight to LA and I'm sure I saw your David in the queue. Does this mean you've changed your mind about Pals Forever? L xx

Alice stared blankly at the screen for a few moments. On the one hand, she was pleased and relieved that apparently there was nothing going on between David and Layla, but on the other it was final confirmation that he was doing what he had said in his letter. It wasn't a bluff or a cry for help. He really was going through with it. The lure of Hollywood had totally transformed him from the man she had thought she knew. She stood there for a good few minutes but then, as the initial shock diminished, she began to feel almost a sense of relief. She wasn't happy with the callous way he had done it, but his departure from her life was for the best, and it had been achieved without any long drawn-out arguments or unpleasantness.

Long-term, this actually made things much less complicated for her. She was now free to take a job anywhere she wanted, without having to worry about the impact it might have upon his life. And in the short term, David's departure didn't need to change anything either. She would leave here and go to the Mona Lisa hotel tomorrow night – on her own, but so what? – and she would move into the little house in the village on Saturday. She had her rental car and she was self-sufficient, so she could have a long, leisurely holiday in Tuscany on her own terms.

She reached for her phone and tapped out a reply to Layla.

> Hi Layla. No, it's just David. I'm staying here and I'm definitely out of Pals Forever. Have a good flight and hope to see you again before too long. Alice xx

After an hour or so, as it was still relatively early, Alice went downstairs and out onto the terrace for some fresh air and a drink. She helped herself to some of Conrad Chesterfield's champagne from an open bottle in an ice bucket and took a big mouthful, barely tasting it. There was nobody else out there so she took a seat, leant back and did her best to relax, watching the bats twisting and turning acrobatically in the purple of the evening sky. In the distance, she heard a dog bark and immediately thought of Guinness the Labrador – and his master. At least, she told herself, she could now think about Matt without feeling she was being unfaithful to David.

After a few moments she got up, walked to the end of the terrace and leant on the balustrade, looking out over the gardens and the vines towards the dark outline of the tower on the hill, silhouetted against the last remnants of the sunset. As she did so, a little light came on, right up near the top of the tower, and she imagined Matt sitting there, with his faithful hound at his feet, maybe with a drink in his hand just like her. Of course, she reminded herself, for all she knew there was every chance that beside his dog there would also be a wife or partner.

'Hi, Alice, how was your trip to Florence?'

She spun round to find Richie standing there. Without Carrie. She pasted on a smile.

'Oh hi, Richie – it was great, thanks. How about you guys? Everything settled for the new series now?'

'Sort of. It's all been handed over to the money men to fight it out, but it looks as though it's going ahead.' He moved a step closer to her. 'It won't be the same without you.'

'It'll work out. I'm sure it'll be a great hit.' She affected an air of confidence that she didn't really feel. 'You'll be picking up awards on stage at the Emmys next year, you'll see.'

'I wish… but it won't be with you.'

She took another mouthful of champagne and let it slip slowly down her throat. Now that David had removed himself from the scene, had the way she felt about Richie after five years of separation changed? It only took her a few short moments to realise that the answer was no. Whether the thoughts of Matt she could now admit to harbouring in the back of her mind contributed to the decision or not, she was able to reply to him with absolute assurance.

'No, it won't, Richie – and you and I won't be hooking up again. I've thought about it like I promised, but that's just the way it is. I want us to stay friends, but that's all.'

'Are you really sure?' He sounded deflated.

'I'm sure. Besides, you're on your way back to Hollywood and I'm staying in the UK. It would never work.'

Light spilled out onto the terrace behind him and Carrie appeared. Alice gave her a wave.

'Hi, Carrie, come and have a glass of champagne.' As she walked towards them, Alice lowered her voice and glanced across at him. 'Just let it go, Richie.'

Chapter 12

Alice didn't sleep well and she woke up feeling drained. Last night she hadn't mentioned David's departure to Richie or Carrie and she got the impression they were unaware he had left. She knew she wanted to talk to Millie about it, but first she wanted to get outside into the open air, so she decided to go for a final run. She pulled on her running gear and followed the same route out of the gate and up the road, but this time there was no sign of the Land Rover or of Matt and his lovely dog. Nursing a feeling of disappointment, although it was a lovely morning and the views over the Chianti hills were as delightful as ever, she returned to the villa, showered and went down to look for Millie. She found her having breakfast all alone out on the terrace. Antonia and the others were nowhere to be seen. Millie gave her a cheery wave as she spotted her and Alice did her best to respond in kind.

'Hi, Mil. All on your own?'

'Antonia left half an hour ago. I imagine you were out on your run. She told me to give you her love if I saw you.'

Alice didn't mention what Antonia had told her the previous night, as she had been asked to keep the news of her resignation to herself for now. 'She's a lovely lady. We

had a great time at the Uffizi and then a super meal.' Pleasantries over, she leant forward. 'Listen, Mil, something's
happened.' She went on to relate in detail everything
about David's departure and the note he had left on the
bed. To her amazement, Millie didn't look too surprised.

'How awful for you, Al, but I was wondering how
things were between you and David. Every time I looked
at him, I could see he couldn't keep his eyes off Layla. I'm
surprised you didn't notice. It was pretty clear to me he
was star-struck, maybe more.'

This made Alice pause and take stock. Now that Millie
had brought it to her attention, it seemed obvious. How
could she have been so blind? Clenching her fists under
the table, she returned her attention to her friend.

'Now that you mention it, I suppose I can see it…
but it's too late. Anyway, according to the text I got from
Layla last night, she's nothing to do with it. She sounded
surprised to see him on the plane and was more concerned
that this might mean I had had a change of heart about
the new show.'

'And have you?' Millie was looking hopeful.

'Nope. Zoë's in, so I'm out.' Paolo appeared and she
asked for a cappuccino, before returning to the matter in
hand. 'As far as David's concerned, like I told you back in
London, this holiday was supposed to be make or break
for us. When all's said and done, he's just accelerated the
process. I should be pleased.' She was glad to hear her
voice sounding resolute.

'So are you going to stay here in Tuscany for the rest
of the month, even though he's gone off?'

'Yes, definitely. I love the area and it'll be a good break.'

'Is that just because of all the art and stuff or is there another reason?' Millie gave Alice a little grin. 'Like another man, for example?'

'Why would there be another man?'

'Carrie was telling me about the guy you met yesterday. She said he was ever so good-looking and she thought you were into him.'

Alice flushed in spite of herself. 'She said what? All I did was pet his lovely Labrador and giggle at him after the dog jumped on him.'

Now it was Millie's turn to giggle. 'Yes, she told me where it landed on him. So, assuming the dog didn't do any irreparable damage to his bits, are you interested in the man?'

They had been close friends for ten years, so Alice told her the truth. 'In one word, yes – although I barely know him and he seems a bit distant. Somehow, he's made a really strong impression on me in such a short period of time. Because of David, I've been trying not to think about him too much. Now that I'm free, though, I'm pretty sure that nothing's going to happen. He's nice, he's friendly, but there doesn't seem to be any more to it as far as he's concerned. I presume he's got a wife or partner already and that's that.' She gave a little sigh. 'Shame, really.'

'I don't think I've ever seen you like this, Al. You've always been the sensible one and now you sound like a lovesick teenager.'

Alice nodded ruefully. 'Don't remind me. I need to try to get my head round it. Maybe it's just because he's one of the first men I've met who hasn't tried to hit on me, and that makes me want him more. God knows what's going on inside my brain. But, irrespective of all that, Chianti is as good a place to be as any. I love Tuscany and, with my rental car, I can get to Florence or Arezzo or Siena in less than an hour from here. In fact, if I feel like it, the coast's not that far either – and Rome's only three or four hours away, come to think of it. No, it's a good location.' She caught Millie's eye. 'Whether I meet up with him again or not.'

'Well, you're not the only one who's going to be around. Paolo told me that Conrad Chesterfield himself is coming over this weekend and staying all month for a holiday. Maybe you could slip up here and poison his food or something.'

An idea came to Alice. 'You don't suppose Zoë's staying on as well? Maybe the two of them are having an affair – that would explain why he lets her get her own way, after all.'

Millie wrinkled up her nose and lowered her voice, even though they were still alone outside. 'He could do better... Besides, if she were to stay on, she'd find herself here along with Conrad's wife, and at least one of his daughters and her family – Paolo told me they're all coming. No, Zoë says she's got business in London and she's on the same plane as me at two o'clock. In fact, we're sharing a limo to the airport in an hour or so.'

'Damn! Bang goes another great theory. I thought I was Hercule Poirot for a moment there.' Alice finished her coffee and stood up. 'Well, I'd better go and pack. Have a good flight back, Mil, and I'll be seeing you.'

'I'm going to miss you, Al.'

'And I'll miss you too, but I promise I'll see you again before too long. Good luck with everything.'

'And forget about David. He's not worth it.'

They hugged warmly and Alice went back to her room. As she had no special plans for the day, she decided to do her best to follow Millie's advice and forget about David by taking a little tour of the Chianti region in her car. Before leaving, she asked Paolo where he thought she should go and he suggested a number of places, including several vineyards that did tours and tastings, the fortified medieval church at Pieve di Spaltenna, and a nearby castle housing some murals by lesser-known Renaissance painters. She thanked him for the information and for looking after them all so well, and he looked pleased.

'It was good practice – you've maybe heard that Signor Chesterfield is coming tomorrow with his family. He's a demanding boss and it's been good to make sure we've got everything running smoothly for him.'

By now Alice had worked out that Paolo was effectively in charge of the household and she could imagine the responsibility he felt with the owner about to arrive.

'I'm sure he'll be delighted. We certainly all were.' She had a final thought. 'By the way, I've been meaning to ask: why's this place called villa of the wasps?'

He pointed across the hall to a little plaque on the wall that she hadn't noticed before. 'We think that might be the coat of arms of the original owners of this place, although it's all a bit of a mystery. This villa was built back in the early eighteenth century, but they say it's on far older foundations, maybe even medieval, and the shield might even date back seven, eight hundred years.'

Alice went over and studied the battered old shield more closely. It was predominantly deep red, with a diagonal blue stripe running across it. All the way up the stripe were little gold insects. They looked more like moths at first sight, but on closer examination she could see a sting in the tail. She glanced back at Paolo.

'I'm not sure I've even seen a single wasp since I got here. Bees, yes, but not wasps. I wonder how the villa got its name. And you don't know the family name either?'

He shook his head ruefully.

—

Alice had a most enjoyable day, and she was surprised to find herself feeling more cheerful as the hours went by and the shock of David's exit from her life began to fade. She drove around the region more or less at random, stopping here and there in charming little medieval hamlets and villages, relishing just wandering about, soaking up the atmosphere of antiquity that Tuscany evoked in her. She added another couple of sketches to her collection and looked forward to trying to transform them into oil paintings once she was back home again. Although she inevitably encountered cars, TV aerials, electricity pylons and other signs of the twenty-first century, the area was still remarkably untouched and steeped in history. She kept coming upon little chapels, wooded hillsides and medieval farmhouses that could have appeared in so many works of art by famous Tuscan artists from Duccio to Paolo Uccello. The fact that she was on her own didn't bother her – in fact, not having David getting bored alongside her was a bonus, or so she told herself. As for *Pals Forever*, although she couldn't say she had no regrets, she knew she was doing the right thing in refusing to work with the irascible director. She didn't need to do it, so why put herself through all that again?

She stopped for a focaccia sandwich at lunchtime in the stunning little town of Monteriggioni. Perched on a hilltop and surrounded by commanding stone walls punctuated by no fewer than fourteen towers, Monteriggioni was mentioned in Dante's *Divine Comedy* and was justly famous. Today it was absolutely packed with visitors and Alice only just managed to squeeze her little Fiat into the last available space in the car park. She entered the town through an arched gateway and found herself in the midst of a host of other tourists. Fortunately, most of them were sitting at tables by this time, eating and drinking, hugging the shade.

There were relatively few people inside the ancient Romanesque church of Santa Maria. Alice sat down in one of the pews for some minutes, savouring the welcome cool after the heat outside, and admired the simplicity of a construction that was now over eight hundred years old. As so often in places that had been in existence for so long, she felt an overwhelming sense of wonder at the thousands upon thousands of people who must have visited here, worshipped here, and been christened, married and, in many cases, buried here. It confirmed just how insignificant the superficial world of celebrity really was, and this just reinforced her conviction that her decision to say no to *Pals Forever* had been the right one. As for David, she was ever more certain that his sudden departure was a blessing in disguise, a lucky escape. The next chapter of her life was starting now, with no looking back.

She finally arrived at the Mona Lisa hotel towards the end of the afternoon, feeling hot and sticky, and the sight of the swimming pool had considerable appeal. In fact, the whole place was most appealing. It was set in magnificent gardens in a densely wooded valley, surrounded by lines of cypresses and, inevitably here in Chianti, row upon row of vines. It was a surprisingly small villa – by Tuscan standards – and her room was in the recently restored former outbuildings, but still very luxurious. It was light and airy, completely painted in white – even the massive beams and joists supporting the roof – while the floor was composed of terracotta tiles laid in a herringbone pattern. Her bed was enormous, but she knew she was only going to use a small portion of it. Interestingly, the sight of her bed took her mind to Matt, rather than David, and she couldn't help wondering – yet again – whether she would see him over the next few weeks.

As she had said to Millie, she was at a loss to explain how a man she barely knew had been able to affect her so deeply. Over the years of *Pals*, the script had decreed that a number of cast members, herself included, had been afflicted by sudden attacks of love at first sight. These had led to often hilarious situations which had all, without exception, ended in tears. Of course, *Pals* was fiction and this was real life but she couldn't help wondering whether her own inexplicable infatuation with this man would also end in crying.

The pool was an 'infinity pool', set into the sloping hillside with no raised lip on the far side, so she was able to float around like a seal, with just her chin above the water, and look straight out over the beautiful Tuscan countryside. Two massive old umbrella pines leant drunkenly over the water, providing welcome shade – although at the expense of shedding pine needles in the water. Having had a pool in her garden back in her Hollywood days, she wondered how often somebody had to come along here with a net to skim the surface. Still, on a boiling hot day like today, she was glad of the shade. As she floated lazily about, she wondered whether the Mona Lisa had really been painted here and if it really had been a portrait of a woman, rather than a convoluted self-portrait by a self-absorbed painter. Either way, it was exciting to imagine that maybe Leonardo da Vinci himself had once looked out over this exact same view. The thought was stimulating and helped to raise her spirits further.

Dinner was served on the terrace outside the old villa and, unlike the terrace at Villa delle Vespe, the view from here was downhill and across the valley, rather than up towards Matt's tower. The whole terrace was bordered by a dense bed of rosemary and the aroma was intoxicating. Along with the scent of the flowers came the inevitable background buzzing of the bees and she felt sure there would be honey on the breakfast table the next morning. Beyond the bushes were gnarled olive trees and then more vines, stretching away until they were replaced by dense woodland.

She ordered a glass of the villa's own Chianti Classico and took a sip, relaxing after what had been a fascinating day. That feeling didn't last long.

'Hi, Al. Millie told me you'd be here.' She looked up in surprise to find none other than Richie standing at her shoulder, a nervous grin on his face. 'Pleased to see me?'

For a moment she was genuinely speechless, but she managed to collect herself. 'Amazed is more like it. What on earth are you doing here, Richie? I thought you and Carrie were on your way back to the US.'

'She is. I'm not. Millie told me about David going off and leaving you, and I wanted to stay on and talk to you.'

'So Carrie's gone home on her own?'

'The fact is, Al, I've dumped Carrie. I wanted you to be the first to know.'

'You've done what?'

'We broke up… on the way to the airport, actually. I left her there and she should be on her way back to the States by now.'

'You did what? That's appalling, Richie. She seemed like a nice girl.'

'Yeah, she's nice, but she's not you. But don't worry about her, she's a big girl. She'll be okay. It's you I want, Al, honestly.' He was staring nervously out over the hillside, unwilling to meet her eye.

Alice just sat there in amazement. This certainly was a very different Richie from the one she had known five years ago. Yes he was looking good, yes he was communicating and interacting far more than before, and he no longer had bags under his eyes and a lingering aroma of cannabis about him, but that wasn't the main difference. Even at his lowest, he had never been unkind. The Richie she had known would never have dumped a girlfriend in such cavalier fashion. He really had changed, and she realised she didn't like this new version of her former boyfriend one bit. Suddenly, the little spark of attraction she had felt stirring inside her when she had first seen him again was completely extinguished – and that had nothing to do with any possible, if unlikely, future connection she might be able to forge with Matt. In consequence it was remarkably easy for her to make her position absolutely clear to him.

'You shouldn't have done that, Richie, and you certainly shouldn't have done it for my sake. Like I said before, it's all over between you and me, and I've moved on. You need to do the same.'

He looked back at her sharply. 'You've moved on? Does this mean there's somebody else?'

Alice was now faced with a dilemma. Her natural instinct was to tell the truth, but that would mean admitting that she no longer had a man in her life, which might just encourage him. Instead, she decided to ignore the question and spell it out to him as clearly as possible.

'Anything there was between you and me is long gone, and you've got to accept that there's no future for us together. Find yourself a new girl – there must be thousands of them out there just clamouring for you – and you'll be fine. Just forget about me, will you? At least, I hope we can stay friends, but that's as far as it goes. Okay?'

She deliberately didn't invite him to sit down and he stood there, looking blank, before finally accepting the inevitable.

'So what you're saying is that it's all over as far as you and I are concerned?' She nodded firmly and saw him take a deep breath. He held out his arms towards her. 'Okay. One last hug for old times' sake?'

She couldn't begrudge him that, so she rose to her feet and gave him a hug and a kiss on the cheek. She felt his arms tighten around her for a moment, but she gently disentangled herself and sat back down again. 'Are you staying here tonight?'

'I was going to but I wanted to talk to you first. If this is the way it is, I think I'm going to leave. There's an early flight out of Florence tomorrow morning, so I'll head for an airport hotel. Goodbye, Al.'

And he left.

She enjoyed an excellent meal, but if asked afterwards to describe what she had eaten, she would have struggled. It had been a stressful twenty-four hours and her head was full of conflicting thoughts. There was David, the man she had once thought she loved and who had behaved so shabbily, and then Richie – another man for whom she had once had strong feelings, but had now rejected. And of course she couldn't stop thinking about Matt, who was almost certainly unavailable. The overriding sensation running through her was one of annoyance. As Millie had said, she had always been the grounded, sensible one – and now? What on earth was going on? If any of the diners at the neighbouring tables heard her grumbling to herself, they were polite enough not to comment.

Back in her room, she sat on the bed and did something she hadn't done for quite a few years. She dug out her iPad and pulled up an old episode of *Pals* to watch. It was the one where she and Richie's character had first hooked up and fallen in love. Polly the flirt had been unusually serious in this one and she remembered how easy it had been for her to appear infatuated with Richie. Indeed, it had been during the filming of this episode that she had admitted to herself that she had feelings for him off-set as well as on it. She paused it on the scene of their first kiss and stared at the screen blankly for some minutes, thinking back over what had been and what might have been. In spite of the apparent love in their eyes, it had all ended badly – on-screen and off.

But then a funny thing happened. As she stared at the screen, Richie's face somehow morphed into Matt's and she found herself wondering how a relationship with him might end. Was the growing attraction she felt for the man in the tower destined to end in tears, just as her previous two relationships had done? In spite of the beautiful surroundings, her heart sank. She was still sitting there, deep in her thoughts, a few minutes later when the iPad, deciding she was no longer interested, switched itself off, and by that time there were tears at the corners of her eyes. It had been an eventful week and there was no way of knowing how the rest of her stay in Chianti was going to pan out. What would happen over the next four weeks?

Chapter 13

In spite of her swirling thoughts, Alice slept remarkably well and got up late next morning. After a swim in the pool and a sumptuous breakfast, she drove back to the village at noon and met Signor Innocenti at the little house. Everything looked clean and smart inside, and there was even a lovely bunch of freshly picked flowers in a vase on the fine old kitchen table. What looked like a brand-new sofa was positioned in the lounge area, as well as a big flat-screen television, but most of the rest of the furnishings were old and, in some cases, almost certainly antique. She smiled as she spotted a print of the Mona Lisa hanging on the wall. He proudly showed her the selection of utensils in the kitchen cabinets and opened the fridge to display a bottle of what looked like Prosecco as a welcome present.

Upstairs, she was delighted to see a fine old wooden bedstead in the larger of the two bedrooms and a brand-new bed in the other room, both fully made up. The bathroom was spotless and, all in all, the place was perfect. She thanked him warmly and he left her with some helpful advice.

'My phone number's on the fridge door – do, please, call if you run into any problems. As some things are brand new, there are bound to be a few surprises. As far as food is concerned, there are lots of shops in Greve, which is only ten minutes by car, and the bakery here in the village sells a bit of everything, so you shouldn't starve. If you feel like treating yourself, Giovanni's restaurant in the village serves remarkably good food. Don't be put off by the appearance of the outside. It's a good place.' He explained where the shop and the restaurant were and left her to it.

Alice checked the time on her watch: it was almost a quarter past twelve and she knew that shops here in Italy often closed at twelve thirty, so she hurried off to buy some supplies. The bakery stocked a limited selection of essentials, mainly consisting of canned vegetables, tuna and other long conservation products, so she resolved to do a run into Greve in Chianti later on that afternoon to stock up. While she was in the shop, she bought a freshly baked big round loaf of the traditional Tuscan bread she had come to love. The beauty of this product, apart from the taste, was that she knew from experience it would last for as long as a week and, seeing as she was now on her own, she would need that long to get through it. She also bought a slice of pizza for lunch and, on an impulse, she added a delightful-looking little strawberry tart. After all the trauma of the past few days she thought she deserved a treat.

Back at the house, she opened the bottle of wine from the fridge, discovering that it wasn't Prosecco after all. It was a local sparkling wine from just a few kilometres up the road and, ice-cold from the fridge, it was very drinkable indeed. After pouring herself a glass, she took the slice of pizza and went out into the back garden. All the builder's rubbish had been cleared away and a wooden bench positioned in the shade of the branches poking over the wall from the neighbour's walnut tree made an excellent place to sit and have her lunch. Apart from the twittering of little birds high above her, it was quiet and peaceful there, and she settled down contentedly, letting her mind roam.

Settling into the little house had cheered her and she was determined to enjoy her holiday. She would be here for almost four weeks and, with David out of the equation, she could go wherever she liked. The only constraint on her was the interview at the auction house in a few days' time. She had booked a flight from Florence, going out early next Thursday morning and coming back on Friday afternoon. That way she would be able to spend the night with her mum, whose holiday in Cornwall would be starting the next day. If the auction house offered her the job, she imagined she would be free to continue her holiday here until that started, presumably in early or mid-August. Of course, if they didn't offer her the job, she would need to dedicate time over the next few weeks to trawling the internet for suitable alternative positions. So far none of her other applications had produced positive responses. Still, she told herself, it was mid-summer and no doubt lots of decision makers were on holiday. Besides, she had the safety net of enough in her savings account to keep her afloat for a good long while, until she managed to find a position that really appealed.

On a personal level, things were no clearer. If she managed to meet up with Matt once more and things developed between them – if he was unattached – she would no doubt want to stay around here. Of course, if she never saw him again or if he proved to be in a relationship already – or just not interested – then she could go anywhere. Those, she realised, were a hell of a lot of ifs. With a certain degree of surprise, it occurred to her that this was virtually the first time in her adult life when she found herself without any pressing commitments. She was free to do whatever she wanted. There was just one downside – she would be doing it on her own. For now, that wasn't a problem, but maybe four weeks might be pushing it. Time would tell.

She spent the afternoon unpacking, reading and checking the internet for possible places to visit, before driving into Greve in Chianti to stock up on food, washing powder, and some wine and water. It was a pleasant little town with a variety of shops and restaurants, and a beautiful triangular central piazza, and she resolved to come back to do a bit of exploring soon. It was as she was walking around the perimeter of the piazza, hugging the shade, that she had an unexpected encounter. She heard footsteps behind her and felt a light tap on her shoulder.

'Alice – it is you, isn't it? Even from the back I recognised you.'

She wheeled round to find herself looking straight into a pair of familiar light-blue eyes and her spirits soared.

'Hi, Matt, fancy seeing you here.' She glanced around. 'No Guinness?'

'No, I left him at home. A lot of the shops don't allow dogs and he isn't used to being tied up. The last time I left him outside a shop he howled the place down.' He looked pleased to see her. 'Are you shopping?'

'That's right. I've rented a little place for a month.' She thought she saw a spark of interest on his face as he heard the news. 'I need to stock up on supplies – including wine.'

'Well, you've come to the right place for that.' He glanced at his watch. 'Got time for a coffee?'

'Yes, of course, although I think I'll just have something cold. It's absolutely boiling today.'

He led her across to a cafe with tables outside on the square, sheltered from the afternoon sun by the buildings ringing the piazza. He ordered a *caffè freddo* for himself and insisted on treating her to one of the establishment's home-made ice creams. On his advice, she went for strawberry and *meringato*, which was a heavenly mix of creamy vanilla and chunks of meringue. With it, she asked for a glass of sparkling mineral water and sipped it as they chatted. She was dying to ask him about his situation and whether there might be a special someone waiting for him back at the tower, but she curbed her impatience and they talked about generalities. It was just lovely to be with him. For his part, he also refrained from asking anything personal, so by the time she had finished her ice cream, she had learnt that she always had to make sure she chose the Chianti with the little black cockerel on the label, which showed it was the good stuff from around here, and that in Greve there was no shortage of good wine on sale... but nothing that related to him. It was informative, but hardly intimate.

As they talked, she studied him surreptitiously and her eyes were drawn to the third finger of his left hand, where she saw no ring. Of course, this didn't prove anything these days, but it was maybe a step in the right direction. And the direction in which she wished to travel – she now allowed herself to admit without a sense of guilt – was towards him. The attraction she had been feeling for him was continuing to grow and she knew she wanted to get closer. For his part, he was definitely looking and sounding more interested in her, and that initial awkwardness she had sensed was no longer evident.

As he told her about the best places to buy wild boar pâté, fresh vegetables and the tastiest cantuccini biscuits, she just soaked up his presence and liked what she found. He was intelligent, attentive and good-looking – and, wonder of wonders, he genuinely appeared not to know who she was. She felt a thrill at the thought that, just for once, she had met a man who was interested in Alice, rather than Polly.

All too soon, he looked at his watch again and stood up. 'I'm sorry I have to dash, but I've got a load of things to do and I'm very conscious that Guinness might be chewing his way through my furniture while I'm away.' He gave her a little grin that warmed her heart. 'He doesn't like being left alone.'

'Who does?' Although hadn't she just decided that she was perfectly happy to stay here on her own for a whole month? To her surprise, she saw the grin disappear from his face.

'Sometimes being on your own can be good.'

He didn't elaborate and just shook her hand rather formally. Before she could say any more, he waved goodbye and headed off across the square. She sat there and sipped the last of her water, full of mixed emotions. On the one hand, she was delighted to have run into him, and to have found him receptive and interested, but the fact remained that she knew no more about him now than she had done before. It was as if he was steering clear of any kind of intimacy. He hadn't asked where she was going to be living or arranged to see her again. It had been a pleasant interlude, but the net result was the status quo. The only plus point was that it sounded as though there wasn't a special someone back at the tower waiting for him – otherwise why worry about the dog eating the furniture? It wasn't much, but it was a glimmer of light.

She followed his advice and bought two bottles of Chianti Classico and a couple of bottles of white wine from a store dedicated to locally produced wines. By the time she had filled her bag with other supplies, she had a hard time staggering back to the car with all her shopping. Back home, she unloaded the food into the fridge and decided to go for a walk, rather than a run, as the temperature was very high. Because she was already familiar with it – or so she told herself – she retraced her steps up the hill, past the entrance to the villa of the wasps and onwards up the road. When she got to the track leading off to the left towards the old tower, she had no hesitation in heading in that direction, but there was no sign of man nor dog. She paused by the gate and even toyed for a moment with the idea of pressing the bell, before telling herself that would just be far too needy. Instead, she returned home feeling frustrated, but also annoyed with herself for the way this Matt thing was starting to obsess her.

Over the next couple of days, she repeated the process, but each time without success. In fact, she didn't see a single person or vehicle as she walked, or ran, up and down the road each morning. It became a recurring disappointment and she couldn't help feeling almost abandoned. After seeing Matt in Greve, she had been hoping to bump into him again as soon as possible, but he had disappeared and she almost wondered if this was on purpose. She did her best to ignore him but found it impossible. Her brain stubbornly refused to give her peace.

Each time she passed the entrance to the villa of the wasps, she wondered if Conrad Chesterfield had arrived and, if so, in what sort of mood? Hopefully she wouldn't run into him, seeing as she had turned down his job offer. She dropped into the cafe every morning around nine o'clock for a cappuccino and chatted to Rita behind the bar, who was quickly becoming a good friend. Needless to say, the Englishman living in the tower came up in conversation, but Rita confirmed that he hadn't been in for a few days. Helpfully, she suggested he might have gone away on holiday. The irony was not lost on Alice that she might have chosen to take her holiday here at the exact same time as he and his canine companion had decided to go off somewhere else. She managed to choke off a snort, but it was one of annoyance at herself for what was becoming a fixation.

Determined to try to put the Matt thing behind her, she set off on a series of visits to places of interest in the area and it was while she was in the ancient little church of San Leolino – with its delightful cloister, just outside the charming hilltop town of Panzano – that she made a discovery. After admiring the stunning glazed terracotta works by Giovanni della Robbia and a magnificent fourteenth-century triptych above the altar, she went out into the tiny cloister and came upon a carved stone slab on the ground with a familiar crest on it. Although worn smooth by the passage of thousands upon thousands of feet over many centuries, there could be no mistake – it was the same coat of arms with the wasps that she had seen on the wall of Conrad Chesterfield's villa. Unfortunately, the name on the stone was now illegible and the date in Latin numerals equally indecipherable. Could it be that this slab commemorated or even housed the tomb of one of the forebears of the person responsible for building the villa? She took a number of photos and resolved to research it further.

One evening she decided to try the restaurant in the village that Signor Innocenti had mentioned. As he had warned, the exterior didn't look promising. It was in a side street off the square – barely a three-minute walk from her home – and the building looked extremely old, maybe even medieval. It was pretty clear that nothing much had been done to the façade over the intervening centuries since its construction, and it looked a bit down-at-heel, with lizards living in cracks in the wall and what looked like a remarkably healthy sapling growing out of the roof. However, once inside the door, she realised that her landlord had been dead right. The dining room was clean, bright and unexpectedly smart. Rather like her own little house, the restaurant had a garden at the rear, but this one was considerably larger than her little patch of dry grass and weeds, and it was full of tables where people were having dinner.

She received a cordial welcome from the middle-aged man behind the bar – quite probably Giovanni himself – and a waitress showed her to a small table in the corner of the garden, from where she could sit back and observe the other diners. At this time of the evening the whole area was already in the shade and the temperature outside was perfect. As she sipped a glass of the same excellent sparkling wine that Signor Innocenti had given her, she checked out the occupants of the other tables. As her eyes roamed around, they encountered another pair of eyes trained upon her. These belonged to a young red-haired woman who gave her a quizzical – but not unfriendly – look, followed by a hint of a smile, and then turned her attention to the menu.

Alice was familiar with the scenario, although she had got out of the habit of being recognised – it was just about the first time since arriving in Chianti that she had encountered somebody who presumably thought she had spotted Polly the flirt. At least, she told herself, it was a woman, rather than a man, so she was unlikely to be pestered. The woman was sitting at a large table set for eight people, opposite a man in a pink shirt, who had his back to Alice. Evidently, the rest of the party still had to arrive.

The waitress brought the menu, written on a blackboard that she held up, so that Alice could decide what to have. There was a lot of choice, but she finally ordered mixed bruschetta as a starter and then her favourite, *fritto misto*, as a main course. This delightful mix of lightly fried prawns, octopus, squid and whitebait was a dish Alice often chose when she was in Italy. Whether it was thanks to the oil in which they were fried, the amazingly light batter coating them or just the excellence of the raw materials, it had been delicious each time and it had become her go-to choice.

She was sitting back, looking forward to a good meal, when the rest of the party on the big table in the middle arrived and her evening suddenly took a most unexpected turn.

Hearing the voices of the new arrivals, she glanced up and did a double-take as her heart sank. Leading the group was none other than Conrad Chesterfield, her erstwhile boss, the man whose offer of employment she had just refused. With his sleek black hair and upright stance, he looked ten years younger than the sixty-year-old she knew him to be. At his shoulder was his stunningly attractive wife, Amber, along with a younger couple and their two little children. They hugged the red-haired woman and her partner, and they all sat down. As they did so, the waitress arrived with Alice's starter and by the time she had moved away, Conrad Chesterfield's group were all chatting animatedly – and Alice was relieved to see that he and his wife were sitting with their backs to her. She did her best to make herself inconspicuous, resolving to make this the fastest meal in the history of eating so she could get the hell out of there just as soon as she could.

Her plan failed.

The red-haired woman who had recognised her earlier was leaning towards Conrad Chesterfield, talking into his ear. Seconds later, just as Alice took a big mouthful of Tuscan bread, topped with sumptuous tomatoes and dowsed in olive oil, her former boss swivelled round and looked across at her. Recognition dawned on his face and she gave him a nervous little wave, doing her best to chew and swallow as fast as she could. To her relief, he smiled and rose to his feet.

He came striding across, hand outstretched, and she jumped up to meet him, hastily wiping the olive oil off her lips and fingers. 'Alice, great to see you again.'

'Mr Chesterfield, good evening. Paolo told me you were coming over.' She would dearly have liked to grab her glass of wine and drain it in one, but she resisted the temptation, deciding the best thing to do would be to clear the air as far as *Pals* was concerned, but he got there first.

'Call me Conrad, please. We're on holiday. Sorry you aren't going to join us for the new show. Quite understand.' His words were as staccato as ever. 'You've chosen a different career path. Congratulations are in order, right, *Doctor* Butler?'

Alice was impressed. It came as no surprise to find he was well-informed. 'Thank you... Conrad. Yes, I'm sorry not to be part of *Pals Forever*, but I've got an interview in a few days' time for a job in the art history field, my speciality.' She glanced across towards their table. 'But please don't let me drag you away from your family. I've rented a little house in the village for the rest of the month, so maybe we'll meet up again some time.'

'Excellent. Come up to the villa some time. Meet the family properly. My two daughters are over there. I'll give you a call. Well, enjoy your meal, Alice. Good to see you.'

As she sat back down again, she reflected that he had been unexpectedly nice but, then, she had always got on pretty well with him, right up until the last few months five years ago, when it had all turned sour. It was with a considerable sigh of relief that she reached for her glass and took a big mouthful before returning to her bruschetta.

Chapter 14

She was woken at three o'clock in the morning by her phone. She opened her eyes and reached for it, wondering if it might be David, as she relished the prospect of giving him a piece of her mind. To her extreme annoyance, it was Richie. She dismissed the call, gave an infuriated sigh and lay back down again. She was just drifting off to sleep five minutes later when the phone bleeped and she saw that it was a text message from him. She was about to delete it and turn off the phone when a couple of words attracted her attention: *so stupid*. Propping herself on her elbow, she read it through. It was short and far from sweet.

> Hi Al, I've been so stupid. Carrie got her revenge for being dumped and it affects us all – and the studio. Check out this link. The story's all over the internet and it'll be in the papers tomorrow. I'm really, really sorry. R.

She clicked on the link and felt a wave of anger wash over her. This website – just about the most popular Hollywood insiders' website – was full of talk of *Pals Forever*, and on the very first page there was a photo of Layla and Alice, both wearing bikinis, lying on sunbeds by the pool at the villa. Carrie must have taken the shot one day the previous week. The caption underneath read: *Layla and*

Alice say no to new show, in spite of looking hotter than ever.
Alice nearly threw the phone across the room in fury, but
she controlled herself and read through to the end.

There was no getting away from it: Carrie had done a
thorough job of spilling the beans. She had even managed
to take a most unflattering photo of Richie with a glass of
wine at his lips, no doubt intended to give the impression
he had a drink problem. That didn't bother Alice in the
slightest – in fact, if it had been a photo of him lying
in a cowpat, she wouldn't have minded. How could he
have been so stupid as to bring a woman he had, by his
own admission, only known for a matter of a few weeks
to a sensitive meeting like this and then, to compound
his stupidity, dump her so callously? She even wondered
whether this article might have been Carrie's plan all
along. Maybe, rather than working in public relations, she
was in fact a journalist who had cynically used Richie for
her own ends. Wherever the true blame lay, the result was
infuriating.

Alice lay back in the darkness and seethed. There was
no doubt Carrie had got her revenge and, after the way
Richie had treated her, Alice couldn't blame her for that
although she resented the way she and Layla had been
dragged into it. She wondered what Conrad Chesterfield
would say when he saw the article – and he would, holiday
or no holiday. As far as she knew, no press release had
yet been circulated to announce the cast or to give any
advance information about the premise of the new show.
Of course, there was the chance Conrad might look upon
it as 'there's no such thing as bad publicity', but he might
take the opposite view and go ballistic. Alice consoled
herself with the thought that at least she was now out

of all the dog-fighting, and this finally allowed her to get back to sleep.

When she got up, she turned on the TV as she made herself a cup of tea and almost choked on it as that same photo of her and Layla, both wearing very little, appeared on the screen. If even Italian television had picked up the story, then there could be no doubt that it had gone viral. She watched as their 'Hollywood correspondent' went on to repeat almost word for word what Alice had read in the middle of the night and, needless to say, a series of photos flashed up on the screen of her wearing her revealing 'Polly' outfits. The cat was well and truly out of the bag and now, after five years of trying to lay Polly the flirt to rest, here she was again.

Alice was furious.

Still seething, she set off up the hill at a fast pace, muttering dire imprecations under her breath as she went along. By the time she got to the gates of the villa, she was sweating profusely and when she reached the top, she was gasping. She stopped for a rest in the shade of an umbrella pine and leant forward, her hands on her thighs, sucking in lungful after lungful of air, as sweat dripped down her nose and onto the bone-dry pine needles at her feet. Such was her state of physical and mental turmoil, she didn't hear the approaching footsteps until they were upon her and she received a hefty push on the bottom, almost knocking her over. She straightened up, fists clenched, and swung round, ready to defend herself, but then the culprit gave a happy whine and launched himself at her a second time, standing up on his hind legs and scrabbling at her waist with his big front paws. Unclenching her fists, she caught the dog's big head in her hands and ruffled his ears.

'Guinness, how good to see you.' And it was. And even better was the sight of his master only a few yards away, hurrying towards them. As Matt approached, he called out to the dog.

'Guinness, get off! No jumping up. We've been through this time and time again.' As Guinness gave no sign of obeying, Matt addressed her directly, 'Hi again, Alice. I'm sorry about Guinness. He's clearly very pleased to see you. Just push him away.'

She gave him a big smile in return and was delighted to see an answering smile from him. He was wearing shorts and a T-shirt, and he looked fit and extremely appealing. 'Good morning, Matt, it's good to see you and Guinness.' She almost told him she'd been looking for him at the cafe the past few mornings but managed to stop herself in time. That would have made it sound as if she were stalking him. 'And I don't mind him jumping all over me in the slightest.' And, she found herself thinking, if his master felt like doing the same, she wasn't going to object. But he clearly didn't. He just stood there for a few moments and she could see that he was trying to think of something to say. When he finally found his voice again, it was hardly romantic.

'You look absolutely boiling.'

Alice followed the direction of his gaze and saw that her light-grey top was now mostly dark grey and sweaty – and plastered tightly across her chest. As a look, it was revealing rather than stylish, and his eyes remained trained on her body for some seconds before he raised them again.

'Did you sprint up here?'

Doing her best to sound unflustered, even though the feel of his eyes on her had given her goose pimples, she nodded. 'A bit too fast, really. I was feeling annoyed and that made me overdo it.'

'That happens to me all the time. I even outrun Guinness on occasions when I'm really angry. Can I ask what you have to be annoyed about?'

His tone was quite innocent, so maybe he hadn't seen the news yet or maybe he still didn't recognise her. Certainly, with sweat pouring down her cheeks, her face the colour of the tomatoes on last night's bruschetta and wearing her soggy running kit, she was a world away from those photos of her by the pool in her bikini or Polly the flirt in her provocative tops. She decided not to enlighten him as to her identity or the source of her annoyance.

'Oh, just stuff. A friend did something really stupid.'

'I bet it was a man. We do stupid stuff.' He hesitated for a moment or two. 'It's really good to see you again. I've been away for a couple of days and I was hoping to bump into you when I got back.'

'It's good to see you, too. Now that I'm a resident of the village for a few weeks, hopefully we can meet up again. I'd like that.'

A smile appeared on his face. 'I'd like that, too. Maybe tomorrow?'

Alice shook her head with real regret. 'Not tomorrow or the next day, I'm afraid.' She saw his face fall and felt a little tremor of satisfaction. It really looked as though he'd miss seeing her. 'I have to go back to the UK for an interview tomorrow and then I'm staying with my mum for the night. I'll be back late on Friday, so hopefully I'll see you at the weekend? The little house I've rented is just a short way from the piazza. Rita at the bar knows where it is.'

'Fantastic, I look forward to it.' He glanced at his watch. 'Anyway, Guinness and I need to get back. Virgilio's coming over and we've got a busy day ahead.'

'Virgilio?'

'My next-door neighbour – you met him last week. He's spent his whole life as a farmer here and he's my agricultural guru. What he doesn't know about vines and olive trees isn't worth knowing. He lives on the farm just beyond my property and he's been a mine of information.'

'Well, don't let me hold you up. Hope to see you at the weekend.'

'Absolutely. Guinness, come on, we're off.'

He turned away, and the Labrador dropped back down onto four paws and followed him, leaving Alice almost regretting having the interview tomorrow. Matt had definitely sounded interested, and judging by the way he had been eyeing her, maybe there really was a spark there. As she set off back down the hill again, this time at a much more moderate pace, she knew she was very much looking forward to seeing him again.

Back at the house, she showered and changed, and settled down to check her emails and messages. Unsurprisingly, after Carrie's bombshell, there were a lot of them. One was even from her mum, asking if she had seen the news. Alice replied, trying to make light of it and telling her that she was looking forward to seeing her the following day. The others were from a variety of people – among them, a long grovelling one from Richie, addressed to her and all the others who had been at the villa last week. She nodded to herself as she read how Carrie had been so furious at his treatment of her that she had taken her story and her photos to a friend in the media. Alice didn't reply. Somehow she felt sure even Benny would have been impressed at her choice of vocabulary if she had done. Instead, she deleted the email and did her best to put that imbecile Richie out of her mind.

There was also a message from Antonia that made interesting reading. Although it was brief and she didn't go into detail, she confirmed that the outcome of her meetings in London over the past few days was that she and two other partners were setting up a brand-new production company. There was a throwaway line towards the end indicating that they might even have a job for Alice in the future. Although all Alice's efforts were concentrated on tomorrow's interview in London, it was reassuring to know that she might still have a second chance to get back into TV, if she ever changed her mind or if the auction house job didn't work out.

Chapter 15

Alice got up early next morning and drove to Florence airport, leaving her car in the parking lot. The flight was uneventful and the temperature in London about ten degrees cooler than in Tuscany. She was at the auction house in good time for her two o'clock appointment, feeling a bit nervous but hoping for the best.

It soon transpired that her hopes were misplaced.

She was shown into the office of the stern-looking lady from the original interview panel, who was sitting at her desk with Tobias double-barrelled standing at her shoulder and looking chronically embarrassed. His female colleague had no such qualms. She reached into a drawer, produced a copy of one of this morning's gaudier tabloids and pushed it across the desk towards Alice.

'Your fame precedes you, Dr Butler.' Her voice was sour, but with just a hint of barely concealed gloating in the background. 'I'm sorry to bring you all the way from Italy for this, but it only came to our attention this morning and, of course, it was too late to contact you. I'm instructed to thank you for your interest in our firm but to tell you that we have offered the position to another candidate.' She tapped the newspaper with a chubby finger. 'I'm afraid this is not the sort of image we wish to portray here.'

Her finger had landed on that same damn photo taken by Carrie – alongside it, in case the reader didn't immediately recognise the British star of *Pals*, the newspaper had put together a little collage of thumbnails of Alice back in her Polly days. Needless to say, the photos they had chosen were mostly those in which she was wearing scanty outfits. Alice looked up again and was about to launch into a spirited defence of herself, but the expression on the woman's face said it all. She wasn't getting the job and that was that. She met the woman's gaze and nodded a couple of times.

'I understand. I think you're making a big mistake, but I thank you and your colleagues for your time. Goodbye.' She turned on her heel and marched towards the door. Tobias double-barrelled hurried around to open it for her and he followed her out. Closing the door behind him, he gave her a sympathetic look.

'I'm very sorry, Dr Butler. Believe me, I tried to fight your corner, but it was a lost cause, I'm afraid. It was two against one and I lost.' As they walked back along the corridor to the stairs, he lowered his voice. 'Between you and me, we all know you were the better candidate for the position. I'm sorry.' He looked so miserable, Alice almost gave him a hug. Instead, she held out her hand and did her best to rise above it.

'Thank you, Tobias, that's kind.'

They shook hands and she left.

At her mother's house in Crouch End she drank a lot of tea and received a lot of sympathy. As the afternoon progressed, Alice gradually recovered and managed to stop imagining ways of murdering both Carrie and Richie – preferably slowly and painfully. The one good thing about this disclosure was that she had barely had time to think about David and his betrayal, and she was genuinely able to tell her mother that she was glad their relationship was over. Interestingly, her mother revealed that she had never liked him much anyway.

A bottle of Chianti Classico, bought that morning at Florence airport, further helped to restore Alice's equilibrium, and she started telling her mother about the house she had rented, the village, the local restaurant and the beauty of the surrounding countryside. As the bottle emptied, she eventually found herself talking about Matt and his dog, and she spotted considerable interest on her mum's face.

'So, are you telling me he lives alone in an old tower with just a dog for company? What's wrong with the man?' Her mother's brow furrowed. 'You don't think he's some sort of crazy person, do you?'

'He's no crazier than I am.' Alice omitted to mention that she had just spent several hours in the afternoon dreaming up ways of wreaking mortal revenge on Richie and Carrie. 'I honestly have no idea whether he lives alone or not. For all I know he might be married with six kids, but somehow I don't think so.'

'And is he renting the tower or does he own it?'

'According to Paolo, the guy who looks after the villa, he owns it.'

'And would I be right in thinking that medieval towers in Tuscany don't come cheap?' Alice nodded. 'So where did he get all his money from?'

'I've only just met the guy, Mum. I can hardly start asking that sort of thing. Maybe he won the lottery or something. Maybe his parents were loaded. I don't know.'

'So, what are you planning on doing about him?'

'Well, I'm hoping to see him again, obviously. After that, we'll just have to wait and see if anything develops.'

'And you really don't think he knows who you are?'

'I honestly don't. Of course, it's possible that by the time I get back he may have seen my photo in the news but, as of yesterday, no, I don't think he has any idea.' She looked over at her mum and grinned. 'If I'm honest, I suppose that's also part of his attraction. For years now I've been fighting to get people to see beyond Polly and her low-cut tops. At least if he does like me, it's got to be for the real me, not a fictitious TV character.'

She flew back to Florence on Friday afternoon and picked up her car at the airport. She had arranged to meet Teresa from the Uffizi Gallery for a drink before driving back home and she was lucky enough to find a parking spot in the centre of town, not far from the station. She walked into the *centro storico* via the San Lorenzo market, pushing her way through the crowds, her bag firmly clutched in both hands. As ever, the shops and stalls lining the streets sold all manner of things, especially souvenirs and items for tourists, ranging from T-shirts to umbrellas – not that umbrellas were likely to be wanted in today's baking heat.

She stopped at one stall and bought her mum a new purse, and then found a lovely old-style hardware shop and bought a good corkscrew to replace the one in her little house, which looked as though it was not long for this life. She also bought a little packet of wedge-shaped corks so she could seal wine bottles after opening them, thus avoiding waste or being forced to drink a whole bottle in one go. As she had discovered to her cost after opening

Signor Innocenti's bottle of sparkling wine, there was no way that sort of cork would go back in again once it had come out and expanded.

Well pleased with her purchases, she headed for her meeting with Teresa. As she passed a little shop dedicated to pet supplies, something caught her eye. It was a smart-looking red dog collar with the words *dog* and *cane* embossed on it in a never-ending loop. On an impulse, she stopped to ask the man if it would fit a Labrador and when he confirmed this, she bought one for Guinness. This, she told herself, would show Matt that she had been thinking about him – or his dog, at least.

She met up with Teresa in the same cafe as before, and they sat in the shade for a drink and a chat. Since she was driving, Alice opted for an ice-cold mineral water, while Teresa ordered a glass of Prosecco. It was a lovely way to end the day and they chatted about all sorts of things. Needless to say, they also discussed Renaissance art, and this reinforced Alice's sense of disappointment and frustration that Carrie's revenge photos had robbed her of the chance to begin her career with the auction house. When she told Teresa the sad tale of how her hopes of that job had been torpedoed, she read sympathy on her friend's face.

'That's their loss, Alice. Try not to let it bother you.'

After an hour or so, Teresa had to go. 'My husband and I are invited out for dinner tonight, so I need to get off. Maybe we could meet up with you one evening and I can get to know your other half?'

Alice shook her head. 'I'd love to meet your husband, but there's no other half now, as of a few days ago.' She shook her head in response to Teresa's interrogative look. 'It's a long story. The more I think about it, though, the more I realise that it isn't tragic. I'm definitely better off without him. So it's just me – at least for now.'

'And nobody waiting in the wings? I always imagined you'd be fighting the men off. I was watching a repeat episode of *Pals Across the Pond* the other night and you looked so great. You still do.'

Alice acknowledged the compliment but added a qualification. 'Thanks, that's really good to hear, but don't forget that the girl you were watching was Polly. I loved her at the time, and I have a lot to thank her for, but she still keeps on bobbing up now and then. I've been trying to separate myself from her for years, but her spectre comes back and bites me on the bum from time to time – like yesterday in London, for instance. No, I'm happily on my own for now.'

Was that really true?

Chapter 16

As she set off on her morning run the next day, she had to smile at herself. There was no doubt she had spent almost as long getting ready for a half-hour run as for a night out. She was wearing a freshly washed top and a new pair of shorts bought specially in Florence the previous day, and she had even spent a ridiculously long time plaiting her hair. She hoped her efforts would not be wasted but, as it turned out, she could have saved herself the trouble. Although she took her time jogging up the road past the entrance to the villa and back again, there was no sign of Matt or Guinness the dog. By the time she got home and stood under the shower, she was feeling disappointed – and just a bit silly.

Determined to give it one more try, at nine o'clock she went out to the cafe to see Rita and have a cappuccino and one of her gorgeous doughnuts. It was as she was sitting outside, enjoying the relative cool of the morning, that a familiar vehicle pulled up on the far side of the little piazza. Seconds later, a big black arrow came flying across the square and did his best to climb onto her lap.

'Ciao, Guinness.' He appeared delighted to see her, and he redoubled his efforts to reach up and kiss her. A few seconds later his master appeared but, alas, didn't try to emulate his dog. He stopped by her table and looked down with a little smile on his face that immediately resulted in a big grin appearing on hers.

'Hi, Alice. Have you been for a run this morning? Guinness and I went for a twenty-kilometre hike yesterday and I'm feeling lazy today.'

'Hi, Matt. Guinness, get off, you weigh a ton.' With the bribe of a little piece of doughnut, she persuaded the dog to settle on the ground at her feet. 'Yes, I needed a run after two days in London.'

'How did the interview go?' So he had been listening. 'Was it for a job?'

'Yes, but I didn't get it.' She had no intention of going into detail about why it had gone wrong.

'Shame. Still, I'm sure there'll be others. Can I get you anything? I'm getting myself a coffee.'

'No, I've got all I need, thanks – besides, I owe you a drink. Come and join me.'

He glanced down at his dog who was now stretched out on his back at Alice's feet, four paws waving in the air, grunting happily to himself. 'It looks like Guinness has already settled in. I'll just get a coffee and be right back.'

He returned seconds later with a little espresso in his hands and took a seat on the other side of the table. 'So, can I ask what sort of job you're looking for?'

'Art history. It was in an auction house in London.' She went on to tell him about her studies and he looked impressed.

'So it's *Doctor* Alice I'm talking to. Good for you. But you don't look like any art historian I've ever seen.'

'Too young?' She rather hoped this might elicit some sort of compliment from him, which would at least signify that he had noted her appearance, but she was to be disappointed.

'I don't know… maybe if you had glasses – on a chain hanging round your neck. A cardigan would probably help as well.' She was delighted to see him grinning and maybe sounding a little bit cheeky.

'I must remember to add a cardie to my wardrobe.' She did her best to put him on the spot in return. 'And what about you, Matt – what do you do, apart from going for long walks with your lovely dog and pottering about in the garden?'

'That's about it, really.' She hoped he'd say more but she waited in vain for almost a minute, before deciding to give it one more try.

'And when you aren't walking and gardening?'

'It's quite a bit more than a garden, really. I mend a few fences, chop down a few trees, and look after my vineyard and my olive trees.'

'That sounds a bit technical. Do you have an agricultural background?'

He laughed. 'Very much the opposite. I'm a city boy, born and bred. All I know about farming comes from the internet and from Virgilio. With his help I've taught myself to prune the vines and the olive trees, and so far the results are looking pretty reasonable.' He swallowed the last of his espresso and stood up. 'And now I'd better get back to my vines.'

It was pretty clear he didn't want to talk about what he did, but it would have been nice to sit and chat a bit longer. A feeling of disappointment came back again, but she suddenly remembered the dog's collar.

'By the way, I was in Florence yesterday and I picked up something for Guinness. If you can wait two minutes, I can pop back and collect it for you.'

'That was kind of you. Where is it – back at your place?'

'Yes, it's just a few doors along that road over there, beyond your car. I'm here until the beginning of August.'

'In that case Guinness and I will come over with you.' Seeing her heading for the café door he added, 'And don't worry about my coffee. I've already paid for it. Don't worry, I promise you can buy me a coffee next time.'

'Next time' sounded good to Alice and she gave him a smile before ducking her head through the doorway and waving goodbye to Rita, catching a distinct twinkle in the old lady's eye as she saw the two of them set off together. Alice resolved to break the news to her the following morning that it wasn't necessarily what it looked like. They walked back across the piazza, with Guinness trotting alongside his master without the need for a lead. When they reached her road, she pointed along to number 5.

'It's the one with the green door. Do you want to come in or will you wait here?'

'We don't want to disturb you. Guinness and I can wait here.'

Alice nodded and set off for her house to get the collar. However, Guinness clearly hadn't understood the plan, as he came running along after her and, as she opened the door, he slipped inside. Alice looked on indulgently as his Labrador appetite for food led him unerringly to the fridge, where he wedged his nose against the crack of the door and wagged his tail hopefully.

'Sorry, Alice, he's always been a nosy dog – especially if there's food involved.'

Alice looked round to see Matt at the front door and felt a naughty shiver of lust at the thought of inviting him into her house. No sooner did the thought occur than the realisation dawned that a large black Labrador would be on hand to observe any developments. A sudden vision of the dog, head tilted to one side as she and Matt collapsed into each other's arms, banished the shiver of lust and replaced it with a grin. 'Come in, by all means. Guinness doesn't stand on ceremony and that's just fine.'

She hurried upstairs to her bedroom, where she had left the collar, but neither the dog nor his owner followed her – which was probably for the best. She picked up the little brown paper bag and took it back downstairs.

'Here, Matt. I hope you like it. Seeing as you're English and we're in Italy...'

He opened it and a genuine smile appeared on his face. 'That's so kind, but you shouldn't have. I'm sure my *cane* will love it.' She saw him glance around the room. 'This place is really nice, and it's a damn sight tidier than mine.'

Alice saw the opportunity to do a bit of digging. 'Haven't you got somebody to do the housework?' His answer wasn't what she wanted to hear.

'No, there's just us. There's no need.'

Us – plural, so there was somebody else living there with him after all. Although she had feared this might be the case, she had been hoping against hope and now felt a wave of disappointment. She was debating whether she could ask for more information, without sounding too intrusive, when he saved her the trouble. His smile broadened as he reached down to ruffle the dog's ears.

'Living alone with a dog makes life dead easy. Guinness doesn't mind if I don't do the housework, and a bit of clutter around the place doesn't bother me.'

Alice had to fight the temptation to sigh with relief. So he did live alone, which presumably indicated there was no wife or partner lurking in the background after all. She felt a surge of excitement. 'I was telling my mum about you yesterday and she asked if you were a crazy man living all alone with just a dog.' She realised her mistake too late. Why on earth had she told him she had spoken to her mum about him? Talk about needy...

'I don't know about crazy, but I don't mind being alone.' His tone became more sombre, as he repeated the remark that had surprised her the other day at the cafe in Greve. 'Compared to some people I've come across over the past few years, my own company is far preferable. Besides, you're never alone with a dog.'

'I can imagine. He's a great dog.' She caught his eye for a moment. 'To be honest, I find I'm quite happy being on my own as well.'

'You're really all on your own? That surprises me.' Was this just a throwaway remark or might it be a sign of interest?

She decided to keep it light and avoid mention of David. 'I would think it's par for the course for an art historian – with or without a cardigan.'

'If you say so.' He headed for the door. 'Thank you for the collar. Guinness will be wearing it next time we meet. See you, Alice, and thanks again.'

He gave a low whistle, and he and his dog were off.

Later that morning she got an email that took her by surprise. It was from Claudio.

She had met Claudio three years earlier, when she had spent the month of July in Italy researching her doctoral thesis. He was a lecturer in medieval history at La Sapienza in Rome – one of the oldest universities in the world – and she had been out to dinner with him a few times before her return to England. They had corresponded sporadically over the following few months – mainly about academic matters – but then contact had ceased. He was a nice guy and, as he was an expert on the Renaissance, he had helped her considerably. In his email he told her he was spending the hot summer months of July and August in the relative cool of the high southern Tuscan hills near Monte Amiata. He had just seen her photos in the news and wondered if she was still in Tuscany, in which case he suggested meeting up.

Alice hesitated before answering. On the one hand, it would be good to see him again – to have a bit of company and to be able to talk shop for a day – but she had got the impression three years ago that his interest in her had been more than just academic and she didn't see him that way. Yes, he was intelligent, yes he was a fairly good-looking guy, but there was just no spark there as far as she was concerned, and she wouldn't want to build up his expectations only to dash them. Even if so many of the men around her seemed incapable of behaving properly, that was no reason why she should follow suit. Still, lunch with him sounded safe enough and a bit of company would be rather nice, so she replied, telling him she was near Greve in Chianti and asking where he would like to meet up.

She spent the rest of the day in the ancient city of Arezzo that perched on a steep hillside and boasted a wealth of historic buildings. It took less than an hour to get there by car and she had a most enjoyable afternoon walking around the *centro storico*. Her first stop was the cathedral, whose fairly plain outside belied the treasures within, and she stayed there for quite some time. After all, it wasn't every day she was able to study works by greats such as Donatello close up and personal. From there she moved on to the much smaller, but even older, Basilica of San Francesco, where the stunning array of frescoes by Piero della Francesca almost took her breath away.

Finally, outside in the cloying heat once more, she headed for the quaint sloping Piazza Grande, took a seat at a table under the arches, and ordered a lemon sorbet and a glass of mineral water. From there she had a spectacular view out over the brick-paved square, framed by a stunning array of thirteenth-century buildings that were bristling with arches and crenellations and full of unmistakable Tuscan character. Although crawling with tourists, it was still mightily impressive. In particular, she was fascinated to see the colourful shields of the city's former rulers mounted on the walls all around the piazza, painted with the coats of arms of local families. She studied them intently but, alas, could see no trace of any wasps.

When she got home again, she was feeling quite hungry, as she had skipped lunch, so she decided to treat herself to dinner at Giovanni's restaurant. As she was walking across the piazza on her way there, her phone bleeped and she saw that it was a message from Claudio. He was offering to drive over to see her. When she got to the restaurant, she checked whether they were open at lunchtimes and sent him a message telling him any day was good for her and suggesting they meet here at the restaurant at noon on the day of his choice. That way he wouldn't actually be coming into her house and this would help to keep things a bit less intimate, just in case he was still keen on her.

That evening, to her relief, there was no sign of Conrad Chesterfield or his family in the restaurant and she enjoyed a fine dinner of grilled trout accompanied by a wonderful mixed salad. At the end of the meal, even though she had had a sorbet in Arezzo, she allowed herself a silky-smooth panna cotta, topped with fresh strawberries and blueberries. By the time she walked back home across the square, she was feeling happy and relaxed. Matt was beginning to thaw and David and Richie were gradually receding into distant memories, and she felt an increasing sense of calm. As she watched the antics of the bats wheeling around the orange streetlights, she reflected yet again that her decision not to head back to Hollywood had probably been the right one. Why trade this sort of peace and quiet for the bright lights? It didn't get much better than this.

Or rather, the only way it could get better than this would be if a certain someone were to show a bit more interest. And whether that would happen or not was still anybody's guess.

Chapter 17

She met Claudio a few days later. He was already waiting outside the restaurant when she got there and he beamed as he caught sight of her.

'Ciao, Alice. It's great to see you again.'

She went up to him and kissed him on the cheeks, then stepped back and studied him more closely. He now had a close-cropped beard and different glasses, but he still looked very much the same as the last time she had seen him three years earlier.

'Ciao, Claudio. It was lovely to hear from you. Thanks for coming to see me.'

They went into Giovanni's restaurant and sat down outside, in the garden. It was another hot day, but the sky was overcast and she wondered if bad weather might be on the way. Not that she could complain – she had only had a couple of wet days in over two weeks. They chatted about her life and his and he congratulated her warmly on getting her doctorate before giving her his big news.

'I'm getting married in September.'

Alice looked up with interest. 'Congratulations. And who's the lucky girl?'

He went on to tell her all about his bride-to-be and Alice told him how happy she was for him – not least as this now removed any fear that he might have been harbouring amorous intentions. As a result, it was a lovely relaxing lunch and at the end of it she invited him back to her house for coffee and a chat. They sat on the bench in the garden and spent a happy hour or more talking about medieval history, and she mentioned the enigma of the shield with the wasps on it. To her delight, she spotted a flicker of recognition on his face.

'On a diagonal stripe, you say?'

'Yes, on a field of deep red. The wasps are a gold colour and the stripe blue.'

'Give me a moment.' Claudio pulled out his phone and busied himself for a few moments before giving a grunt of satisfaction and passing it across to her. 'Look familiar?'

It certainly did. There could be no doubt about it – the red background, the stripe, the insects – yes, this was the same one. She nodded emphatically.

'That's it, I'm sure.'

'I thought it sounded familiar.' Claudio took the phone back from her and explained. 'I knew I'd seen it before. It belonged to the Vespucci family. The wasps are a play on the word *vespa*, wasp in English. Does the name Amerigo Vespucci ring a bell?'

Alice's eyes opened wide and she nodded. 'The man who gave his name to America?' She hesitated. 'I never did know whether he discovered it or whether that was down to Christopher Columbus.'

Claudio laughed. 'Academics have been arguing about that for hundreds of years – or at least the naming part of it. Forgetting for a moment that it's pretty certain the Vikings, cod fishermen from Europe and maybe even the Chinese got there first, it's generally accepted that Columbus discovered what he thought was the Spice Islands in 1492, even though what he had in fact found was the Bahamas. Subsequently, he made it as far as Cuba, but he only actually reached mainland America in 1498 – and that was Venezuela. Although there's a public holiday in his name in the USA, the fact is that Columbus never set foot in North America.'

'And Amerigo Vespucci?'

'There's just as much myth and mystery surrounding him. He was born in Florence, and went off to work in Portugal and then Spain as an explorer and cartographer. Nobody knows for sure how many times he went to the Americas, or if he ever reached North America, although that looks highly unlikely. But he was the first to speculate that what had been discovered might be a whole new continent. His maps were used by a German cartographer called Martin Waldseemüller, who published his definitive world map in 1507 and was the first person to coin the name America. He did this out of respect for Amerigo Vespucci, and it stuck.'

'And do you think Vespucci might have lived in the Chianti region?'

Claudio shook his head. 'I doubt it. I'd have to check, but I'm almost certain he spent most of his life in Spain and he died there. Maybe some descendant adopted the coat of arms and settled in Chianti some years later. If I find anything else, I'll be in touch.'

Alice beamed at him. Her academic interest had been tickled by this mystery and she decided to do her best to discover the truth of it. It occurred to her that Conrad Chesterfield, as an American, would no doubt be fascinated if it emerged that his Tuscan villa had such a connection with the origins of his home country.

It was a lovely afternoon and she enjoyed Claudio's company and had a great time talking about her chosen subject. When the time came for him to leave, she accompanied him up the road to the piazza where he had left his car, gave him a warm hug and kissed him on the cheeks, wishing him well for the future.

There was just one problem.

As she stood there, watching him drive off, she happened to glance back in the opposite direction and saw the unmistakable shape of an old Land Rover pull out of a parking space outside the bar and disappear around the corner. Although it was a hundred yards away, she got the distinct impression that the driver's eyes met hers for a second before hastily looking away. She stood there blankly, wondering if Matt had seen her kissing Claudio – albeit chastely on the cheeks – and whether he had jumped to any conclusions. The rational part of her brain told her it didn't matter anyway, but the less rational side was immediately seized with frustration that she might, unwittingly, have convinced him that she had found another man. She shook her head in annoyance.

That evening there was another storm, complete with spectacular flashes of lightning and deafening claps of thunder, and she sat in her lounge, reading the book that Millie had left her – the misogynistic *The Playboy and His Women*. She couldn't avoid the uncomfortable parallels she found herself drawing between the behaviour of the selfish hero, Justin – with his cynical and predatory attitude towards women – and so many of the men she had met in her life, starting with David and Richie, not to mention Harry. Grudgingly, she had to admit that the book was well-written and, while the subject might be unpalatable, it was a fair reflection of much of her experience so far. But now, she told herself with a flash of self-awareness, was she maybe behaving just like that towards Matt? She knew she had been obsessing about him, just like the character in the book, so might this just be lust? Was the fact that she felt her heart flutter every time she saw him just a hormonal reaction or could there be more to it than that?

The question continued to occupy her mind on and off all night. The noise of the storm kept waking her up and, whenever she did, she was almost immediately assailed by these same thoughts. Finally, somewhere around the middle of the night, the storm stopped as suddenly as it had started and she fell asleep, not waking until almost nine o'clock.

She rolled out of bed and glanced out of the window. Puddles filled the back garden, and she could hear the persistent sound of water dripping from the eaves and the gutters, which had overflowed. The patch of sky directly above her, however, was now cloudless and bright blue once more. It felt blissfully cool in comparison to previous days, so she went downstairs, made herself a cup of tea and set off on her morning run before the temperature climbed once again.

As she crossed the piazza, she looked over towards the bar but saw no sign of Matt and his dog, so she headed up past the villa, constantly having to swerve from side to side to avoid the streams of water running down the road after last night's downpour. It was a sparkling clear day after the rain and she relished the relatively fresh air at this time of the morning. It felt good to be alive. The only downside was the fact that she saw no trace of Matt or Guinness on her way up and, even though she jogged along the gravel track at the top as far as the gates to the tower, it was without success. She wondered whether he had been put off by the scene involving her and Claudio or if, quite simply, he had just not felt like coming out.

But then, as she was almost back home again, just where the road entered the village, she heard a vehicle behind her and turned to see the Land Rover coming towards her, with man and dog in it. Her heart gave that same flutter of attraction, lust or whatever it was, as he came to a halt alongside her.

'Good morning, Matt. I'm a bit later than usual today. Hi, there, Guinness.'

The jubilant Labrador, proudly sporting his new collar, stood with his front paws on the top of the door to say hello, while his master looked up at her.

'Couldn't sleep because of the thunder?'

'Pretty much.' She didn't tell him about the thoughts of him that had been plaguing her. 'But it's cleared the air wonderfully.' *That's the way, girl*, she told herself, *talk about the weather. That's what we English do, after all.*

'All I can say is I'm glad I had a lightning conductor installed. The tower's pretty exposed up there. Feel like a coffee? Guinness and I would enjoy your company.'

The idea of a coffee with Matt did sound good, although dripping with sweat wasn't necessarily the look she would have chosen. Then a sudden thought struck her and she shook her head, patting her thighs to highlight the lack of pockets in her running shorts. All she had was a tiny pouch with just room for her house key.

'I can't, I'm afraid. I've come out without any money.'

'Leave that to me. A cappuccino and a doughnut, isn't it?'

'Well, thank you yet again, that would be lovely, but I can't let you keep on paying.'

'Don't worry about it.'

She jogged along after his car and by the time she got to the bar, Matt was already sitting outside at a table, while

Rita bustled about with a cloth, wiping everything dry. Guinness made a terrific fuss of Alice and then stretched out happily underneath the table. She knew there was something she had to do so, as soon as Rita had brought them their coffees and a doughnut for her, she launched into it.

'I think I saw you yesterday afternoon. Sorry I didn't have a chance to chat, but I had a visit from a good friend from Rome. He's a lecturer in medieval history and he was very helpful to me when I was researching my thesis.' Was that an expression of relief on his face? Surely not?

'He must like you a lot to drive all the way from Rome to see you.' That definitely sounded like fishing.

'He's on holiday in Tuscany and he came to tell me he's engaged to be married in September. We had lunch together and then talked history all afternoon.' Confident she had got the message across, she reached for the doughnut. As she did so, a black nose materialised at her side and rested on her thigh, while a pair of mournful brown eyes stared longingly up at her – or more precisely, the doughnut. 'Is it all right if I give Guinness a bit of doughnut?'

'By all means. He gets loads of exercise, so he'll just run it off.'

Matt leant back, and Alice sensed he was relaxing more and more in her company. They chatted for half an hour but he still didn't talk about himself much, except to tell her that he had a 'little place' in London, but that the tower was now his permanent home. He made no mention of a job, but it was clear he must have a regular income from somewhere. She wondered where his money came from but didn't think it appropriate to press him on it.

After a bit, she decided he had relaxed sufficiently for her to do a little digging. 'So why come to Tuscany, Matt?'

'I needed a bit of peace and quiet, and I was getting fed up with London.'

'But you could have gone anywhere, surely?'

'Yes, but my mother's Italian and, seeing as I spoke the language reasonably well, Italy seemed like a logical choice. I'd been to Tuscany before and loved it. As a place to escape to, this region seemed an ideal choice.'

'Why buy yourself a tower? Isn't that a bit extreme in terms of getting away from it all?'

He smiled gently. 'I'd been going through a funny time in my life – it's complicated but I was feeling a bit stressed, a bit harassed, so I suppose the idea of a fortress was just what I needed at the time. Like I said, it was a sort of escape for me.'

'And are you still feeling stressed?' She glanced across but saw little of the rather careworn expression on his face that she had noted before. 'Is something still bothering you?'

'It's far better now. Without going into detail, I'd been getting a lot of grief on social media and I needed to get away. I've hardly used the computer for anything more than emails for years now and I feel a hell of a lot better as a result.'

'When you say "grief", what sort of grief?'

'Everything from ridicule to death threats.' He caught her eye and nodded. 'I know, it's unbelievable the stuff people are prepared to say from behind the anonymity of their computer screens.'

Alice knew only too well just what he meant. Although she had never had death threats, she had regularly received the most barbed insults and even threats of sexual violence, which had led her to do the same and drop out of all social media. She toyed with the idea of telling him, but decided that, as it really did appear he had no idea who she was, she would leave it like that. At least that way she would know that any reaction from him would be towards her as a real person, not to Polly the flirt. She wondered what he had done to attract all this negative attention but, as he seemed unwilling to go into any detail, she decided to relegate that line of enquiry to a later date. The main thing, for now, was that he had started talking.

Attempting to steer the conversation to different territory, she told him what Claudio had said about the possible Amerigo Vespucci connection and was surprised to find that this struck an immediate chord. He picked up his teaspoon, turned it over and used the narrow end to trace the shape of a shield onto a paper napkin. As he drew it, she saw immediately that it was the same design, with the stripe and the wasps, as the coat of arms at the villa.

'Wow, that's it!'

'You sure this is the shield you saw?'

'Absolutely.' She felt a thrill of genuine excitement run through her. 'Where have you seen that?'

'It's etched into a slab set in the wall on the ground floor as you come into the tower.' He looked up at her and she could see excitement in his eyes now. 'Do you think it might have belonged to Vespucci?'

'Well, it's the same shield they found at the villa, so it would make sense, seeing as they're side by side and the villa is supposedly built on medieval foundations. I wonder... I don't suppose I could take a closer look at it by any chance?'

She saw him hesitate again and she waited with bated breath. Finally, he nodded.

'Of course, any time you like. This evening, if it suits you? Why not come along at six and I'll give you the tour? But, be warned, the place is in a terrible mess and there are a lot of steps.'

Chapter 18

Alice spent a lot of the day researching Amerigo Vespucci but was only able to find sketchy traces of his family after his death in Spain in 1512. She did, however, read all about his career and the controversy surrounding just how many times he actually travelled to the New World and how his name became associated with the continent. She gradually put together a brief paper, outlining the facts and pointing to the possible significance of the presence of the coat of arms in Panzano, as well as the villa. This, she felt sure, would be of interest to Conrad Chesterfield. She hadn't heard from him since their brief encounter at Giovanni's restaurant and she seriously doubted whether he would contact her. She decided that she would drop the paper into his letterbox as a little parting gift before heading home at the beginning of August, and leave it at that.

She drove up to the tower at six o'clock and took with her a bottle of the local sparkling wine to which Signor Innocenti had introduced her. She had debated what to wear and had decided not to go overboard, so she had chosen the same simple summer dress she had worn for lunch with Claudio. This wasn't the time to pull out her designer frocks. Even so, by the time she finally decided she was presentable, she calculated she had been in the bathroom for even longer than the fairly lengthy make-up sessions she had had to go through before the shooting of every episode of *Pals*. In spite of this, she kept checking her appearance in the rear-view mirror all the way up to the tower and almost ran into a ditch as a result. For what was, in all likelihood, just going to be a short viewing of a historical artefact, she was far more nervous than at almost any time she had been in front of the cameras.

When she reached the gates, she pressed the bell and after a brief delay they opened automatically. As the car crunched up the gravel drive to the tower, a familiar black shape emerged from the trees and came running alongside, barking excitedly. She pulled up and opened the door, her nerves slightly reassured by the presence of the dog. As soon as Guinness realised it was his new best friend in the driving seat, he nearly jumped on top of her. She scratched his ears and persuaded him to let her climb out, but then he immediately goosed her with his cold wet nose – the dress was maybe a tad short – making her jump and blush with embarrassment. She was just smoothing her dress and endeavouring to calm herself down when she heard Matt's voice.

'Good evening, Alice. You look... a bit different from this morning.' This sounded complimentary but she wasn't going to get too excited yet. She just kept it light, hoping her cheeks weren't glowing too brightly as a result of the Labrador's friendly assault.

'I thought it was time to make a change from the sweaty, unkempt look.' He was wearing jeans and a light blue polo shirt, and he looked good. 'No shorts tonight?'

'Seeing as you're the first female visitor to the tower since my mother at Easter, I thought I should make an effort. Come on in.'

Alice handed him the bottle of wine and digested this snippet of information, as they walked up half a dozen stone steps to the entrance. This was an imposing arched wooden door almost six feet wide, studded with ancient square-headed nails. On either side of the doorway were narrow arrow slits, while the real windows didn't begin until further up the building. The massive stones used in its construction looked as if they had always been there, and Alice got a real shiver of history as he pushed the door open and ushered her into a dark hallway.

'The coat of arms is over here.'

He flicked a light switch and led her across to a stone slab, sculpted in the shape of a shield, set in the wall directly opposite the door, alongside a steep stone stairway. Any visitor to the tower would have been unable to miss this very obvious sign of ownership. She checked it out and confirmed that it was identical to the two other shields she had seen. It was unmistakably the Vespucci coat of arms. She pulled out her phone.

'Would you mind if I took a photo or two?'

'Of course. Go ahead.' She noticed that he retreated several paces, so as to be well out of shot.

Once she was satisfied with the pictures she had taken, he ushered her towards the stone stairway with a word of warning. 'It's a long way to the top, but the view's worth it, I promise. But with all the running you do, you'll probably get there faster than me. Just be careful where you put your feet. Some of the steps are odd heights. Why they couldn't make them all the same, I really don't know.'

'Ah, but I do – or at least I think I do.' Alice rolled out a snippet of historical information she had picked up in the course of her studies. 'I remember reading that medieval castle builders sometimes deliberately did that so that attacking soldiers trying to charge up the stairs would end up flat on their faces.' She gave him a little grin. 'Mind you, that might just be a useful excuse for some pretty shoddy building work.'

She was very conscious that she was wearing a fairly short skirt and he was walking behind her, and this realisation did little to calm her nerves. The first to get to the top was the dog, who scampered effortlessly up the tortuous stone staircase. As they climbed, it got lighter and lighter in there as the window openings set in the substantial walls grew wider. They finally arrived at the top floor, where wide arched windows flooded evening sunlight into the room. Unlike the other floors, where she had seen doorways – presumably leading to bedrooms and so on – this huge area was wide open and it was an unexpectedly large space, occupying the whole width of the tower. There was a lounge area, a dining area and a state-of-the-art kitchen over on the far side. It was a stunning room, and she stood and admired her surroundings for some time before speaking.

'Matt, this place is awesome. Really, it's amazing and you're so very, very lucky to be able to live here.'

He nodded. 'I know. All right, there are times when the stairs are a pain – my mum and dad complained like hell – but I mainly bought it for this room. I spend most of my time up here and I just love it. Here, seeing as we're climbing, let's go the whole hog and I'll show you the roof.'

Over to one side of the room was a much narrower staircase – also made of stone – that climbed steeply and disappeared into the ceiling high above. At the top was a low doorway. He pushed the hefty door open and they walked out into the evening light. The sun was still above the horizon but was already flushing the western sky a delicate shade of pink. Alice stood stock-still and breathed deeply. It was stunning. The whole of the Chianti region was laid out before her, forming a charming tapestry of little villages, vineyards, olive groves, farmhouses and villas – including the villa of the wasps directly below them.

'What do you think?' She heard his voice at her shoulder.

What she thought was that this had to be one of the most romantic views on the face of the earth. She felt a warm, happy glow spread through her, as she let her eyes roam across it. Finally, she glanced towards him.

'I'm speechless, Matt. It's absolutely stunning. Thank you so much for letting me experience it.'

'I'm glad you like it as much as I do. Now, what can I get you to drink?'

'Anything cold. You choose.'

'I'm afraid I won't have any of my own wine until next year, but I have got some of Virgilio's cold rosé in the fridge. I like it a lot. Unless you prefer me to open that bottle you so kindly brought, maybe you might like to try some rosé?'

'Some rosé sounds perfect, thanks.'

They returned to the big living room and she sat down on one of a pair of smart modern sofas. The dog positioned himself on a rug at her feet and when Matt returned with the wine, he sat down opposite her, at least two or three metres away. Well, she told herself, he certainly couldn't be accused of crowding her.

The wine was indeed good and they settled down to chat. Very gradually, she managed to get him to talk more about himself, but she couldn't get a clue as to why he had been suffering so much abuse on social media. Whenever the subject moved in that direction, he skilfully steered it away again and she took the hint. She did, however, make one interesting discovery, which went a long way towards explaining why he had been looking a bit glum from time to time. When he wasn't working on the estate, he admitted that he was trying to write a book, but he was suffering from chronic writer's block. He told her he had been agonising about making a start on it for months, without being able to put a single word down on the page.

'What sort of stuff are you thinking of writing?'

'To be honest, I don't really know and that's what's screwing me up at present. I'm torn between trying to write something lightweight or even humorous and something a bit more meaningful, but every time I think I've decided what I'm going to do, I end up just staring at the blank page.'

'Do you have a background in writing?'

'Sort of. I used to be a journalist, but there's a big difference between a thousand-word article and a book.'

Alice wondered how a journalist – however good at his job – might have managed to amass enough money to buy this amazing historic building, but she sensed he was still reticent to talk. In particular, he didn't say what he had been doing since giving up journalism, so she didn't press him, as it was none of her business – at least until she got to know him better.

'I've been doing a bit of writing myself. It's just a little paper about Amerigo Vespucci and the wasps on the coat of arms. If it's okay with you, I'd like to mention the shield you've just shown me here in the tower and add a photo. Would that be all right?'

'Of course, but preferably without naming names. The last thing I want is a horde of eager tourists or academics pestering me for a look at it. Escaping to Tuscany was so I could live in peace.'

'Of course. It's just for fun, really. I was wondering – once I've done that, could I email it to you, and do you think you could do me a favour and print me off a copy to give to the people at the villa? I don't have access to a printer here. And, of course, take a copy for yourself if you're interested.'

'I'd love that, thank you, and of course I'll run off a copy or two. Just send it over and I'll get onto it.' He dictated his email address and she reflected that, while not a phone number, this was a step in the right direction as far as getting closer to him was concerned.

It was getting quite dark when she glanced at her watch and saw that it was almost eight o'clock. Finishing her drink, she got to her feet and looked across at him. As she did so, the Labrador – who had been snoring happily, occasionally running in his sleep – opened one eye and his tail gave a single lazy thump on the floor. She looked down at him affectionately for a few moments, before addressing his master.

'I'd better get back home. Tell me something, just for curiosity's sake. I've been looking round the room, but I can't see a TV. Does this mean you don't have one?' Maybe this was why he hadn't recognised her.

'There *is* a TV in one of the bedrooms on the floor below, but I hardly ever turn it on. I've never been particularly interested, really, not since I was a kid. I'd rather read a book, to tell the truth. I haven't a clue what's on these days, although from what people tell me, it's mostly rubbish. To be quite honest, over recent years since giving up the day job, I've done my best to avoid social media, newspapers and TV like the plague. I listen to the news on the radio from time to time but, otherwise, I stay away from all that sort of thing.'

'That sounds pretty radical.' Although it was almost exactly what she had been doing. Maybe they had more in common than she had initially thought. It also went a long way towards explaining why he hadn't recognised her.

'I know. I suppose it is, but I have my reasons.' But, clearly, he wasn't going to reveal them – at least not tonight.

They went back down the stairs and he accompanied her to her car, while the dog trotted off into the undergrowth. As she reached the car, she turned towards him.

'Thank you for a lovely evening, Matt. Maybe you might like to come to my place one evening so I can return the favour?'

To her delight, he didn't hesitate. 'I'd like that, Alice, a lot.'

She held out her hand primly but, to her surprise – and considerable pleasure – he leant forward and kissed her gently on the cheeks. She was glad it was twilight, as she felt her face colour. Swallowing hard, she murmured her reply. 'I look forward to it. Thanks again, Matt, and goodnight. Maybe see you in the morning.'

Chapter 19

She didn't see him on her run the following morning but when she got back to her house she found a big white envelope in her letterbox. Inside it were a couple of printed copies of her paper on Amerigo Vespucci, which she had updated and sent to Matt before going to bed last night. Along with it was a handwritten note.

> Hi Alice. Here are the copies you asked for. Really fascinating. I've kept one for myself – I hope that's okay. I'll be in the fields all day, but if you want to contact me, send me an email. Matt

It was hardly a billet-doux, but it was good to hear from him all the same. After showering, and changing into shorts and a fresh top, she made herself a cup of tea and set about composing an invitation to send to him by email.

> Hi Matt. Thanks again for last night. I love your house. Would you like to drop in this evening for a drink? And do bring Guinness. Alice

She toyed with the idea of inserting a little *x* alongside her name, but as he hadn't bothered, neither did she. She was just about to press Send when her phone started ringing. It was an unknown number and she answered cautiously in Italian.

'*Pronto, chi parla?*'

'Hi, can I speak with Alice, please?' It was an American woman's voice.

'Hello, yes, this is Alice. Who's speaking?'

'Alice, hi, I'm Tracey – Conrad's daughter. I saw you in the restaurant last week, remember?'

'Yes, of course! Hi, Tracey.' Alice wasn't sure if this was the red-haired woman or the one with the two children.

'My father asked me to give you a call. We're having a little drinks thing tonight and we hope you might like to come.'

Alice's eyes flicked down to the email she had been composing. Nice as it would have been to have spent time with Matt again tonight, she knew she needed to say yes to this invitation. Apart from anything else, it would hopefully offer the chance to get rid of any lingering bad blood between her and Conrad, irrespective of her future career choices. It would also give her the opportunity to give him a copy of her paper on Vespucci.

'That's very kind, Tracey. I'd love to.'

'Great. Say around six, if that suits you? By the way, there's going to be another special guest here tonight: Felicity Winter.'

Alice was impressed. Felicity Winter was one of the biggest movie stars on the planet. Did this mean Conrad was maybe planning on moving on from TV to cinema? It would be interesting to find out. Alice had never met the legendary star before and she found herself looking forward to the prospect with some anticipation.

'Wow, that sounds great.' A thought occurred to her. 'Is everybody going to be dressed up?'

'We're all on holiday, just come as you like. It's not going to be evening dress or anything like that.' That sounded reassuring, as did the next bit of advice. 'There's just one thing: it looks as though news of Felicity's arrival here has got out. Paolo tells me there are two paparazzi outside the front gate. He advises you to walk up the road and come in through the side gate. He says you know which one, and you have the combination.'

'Thanks for telling me. The last thing I want at the moment is to run into a bunch of paparazzi.' She wondered if Tracey and her father had already seen Carrie's now infamous photos, but there was no mention of this in Tracey's reply.

'Great. Look forward to seeing you, Alice. Ciao!'

'Bye.'

Alice returned to her email, changed Matt's invitation from tonight to tomorrow, and pressed Send.

She drove down to Siena and spent the day there, fighting her way through the crowds of tourists filling the narrow streets. She had been there before, and she loved this charming and historic little city. On an impulse, she decided to go to a hair salon – for the first time in many months – in readiness for tonight. She had enough experience of Hollywood invitations to know that the instruction to come dressed in any old thing was not to be taken seriously. She had no doubt that a world-famous actress and her retinue wouldn't turn up in shorts and scruffy T-shirts. It looked as though her Stella McCartney was going to get its second outing in five years tonight.

Conscious that she would have to walk some way up the road and then along a gravel path to get to the villa, she invested in a nice pair of sandals with just a bit of a heel. They were comfortable and would be a lot more stable than the one pair of 'smart' shoes with fairly high heels that she had brought. While shopping, she also bought some new underwear and told herself that this was just because she needed some, not because of any possible hook-up with Matt. Her brain told her she wasn't even fooling herself, but she had bought it by then.

At six o'clock she let herself into the villa grounds through the side gate and walked up through the olive trees to the house. It felt strange to be arriving here as a visitor after having been a resident. She was about to ring the fine old doorbell alongside the front door when it opened and she found the red-haired woman standing there with a smile on her face and a thousand dollar dress on her back. Alice was glad her instincts to dress up had been vindicated.

'Alice, hi. I'm Tracey.'

'Good evening, Tracey. Thanks for the invitation.' Seeing as she was now nominally back in Hollywood-land, she added a bit of froth. 'And that's a gorgeous dress. I love it.'

Tracey's smile broadened as she returned the compliment and then led Alice through the dining room and out onto the terrace.

'Alice, so good of you to come.' Conrad's voice cut across the chatter and all faces turned in her direction. 'You look just great.'

Thanks to all her years of acting, Alice managed to keep her face from blushing, as she felt herself the object of so many eyes, and she did what she always did in these circumstances. She reminded herself of how she had felt that time on set when she had had to bare all. In comparison, this was just a walk in the park. She went across to shake hands with Conrad and he then made the introductions, starting with Felicity Winter, who was standing at his side with an unexpectedly friendly expression on her face. Alice had never met her before and she was as stunningly beautiful in the flesh as on-screen, even though she wasn't wearing anything extravagant or outrageous. Her dress did shriek class and expense, though – definitely a long way from shorts and a T-shirt.

'Felicity needs no introduction, does she? And, Felicity, you know this is…'

'Polly!' Felicity surprised Alice by reaching out, catching her by the shoulders and air-kissing her noisily, before grabbing hold of her arm excitedly. 'My favourite character in my favourite show. I have box sets of all five series, and I regularly watch them over and over again. It's a real pleasure to meet you in the flesh, Alice.'

Alice was genuinely impressed. It had been five years ago, after all. 'Well, I'm even more pleased to meet a megastar like you, Felicity. I can't tell you how many of your films I've seen and loved.'

At that moment Paolo materialised at Alice's elbow with a tray of champagne. Alice took a glass, thanked him and waved the white envelope she was carrying at him.

'By the way, Paolo, I've found out a lot more about that shield in the hallway. It's all in here.' She turned towards Conrad Chesterfield and held the envelope out to him. 'Paolo showed me the shield when I was here before and I've been doing a bit of research. I'm delighted to say I think I may have found the identity of the man who used to own your villa, or at least the medieval building on whose foundations this one's built.'

She saw interest and maybe something more on Conrad's face. Respect maybe? He took the envelope but made no attempt to open it. 'That's amazing, Alice. So, go on, tell us. Who was he?'

'It's still not proven, but I'm ever more convinced that it might have belonged to the man who gave his name to America.' In the general hush that followed this revelation, she added the name. 'Amerigo Vespucci or, if not him, at least somebody from his family.' She went on to give them a brief summary of what was laid out in her paper and she saw wonder on the faces of the listeners. Then, as she was looking round the group, her eyes suddenly alighted upon a familiar, if unwelcome, face in the background. It was Zoë, but Alice didn't have time to consider the implications of the bad-tempered director's presence at the villa for now.

'Alice, that's simply amazing.' Conrad looked around at his family and then back at her again, his eyes shining. 'So you think my house might have started life belonging to the man who discovered America? That's awesome.'

It turned out to be a most enjoyable evening. Even Zoë was on her best behaviour and came over to deliver air-kisses with every appearance of warmth, although Alice knew of old just how good an act her old director could put on. She was introduced to the rest of Conrad's family, and found them friendly and welcoming. His other daughter, Silvia, and her two little children were very pleasant. Unsurprisingly, her husband was also involved in the TV business.

It soon emerged that they had all seen the results of Carrie's revenge upon Richie, and Alice was mightily relieved to find that Conrad had taken it on the chin. In fact, he didn't seem too worried at all.

'We were going to put out a press release some time soon, but we've been hanging on, seeing as so many people are on holiday. The news coming out like this has caused quite a stir, so it's actually been a better launch than we thought.' He gave Alice a grin. 'But I intend to have a few choice words with Richie about his girlfriends and his behaviour towards them.'

Alice smiled back. No irreparable damage, and Richie getting a smack on the wrists seemed like an ideal solution. She was glad for Millie and the others that Conrad was reacting so pragmatically.

As for Felicity – 'call me Fliss' – the famous movie star, it turned out that she had been best friends at school with Tracey and had regularly holidayed with her since they had been in their teens. As a result she was clearly accepted as part of the family. She parked herself alongside Alice and monopolised her, clinging to her arm and demonstrating an encyclopaedic knowledge of all the twists and turns of the often complicated storyline of *Pals*. Alice was feeling quite overwhelmed by the time Paolo came out to announce that dinner was served. She went over to Conrad and his wife to thank them for their hospitality and take her leave, but they wouldn't hear of it.

'You must stay. Please don't go.'

It genuinely sounded as if he meant it. His wife repeated the invitation with equal sincerity, so Alice thanked them most warmly and sat down to another excellent meal served by Paolo and Rosanna. To her surprise, Fliss took up station alongside her and the two of them chatted all the way through. In the course of the meal, Alice couldn't help noticing that Zoë appeared remarkably relaxed in this company, and the other members of Conrad's family looked similarly at ease with her. Apparently, she had been in London for some meetings but was now here on holiday. By the look of it she and the family were very close and this wasn't the first time she had holidayed with them. This close friendship at least went some way towards explaining why Conrad refused to ditch her.

By the end of the meal, Alice and Fliss had really got to know each other unexpectedly well and the megastar had even talked about the events leading up to the recent collapse of what was her second marriage, although she was only a year older than Alice. She said she was here in Italy for a few days' holiday without a partner and she was enjoying the freedom. Alice gave her a brief rundown of what had happened with David and told her that she, too, was happy on her own. Just how true that was remained to be seen and she avoided mentioning Matt. In fact, they bonded so well that Alice even offered to take her to Florence and show her around, but Fliss shook her head ruefully.

'I'd be mobbed. That's the trouble with being such a recognisable figure. And some of the people can be seriously objectionable. I suppose, as you've been out of it for a few years now, you manage better, but back at the height of *Pals* you must have had the same sort of trouble.'

Alice nodded soberly. 'I certainly did. Most people were nice, but the few that weren't were really scary. And social media was even worse. I still stay well away from it.'

'It can be brutal.'

The dinner party broke up around ten and Alice said goodbye to everybody, with warm thanks to the host and hostess. Conrad thanked her again for the research she had done on Amerigo Vespucci and told her he hoped they could meet up again before the end of the month. With

Zoë now here, Alice reckoned that would be unlikely, but she didn't mind. She felt confident that relations between her and Conrad were now restored and she was glad, even though in every likelihood their paths would never cross again. Although stubborn, he was a good man deep down and she liked him.

Fliss took her arm and insisted upon accompanying her to the gate in the fence and kissing her goodbye. 'I've really enjoyed meeting you and talking with you, Alice. Who knows? Maybe we'll work together some time.'

Alice was about to tell her that her own acting days were over, but it was such an intriguing thought that she couldn't help a little surge of excitement at the prospect.

'That would be amazing. Anyway, I've rented a little house in the village. If you feel like a chat any time, just come down or give me a call and I'll come up and meet you here. It would be good to stay in touch. Tracey's got my number.'

When she got home, she found she had a reply from Matt. Disappointingly, it was to tell her that he would be away for a couple of days, but he hoped they could meet up next week. Suppressing a little sigh, she went up to bed with mixed feelings. On the one hand, there was considerable satisfaction at how well this evening at Conrad's villa had gone, but this was tempered by the knowledge that she would have to wait before seeing Matt again.

Chapter 20

Next morning, she toyed with the idea of taking a different route for her run, just in case the paparazzi lying in wait for Felicity might recognise her, but natural curiosity and the desire to see Matt and his dog again – if they were still about – took her back up the road. She did, however, deliberately camouflage herself for the run in a baggy T-shirt, baseball cap and sunglasses, and kept her face averted as she passed the two men. She could feel their eyes on her as she went past, but she felt confident that was probably more an instinctive reaction to the sight of a woman's bottom in running shorts than recognition of her face.

Up at the top of the hill there was no sign of Matt or the dog, even though she ran along as far as his gates, so presumably he had already left and she felt another little twinge of regret. She had learnt by now that there was a path along this side of the fence that circled the villa grounds and led back into the village by another road, so she carried on along this, rather than risk running the gauntlet of the paparazzi again. Her talk to Fliss last night had reawakened memories of the discomfort of being recognised, and now that she had hopefully achieved a certain degree of anonymity, she was determined to keep it that way.

In the afternoon she took the car and followed a winding wine route through the Chianti hills, admiring the old villas and farms among the vineyards and olive groves, and stopping off from time to time to visit fascinating old churches and picturesque villages. Everywhere she went, she searched for signs of the Vespucci coat of arms but without success. She bought a pecorino cheese from a roadside stand, along with some delicious-looking peaches and a couple of bottles of red wine from a producer selling direct to the public outside his cantina. It was a quiet, restful day and all that was missing was a bit of company – but he was away.

She didn't feel like a run next day so she showered, got dressed and then went across to the cafe for her morning cappuccino and a doughnut. It was another hot day, with no rain forecast for the days to come. While she was sitting outside in the piazza, her phone started ringing. She didn't recognise the number and wondered if it might be Matt, only to discount the idea straightaway, as he only had her email address. She swiped green and answered.

'*Pronto. Chi parla?*'

'Alice, is that you?' Alice recognised the voice immediately.

'Fliss, how great to hear from you.'

'I was wondering if you were doing anything today? Feel like a swim and a chat?'

Alice was impressed. An invitation to chat with a Hollywood icon wasn't something that happened every day and, besides, she had genuinely got on well with her. She immediately said yes, and they agreed she would walk up to the villa and come in through the same side gate as before, at eleven o'clock.

When she got there, Paolo met her at the door and told her that Felicity was down at the pool with 'the others'. As Alice walked through the gardens, she wondered who might be there – maybe Zoë? As it turned out, she was relieved to find only Felicity and Silvia, Conrad's elder daughter, with her family. Her two little girls were splashing about in the shallow end, while her husband was swimming lengths. After greeting both ladies with kisses, Alice dropped her bag on a sunbed alongside Fliss and slipped out of her clothes into her bikini. Fliss gave her an appraising look.

'You've still got it, Polly. You look great.'

'Polly, who's Polly? I think you must be confusing me with somebody else, madam.' Alice gave her a wink and read comprehension on the big star's face.

'Of course, Alice, that chapter of your life's finished now. Still, I'm impressed to see you've been looking after yourself so well.'

Alice headed for the water. She swam up and down a few times before playing beach ball catch with the two little girls for a while and then finally coming back out again. As she dried herself off, she sat down beside Fliss and pointed to the familiar cover of the book the film star had been reading.

'*The Playboy and His Women* – I've just finished reading it. What do you think of it?'

'It's okay – quite interesting, actually. Thankfully, it's more psychological than *Fifty Shades* and there's far less of the kinky stuff.' She pushed her sunglasses up onto her forehead and gave Alice a wink. 'Seeing as I've just heard I'm starring in the screen version, I'm relieved about that.'

'Wow, congratulations. The book has been an amazing hit. I'm sure the movie with you in it will break all records. When's it all happening?'

'Shooting starts in LA in the late autumn. I thought I'd better read the book first, before I learn my lines, so I picked up a copy at LAX as I was getting on the plane and I'm glad I did. It's extremely well-written and there are insights into my character's personality that don't immediately leap out from the screenplay.'

Alice was impressed at Fliss's professionalism – but she was one of the greatest living actresses, after all. 'So is that your homework for the summer?'

'Pretty much, and then I'll have to decide what to do next.' She glanced across at Alice. 'Do you ever wish you'd tried cinema? You're a great actress and you're so photogenic.'

'There was a time when my agent was pushing me to try movies, but I was so busy with *Pals* I never took it any further. Anyway, that was years ago and now I'm pretty much set on a career in art history.'

'Have you got a job lined up?'

Alice shook her head. 'Not yet, but it'll come. I'm in no hurry.'

She saw Fliss hesitate. 'The thing is, Alice, if you were thinking about making a move into cinema – even temporarily – there's a script my agent's been telling me about. It's a sort of *Thelma and Louise* road-trip movie with two women, both desperate to get away from their humdrum lives. If you like, I could put your name forward. It would probably start filming next summer or early autumn.'

Alice was truly flabbergasted. 'Me working alongside you? That would be amazing.' Apart from anything else, it would no doubt provide the sort of massive financial buffer she needed to take a history of art job and still live in comfort. But, more than that, the idea of appearing alongside Felicity Winter, maybe even co-starring? It sounded like a dream come true, although she had no illusions as to the effect it would inevitably have on her private life. Still, she knew she would say yes if they offered it to her. Maybe this was another second chance to renew her relationship with Hollywood.

Fliss looked pleased. 'Of course, the decision wouldn't be mine, but I'd be surprised if they turned you down. I'm sure your comeback would be a major box-office draw.' She reached across, caught hold of Alice's hand and gave it a reassuring squeeze. 'No rush. Just think about it. I'm off to Rome later in the week for a couple of days of meetings and then a few days' holiday. I won't be back in LA until early next week. You have my phone number. Think it over and if you want me to put your name forward, just give me a call.' She leant over and gave Alice a peck on the cheek. 'I'd really enjoy working with you, Alice.'

—

Alice was woken by her phone at seven o'clock next morning. As she picked it up, she was surprised to see it was Layla, presumably back in LA, where it was late at night.

'Hi, Layla, all well?'

'Hi, Alice, I hope I didn't wake you too early. I'm fine, thanks, but I wanted to let you know what's been happening. Millie's been telling me about the way your David just took off for Hollywood and I'm appalled. What a way to behave! And to you of all people!'

'It's okay, I'm over it. In fact, he probably did me a favour. But has something happened?'

'Nothing bad, but I've just had dinner with Millie and while we were sitting there, David appeared. I hadn't seen him since getting back to LA, but he'd obviously been keeping tabs on me.'

'What? Stalking you?'

'Maybe not quite as sinister as that, but he'd been asking around to find out where I would be.'

'And what did he want?'

'It was all a bit weird, really. He just pitched up and hung about by our table, presumably waiting for an invitation to join us and when it didn't come – Millie and I were in the middle of some personal stuff – he just stood there like a lemon and mooched about until I sent him packing.'

'And he didn't say what he wanted?'

She heard a momentary hesitation on the part of Layla. 'According to Millie, he might have been after me.'

With Millie's help, Alice had already worked this out for herself, but she was delighted to hear that Layla didn't reciprocate his feelings. She gave an annoyed hiss. 'What a prat.'

'Quite… Anyway, look Alice, I wouldn't want you to think I've been responsible in any way for encouraging him – apart from giving him the names of a few agents and TV execs, while we were still at the villa, to help with his career. The last I saw of him was at the airport, when I texted you about it. I was in first class and he was at the rear of the aircraft, so I didn't even see him when we got to LAX. If I was in any way responsible for raising his hopes, I'm truly sorry – not to him, but to you. My friendship with you is far too precious to risk for the sake of some man. Please believe me that there isn't anything, there never was anything, and there certainly won't be anything between David and me at any time in the future.'

Alice thanked her warmly and did her best to reassure her that she didn't blame her in the slightest. After chatting a bit longer, Alice rang off and lay back in bed as she digested this information. On the one hand, she was pleased — and relieved — to know that her friend Layla hadn't behaved unscrupulously, but it also just confirmed what a moron her supposedly intelligent boyfriend had become. They had had no contact since the note he had left on her pillow, and that was fine by her. The shock of his sudden departure had gradually worn off and she knew she wanted nothing more to do with him. Besides, now there was Matt... hopefully.

Half an hour later she threw some clothes into the washing machine and sat down to check her messages over breakfast. There were two of them and her eyes were immediately drawn to the first. It was an email from Matt.

> Hi Alice. Feel like a (longish) walk? I've just
> come back from a couple of days in London
> and I need some fresh air. Matt

She replied immediately and they arranged to meet at ten. Feeling buoyed by the prospect of seeing him again, she then checked a text message that must have come in while she was in the shower and saw that it was from Millie, back in Hollywood. It repeated the events at the restaurant that Layla had outlined and ended with the words:

> It was awfully embarrassing and I just wanted
> you to know that it's quite clear Layla had

nothing to do with making David decide to come over to the States. She said she'd give you a call to apologise but, as far as I can see, she has nothing to apologise for. Hope you've hooked up with your mystery man. I want all the juicy details.

Mil

xx

Alice sent her a cheerful, friendly reply, but didn't go into too much detail as to how things were going with Matt – mainly because she didn't know herself.

Chapter 21

At ten o'clock, after spending far too long in the bathroom getting ready for what might be just a walk in the country, she put on shorts and trainers and drove up to Matt's house, doing her best to dominate the rising sense of excitement at the thought of seeing him again. She had toyed with the idea of going up on foot but, seeing as there was a long walk ahead of her, she opted for the car. Her heart leapt as she saw him waiting for her with his faithful hound at his side. Guinness charged over to give her his usual boisterous welcome and Matt welcomed her with the lightest of kisses on her cheeks, which nevertheless sent sparks coursing throughout her whole body. She checked him out surreptitiously and wondered if that might even be just a hint of nervousness on his face. Was he maybe feeling similarly excited at the prospect of a day together?

'Hi, Matt.' She was delighted to hear her voice sounding more confident than she felt.

'Hi, Alice. So good to see you. I've been thinking of you a lot while I've been away.'

That sounded extremely promising.

'I've been thinking about you an awful lot, too.'

'If you can handle a four-hour walk — two hours each way — I thought we could go up to the old monastery at the end of the valley. I've put together a picnic, so we won't starve, and I've brought loads to drink. It's a gorgeous spot, and Guinness and I often walk there. It's very quiet and for somebody like you, with a love of history, it should be interesting. It was founded in the twelfth century by the Cistercians.'

In spite of her love of history, Alice knew that today she was less interested in the ancient monks than in her companion, but it sounded good, not least as it looked like they would have a full day out alone together.

They set off on foot, passing through Matt's meticulously maintained olive groves, before leaving his land and heading along a good track that wound around the contours of the hillside high above the river. A lone cuckoo called from a tree behind them and swallows whizzed to and fro overhead, their cries producing just about the only sounds, apart from the bees. It was enchanting, and even the sight of a large brown-and-yellow snake slithering across the track in front of them didn't lessen her enjoyment. Matt told her it was a harmless grass snake and she took his word for it, although reptiles were far from her favourite animals. The further they walked, the more the valley floor gradually rose up to meet them, until they finally found themselves level with the river. Although it was now little more than a trickle, there was still some water among the stones, and the Labrador wasted no time in leaping in and splashing happily about.

They sat down in the shade of a magnificent old willow and threw sticks into the water for Guinness to retrieve and drop at their feet, barking until they were thrown once more. It was a delightful day in delightful company, and Alice couldn't have been happier. Well, she told herself, a kiss would have been rather nice… She was just debating whether to throw caution to the winds and kiss him, when he stood up.

'On we go, okay?'

Reluctantly, she stood up, too.

As he had predicted, it took almost two hours for them to get to the ruins of the surprisingly large old monastery. It was in a state of considerable decay – barely more than four walls with some empty window openings and rounded arches where doors had once stood – and they appeared to be the only visitors. Matt explained that there wasn't a proper road leading here so, in spite of its antiquity, it had remained off the tourist trail.

'Guinness and I happened upon it pretty much by chance a year ago and I've been back numerous times, not least as there's a decent pool in the river. I presume it might have been something to do with the old watermill and it's deep enough for him to have a real swim, even at the height of summer.' He grinned at her. 'To be honest, I swim here myself sometimes.'

A tantalising image of skinny-dipping in the pool with Matt flashed before her eyes, but it was dashed as they heard the sound of approaching voices. A group of what were unmistakably Boy Scouts came hiking past with their leader, and Alice realised that this place maybe wasn't quite as secluded as she had thought. Instead of going skinny-dipping, they found a spot in the shade where they could sit by the water and have their lunch. He had made ham-and-cheese sandwiches, accompanied by little cherry tomatoes, and followed by fresh nectarines and the same strawberry tarts from the local shop that she already knew well. This was all accompanied by mineral water and rosé wine that he set in the stream to cool – he had even brought plastic wine glasses. Unsurprisingly, the prospect of some titbits for lunch caused the Labrador to forsake the river and concentrate on food. Clearly, he had his priorities. So did Alice. She made sure she was sitting on the bone-dry grass alongside Matt, close enough to feel the warmth of his skin next to her shoulder. It just felt right, somehow.

At the end of her food, she lay back and closed her eyes. A few seconds later, she heard the dog splash back into the water again and then a movement, as Matt stretched out beside her. She was just trying to summon up the courage to roll over towards him, when she felt his hand grip hers and give it a gentle squeeze.

'This is wonderful.' There was a dreamy note to his voice and she felt a wave of affection sweep over her. She turned her head towards him and opened her eyes. His face was barely a few inches from hers.

'It really is, Matt. I can't imagine a better way to spend the day — or a better person to spend it with.'

A little smile spread across his face and he leant towards her. She was just closing her eyes in delicious anticipation, when it felt as if somebody emptied a bucket of water over the two of them. Just as she was catching her breath after the cold shower, a heavy object landed on top of her, before ricocheting across to Matt.

'Guinness! Get off, you little bugger! I'm soaked.' Matt's voice was more frustrated than angry. She knew how he felt.

Alice raised herself onto her elbows and took stock. She looked as if she had just taken part in a Miss Wet T-shirt competition, she was emanating an unappealing odour of Labrador, and there were dirty paw prints across her tummy. Alongside her, a very happy dog was wrestling with his master, who looked even more bedraggled than she did. In spite of the unwelcome interruption to what had had all the makings of a defining moment in their budding relationship, she felt a wave of mirth rise up inside her and she burst out laughing. A second or two later she caught Matt's eye and he, too, erupted into a fit of laughter. The Labrador, clearly puzzled by this bizarre behaviour by the two humans, finally relinquished his master, sat down on the straggly grass and occupied himself with burrowing for an itch somewhere under his armpit.

'I'm really sorry about that, Alice. I've said it before and I'll say it again: Guinness has absolutely no manners.' She saw his eyes run across her body and felt another thrill. 'Are you all right?'

In answer she leant across, took his face between her palms and kissed him softly on the lips. 'I'm just fine. And you?' It didn't just feel good, it really did feel right, and she almost purred.

His eyes were barely a couple of inches from hers. 'Never better. And it's all down to you.' He leant in and kissed her again, before suddenly drawing back. 'Great! That's all we need: Baden bloody Powell and his band.'

She followed the direction of his gaze and saw that the Scout troop had returned and were in the process of pulling towels and costumes out of their backpacks, clearly about to leap into the pool. She and Matt got to their feet, and she rearranged her clothing as best she could – but not before spotting a gangly lad in his teens with his eyes glued to her chest. As they made eye contact, the boy blushed and looked away.

She glanced across at Matt. 'I think we should maybe consider moving camp.'

He nodded and glanced at his watch. 'To be honest, I suppose we should make tracks. I'm afraid I've got to head off to Rome tonight. I'm driving down and it's going to take about three hours, so this means I need to go back home, jump in the shower, change and get away as soon as possible.'

Doing her best to swallow her disappointment, Alice nodded. 'I see. Is this a business thing?'

'A bit of both. Mostly business, but my grandma lives just outside Rome and my mother told me she hasn't been too well, so I thought I'd call in on her this evening.'

While Alice was impressed that he cared enough about his old grandmother to drop in and see her, she knew she would have preferred to spend the evening – if not the night – with him. Still, drawing upon her thespian background, she produced a big smile, reached up and gave him another kiss on the lips.

'I look forward to picking up where we left off when you return – maybe without Guinness's participation.'

On the way back to the tower they talked a lot and she felt she knew quite a bit more about him by the time they got there. However, there still remained the mystery over just what he did for a living or, at least, how he had made his money. After all, as her mum had pointed out, historic Tuscan towers didn't come cheap. Mind you, she reminded herself, in fairness she still hadn't told him about her acting career. It would no doubt all come out in due course, as their relationship progressed – and for the first time she truly believed it would. By now it was mid-afternoon and the temperature was surely well into the thirties. Although they hugged the limited shade on offer as far as possible, Alice was sticky with sweat and very conscious of the lingering aroma of Labrador on her body by the time they arrived back at his home. She told herself it was maybe just as well he was hurrying off, so she could go home and take a long shower.

As they reached her car, they stopped and stood facing each other. She did her best not to let her disappointment show. 'Well, drive safely. When will you be back?'

'I've got meetings tomorrow and the day after, so I should hopefully be back on Friday.'

Alice did her best to ignore the wave of frustration now that she knew she wouldn't see him for several days. 'Would you let me buy you dinner that night?'

He reached out and took her hands in his. 'You don't need to do that.'

'I was wondering about cooking for you but I'm not the greatest cook in the world and I wouldn't want to risk poisoning you. Seriously, let me take you out to Giovanni's restaurant. I'd really like to and, besides, I've already sampled your hospitality.'

'I still don't think you should pay but, all right, if you insist, that would be great.'

'Excellent. I'll book a table.' A sudden thought occurred to her. 'What about Guinness? Is he going to Rome with you? Do you want me to look after him?'

'That's kind of you but it's all arranged – I'll leave him with Virgilio. Guinness often stays with them. They spoil him rotten and he loves them. He'll be fine.'

Accepting the inevitable, Alice released his hands and opened the car door, but then had to take two steps back, as a blast of scorching air came belching out. The Fiat had been sitting in the sun all day and the door handle was almost too hot to touch. As she waited for the interior to cool down a bit, she felt his arms encircle her waist and his lips touch her ear. She leant back against him and sighed happily.

'I'm really sorry I have to go.' His voice was little more than a whisper.

'So am I.' She took a big breath and half-turned her head towards him. 'At least we have Friday to look forward to.'

He kissed her and she felt herself melt but then, all too soon, he pulled back.

'*A venerdì.*'

'*A venerdì.* See you on Friday and hope it goes well.'

Then, mildly surprised that her knees were still working after the effect his lips had had upon her, she left him and his lovely dog, and drove back to the village.

When she got back home, she lost no time in jumping under a long, cool, refreshing shower. It had been a lovely, if hot, day and she was now under no doubt that he liked her a lot, but she could still sense hesitation in him. Was something – or someone – holding him back? He hadn't mentioned a girlfriend or relationships of any kind, but was it credible that a most desirable man like Matt – and no doubt a millionaire to boot – had really been living a celibate life, just like one of the old monks in the monastery in the valley back in the Middle Ages? Was the real reason for going to Rome even business? Maybe there was another woman...

With a snort of frustration – directed more at herself than at him – she pushed the shower control far over to the right and gasped as a stream of freezing water landed on her head. Apart from making her jump, this did at least achieve the desired result, and she managed to start thinking more logically as she stepped out of the shower and dried off. She made a mental note that it would be wise to try to avoid descending into paranoia. It had been a wonderful day and their relationship was blossoming. When she saw him on Friday, she would make a point of finding out just exactly who Mr Matthew Livingstone really was.

But so far so good.

Chapter 22

The following day proved to be far more eventful than Alice could possibly have expected. After yesterday's long walk, she decided not to go for her usual run and instead she strolled across to the cafe for her morning cappuccino and a chat with Rita. It was another hot day, although there was a bit of hazy cloud building, and she wondered if that might indicate that much-needed rain was on the way. As they had walked through the fields yesterday, she could almost hear the parched earth and equally thirsty plants crying out for water. For her part, she couldn't complain. She had been here in Tuscany now for three weeks and had only had a couple of rainy days. It occurred to her that she only had ten days left in the little house and she would soon have to decide what to do next. Of course, she knew full well that much of that decision rested upon what might or might not happen between her and Matt, and she wouldn't see him again until the day after tomorrow.

She had also been thinking long and hard about what Fliss had said about the upcoming movie. Although she was adamant that she wanted to put her five years of study to good use, there was no great rush. None of the universities to which she had sent her CV had been able to offer anything, and none of her other applications had resulted in any more interviews so far, so it was probably prudent to let Fliss put her name forward for the role.

If the producers decided she was right for the part, there would then be time to make the final decision. The downside, of course, would be being catapulted once again into the public eye, with all the aggravation that would bring, but the more she thought about it, the more she felt it worth the risk. The big unknown, of course, was Matt and just how things might develop between the two of them. It would be ironic if she were to fall in love – and she now found herself actually using the word, albeit just in her head – with somebody who lived in Tuscany only to take a job that involved a move to the other side of the world.

Later on that morning, just in case there really was rain on the way, she decided to go for a leisurely stroll up the road and around the perimeter of the villa. She decided to take her sketch pad with her as well, in case anything caught her eye. Then maybe later on she might head up to Florence for a bit more retail therapy.

The walk past the now-deserted villa gates to the top was as lovely as ever, and the cloud increasingly covering the sun meant that it wasn't too terribly hot, although she could feel it was becoming ever more humid. As she reached the woods near the turn-off for the tower, she had a rare treat. Hearing movement and sensing she was being watched, she stopped and scanned the trees, until a movement high up revealed the culprits. A pair of delightful little red squirrels were studying her from the safety of a gnarled old pine and, as she made eye contact with them, they turned and scampered off deeper into the trees, leaping acrobatically from branch to branch until they disappeared. She gave a happy little sigh as she watched them go. She turned left onto the track and spared a thought for Matt, as she approached his gates. He would probably be having his first meetings in Rome about now and she couldn't help wondering yet again just what it was he did.

When she reached the highest point of the fence, not far beyond the gap that the wild boar had torn in the wire, she stopped for a rest in the shade, perching on a fallen tree, from where she had a wide-ranging view down across the villa and its grounds, and onwards through the Chianti hills. Although it was getting hazier by the minute, as the clouds continued to gather, the contrasting colours of the olives, the vines, the fields of ripening corn and the red roofs of the houses dotted about the landscape were glorious, and she felt genuinely lucky to be here. She could see just why Matt had chosen Tuscany for his escape – whatever it had been that had forced him to do so.

She was just about to open her sketch pad when the sound of footsteps attracted her attention and she leant forward to see better. To her left, a head was just appearing up the track on the other side of the fence and she recognised it straightaway. It was Zoë. As Alice looked on, however, it soon became clear that all was not well with the irascible director. She was swaying drunkenly from side to side as she staggered up the slope, and Alice was appalled. They had all had experience of Zoë's tendency to go off on wild binges, from which she would emerge red-eyed, sore-headed and even snappier than normal, but Alice had hoped that these were now all in the past. Such would appear not to be the case after all and Alice shook her head sadly, reflecting that this didn't bode well for Millie and the others in the new series. Then, just as she was considering making a hasty departure before she was spotted, she saw Zoë lurch to a halt and sink to her knees with her head in her hands. Two seconds later, she was flat on her face in the dust.

Alice leapt to her feet. 'Zoë, are you all right?'

Although she shouted at the top of her voice, feeling sure that it would reach Zoë, there was no response as the crumpled form lay there, immobile. Alice looked around wildly but there wasn't another human being to be seen anywhere so she ran back along the wire until she came to the gate she had used before and punched in the entry code, hoping it hadn't been changed. She gave a sigh of relief as she heard a click and the gate swung open. She ran through and back up the slope to where Zoë was lying on the ground, mouthing jumbled words and moaning, her face bright red. It was immediately apparent that it was far more serious than too much to drink – maybe a heart attack – so Alice dropped her sketch pad, pulled out her phone and called the number of the villa to tell them what had happened. It rang and rang and then, just as she was getting desperate, it was answered.

'*Pronto.*' It was Paolo and she had never been so happy to hear his voice.

As quickly as she could, she blurted out what was happening, giving details of where they were, and was greatly reassured to hear him respond in a calm voice.

'Leave it to me, Alice. I'll get onto the emergency services and they'll be along shortly, I'm sure. Stay with Zoë and we'll be with you in a couple of minutes.'

As the line went dead, Alice tucked her phone back into the pocket of her shorts and returned her attention to Zoë. By now, her lips had stopped moving and she was lying on her side, breathing rapidly, eyes closed. Dim memories of first-aid classes when she was a teenager told Alice that this was already pretty close to the so-called recovery position, so she didn't attempt to move her. Instead, she crouched down at her side, gently cradling her head in her hands. She was relieved to see Zoë's eyes open, as she felt her touch, and saw what might have been recognition dawn upon her face. She opened her mouth to speak, but no words came out and Alice did her best to reassure her former tormentor.

'Just take it easy, Zoë. We've called the ambulance and help is on its way. They'll be with us shortly.' She read what could have been comprehension in Zoë's eyes, before they closed again.

Alice crouched there, softly stroking Zoë's hair and hoping the medics would arrive soon. Zoë's breathing, apart from being rapid, was shallow and Alice didn't like it one bit. From time to time she leant down to check that Zoë was still breathing and was surprised not to smell even a hint of alcohol on her breath. Presumably, the staggering had been caused by the onset of the heart attack or whatever it was, rather than booze. That, at least, was one positive to take away from this incident, when it was all over.

A few minutes later she became aware of the sound of a vehicle approaching up the narrow track from the vines and was mightily relieved to spot a quad bike racing up the hill, driven by Paolo, with Conrad perched precariously behind him. As the little vehicle drew up in a cloud of dust, Conrad leapt off surprisingly nimbly and came running across. He dropped to his knees beside Alice and she could immediately see that he was distraught. He reached out and replaced Alice's hands supporting Zoë's head, bending towards her as he did so.

'Zoë, sweetie, I'm here. It's gonna be okay.' His voice was low and charged with emotion. 'Can you hear me, Zoë?'

'I don't think she can, Conrad.' Alice stretched her arms gratefully and stood up again. 'I think she's unconscious. When I got to her, I'm pretty sure she recognised me and I told her help was on the way, but she's lost consciousness since then. Try not to worry.'

He made no comment but just dropped his head even closer to Zoë's, rocking gently to and fro, and Alice saw tears fall from his eyes onto the stricken woman's cheek. She was frankly astounded. It had been clear at the dinner party the previous week that he and Zoë got on well, but she hadn't been expecting such an outpouring of totally genuine emotion. Any further conjecture was interrupted by Paolo, who came up alongside them and gave Alice an encouraging look.

'Pierangelo's waiting for the ambulance by the main gate. He'll bring them up here to the side gate and we'll carry her down on a stretcher.' He patted Alice's shoulder. 'Thanks for reacting so quickly, Alice. The medics will be here soon.'

At that moment his phone rang and he answered it. After a short conversation, he flicked it off and returned his attention to Alice and Conrad. 'That was Pierangelo. The ambulance will be here in five minutes. That's remarkably fast, considering where we are.'

As he spoke, Alice already began to hear the distinctive wail of a siren in the distance, and it wasn't long before a cloud of dust and the crunch of gravel announced the vehicle's arrival along the track. Three minutes later Pierangelo came running up from the side gate, followed by two paramedics in uniform, carrying a stretcher. They knelt beside Zoë and took over from Conrad, who slowly rose to his feet and stared vacantly around, as if in a daze. Alice caught hold of his arm and gave him an encouraging squeeze.

'Try not to worry, Conrad. She's in good hands now.' She saw his eyes gradually focus on her and he gave a hint of a nod.

'Yes, yes, of course.' He rallied. 'And thank you, Alice. Thank God you were here.'

'Yes, a lucky coincidence. I was just walking around the perimeter.' She glanced down at the two paramedics, who were speaking quietly between themselves. After another few moments they reached for the stretcher and gently rolled Zoë onto it, securing her with straps. Finally, assisted by Paolo and Pierangelo, they lifted her up and set off down the hill towards the gate. Alice released her grip on Conrad's arm, retrieved her discarded sketch pad and followed on.

As Zoë was loaded into the ambulance, Paolo explained to Conrad and Alice that it had been by sheer lucky chance that this ambulance and its crew had been in Greve, barely a few kilometres up the road, which explained why they had got there so quickly. Now they would take her back to the main hospital in Florence. Although Conrad wanted to go with Zoë in the ambulance, only one person could travel with her and Paolo volunteered, as he could speak both Italian and English. As the ambulance reversed back down the track, Pierangelo went to get the quad bike, while Alice accompanied Conrad down the path to the villa on foot. As they walked, he barely said a word and Alice could tell how upset he was. She was still at a loss to understand why, though.

Clearly, he and Zoë were good friends, but what made their connection strong enough to bring tears to his eyes?

Back at the villa, Alice offered to go to the hospital with Conrad to help with translating – and just to keep an eye on him. His wife, Amber, was tremendously grateful and even kissed Alice before they set off in a car driven by Pierangelo. During the drive, Conrad continued to stay silent, lost in his thoughts. It was a relief when the car screeched to a halt outside the hospital and they hurried inside. They found Paolo waiting for them by the door with the news that Zoë had been wheeled in for examination and tests, so they would have to sit in the waiting area until called.

He went off to get them all some coffee, while Alice took a seat alongside Conrad. They sat in silence for a couple of minutes before she risked a direct question.

'How're you doing, Conrad? Try not to worry. They'll sort her out, I'm sure.'

He jerked his head up and looked at her, as if surprised to find she was there. His eyes were red and watery. 'Alice, hi. Yes, thanks, I'm sure they'll take good care of her.'

He lapsed into silence again but only for a few moments before beginning to talk, softly and quietly, his eyes once more directed down at his feet.

'She's very, very dear to me. I'd hate it if anything happened to her.'

Alice took the plunge, hoping to get him talking which should, hopefully, raise his spirits. 'Have you known her long?'

'All my life.' His voice tailed off again. As Alice was still wondering what this might mean, she heard his voice again – if anything, now even lower and weaker. 'She's my sister.'

Alice struggled hard to stop an expression of amazement flooding across her face. Even for an experienced actress, it was a tough ask. Suddenly, the whole Zoë enigma was explained. The reason Conrad always stood by his controversial director was because she was family. It all fell into place. But why didn't anybody know? As if reading her mind, Conrad raised his head and looked across at her.

'Nobody knows because that's the way she wanted it. Alice, I shouldn't have told you, so please will you promise me you won't tell anybody else? I know I can trust you.'

Even through her mystification, Alice felt a little surge of satisfaction that he thought highly enough of her to trust her with this secret. She nodded. 'I promise, Conrad. What happens in the hospital stays in the hospital.' She was pleased to see him summon a glimmer of a smile in return.

'Thanks, Alice.' His eyes returned to his feet, as he picked up the story once more. Clearly, he needed to talk. 'She's my little sister. Our mother died while we were still young and Zoë never quite recovered. She was a wild thing, growing up, and she and my father were always fighting. In the end she ran off when she was still in her teens. I didn't see her again for ten years. In that time she got married and divorced twice, and she collected some serious mental scars as a result. When she came to me for help, it was as a last resort, and she was a mess.'

'And so you helped her.'

'Of course, I helped her – she's my sister.' Conrad looked up again. 'I started her off in the business and she did really well. She turned out to be a brilliant director – except for the way she treats people.' Alice saw him shake his head sadly. 'I tell her to go easy on them, she agrees, but it seems to be something she can't control. The results she produces are always great – just look at the success of *Pals* – so what can I do? The thing is, I know what she's been through, what's made her the way she is, and I feel sorry for her.' He shook his head ruefully. 'And, like I say, she's my sister.'

'But why doesn't she want people to know?'

'Pride, I suppose. After everything that's happened to her in her life, she's incredibly low in self-esteem.' This didn't really tie in with what Alice had seen over the years, but maybe it had just been an artificial veneer of confidence. 'She doesn't want people to think she only got where she did because she's the sister of the boss. I get that, so I've always gone along with it. Going off the radar, marrying a couple of times and changing names muddied the waters sufficiently, and so nobody's picked up on it.'

Alice sat back and let this bombshell sink in. It explained so much, but it also firmly dashed any hopes there might have been that the new series might have a change of director. She nodded sagely to herself – no question she had done the right thing in walking away from *Pals Forever*.

Just then Paolo appeared, carrying a plastic tray with coffees and croissants, and he handed them round before sitting down alongside them. They sat and chatted about everything from vineyards to Amerigo Vespucci for almost an hour, before a nurse appeared and announced that one of them could see Zoë, but only briefly. Conrad stood up, braced himself and followed the nurse through a door with a 'No Entry' sign on it. When he came back five or six minutes later, he had a look of relief on his face.

'It wasn't a heart attack, thank God. She's suffering from heatstroke. It was a serious attack and she's badly dehydrated, so they're keeping her in overnight, but the doctor says she'll be fine tomorrow or, at worst, in a day or two.' Then he surprised Alice. 'She asks if you can go in and see her, Alice. Would you do that?'

'Yes, of course.'

He caught her eye for a couple of seconds. 'And, Alice, I'd be grateful if you didn't mention anything about my little indiscretion.'

She gave him a reassuring nod of the head and, not without some trepidation, followed the nurse back through the door and along the corridor. She found Zoë hooked up to a drip, eyes closed and with a weary expression on her face, but looking a whole lot better than she had done out there on the hillside.

Alice went over to the bedside and leant towards her. 'Hi, Zoë, how're you feeling?' She saw the eyes open and readied herself for a caustic reply, but it didn't come. Instead, Zoë reached out and caught hold of her wrist, pulling her gently down until she was able to kiss her on the cheek. As she looked up at Alice, there was genuine gratitude in her eyes.

'Thank you so much for saving my life, Alice. The doctor says if I'd been left there for long, I'd have died.' For a moment there was a flash of the cynical Zoë that Alice had come to know so well. 'Why didn't you leave me to die? That way, you could have joined the others in the new series.'

Alice straightened up in shock. 'Why didn't I do what? What are you saying? Of course, I came running and, of course, I called for help.' She shook her head in disbelief. 'Zoë, you and I have had our differences on set, but when it's a matter of life and death, all that goes out the window. No job's worth a human life and that's for sure. No, I'm pleased I could help and I'm delighted to hear that you're going to make a full recovery.'

'You're so sweet. Thank you, really, thank you.' As Zoë's eyes closed again, the nurse gave a little shake of the head and Alice headed back to the others. She was astounded by Zoë's tender tone, but also appalled by her insinuation that she might, even for a moment, have considered turning a blind eye and leaving her to her fate. If it hadn't been for Conrad's account of Zoë's troubled past, she would have screamed in frustration – instead, she walked out feeling happy, knowing she had done the right thing.

Chapter 23

By the time she got back home it was late afternoon and she was feeling unexpectedly tired after the stress of the day. She went upstairs, lay down on the bed and dropped off to sleep within minutes.

She was woken a good while later by the sudden onset of a torrential deluge outside the open window, thankfully this time not accompanied by thunderclaps. Along with it came a breath of blissfully fresh air, wafting into the room.

She stretched lazily and then checked her emails: there were two, both of them fascinating in their own way. The first was from Matt and it was anything but wordy.

> Hi Alice. Hope you're okay. Can't wait to see
> you. Off to dinner at La Pergola. A venerdì.
> Matt.

She couldn't help grinning. He certainly didn't waste words in his emails. Presumably, he had been in a rush. 'See you on Friday' sounded good and Alice felt another little shiver of love, lust or whatever it was run through her. She also realised she was feeling quite hungry and the idea of dinner in the famous Michelin-starred restaurant in Rome sounded most appealing – especially with him sitting opposite. Still, she would have him to herself the day after tomorrow, which wasn't too long to wait. She sent him a short reply, telling him she was looking forward to seeing him again, and she added her phone number, wondering if he might take the hint and call her. It would be good to hear his voice. There was no doubt about it – she was spending a lot of time thinking about him.

Doing her best to relegate any further thought of him until another time, she checked the second email. Also short and sweet, it was from Antonia and it made interesting reading.

> Hi Alice. I'm coming back to Europe at the weekend and would love to see you. I have some exciting news. Could we meet up in Florence on Saturday? Antonia

Alice was mildly surprised that Antonia was returning so soon, but she knew she would enjoy meeting up with her again and she wondered what the exciting news might be – presumably something to do with her new TV venture. She dashed off a quick reply, agreeing to meet, before her mind returned once more to the possible movie role that Fliss had mentioned. Fliss had said she would be back in LA next week, so Alice knew the time had come for her to make up her mind and tell her.

As she sat there in the gathering dusk, listening to the rain hammering down outside, she knew she had to put her name forward. Of course, they might say no and it might lead to nothing, but she had to give it a go. After all, the chance to appear in a big Hollywood movie alongside a star of Fliss's calibre wasn't the sort of opportunity that came along every day. As for the problems her return to the limelight was likely to throw up and the uncertainty surrounding her relationship with Matt, she would worry about all that if they offered her the part. She composed an email to Fliss, wishing her a happy few days' holiday in Rome, and asked her to put her name forward. As she pressed Send, she wondered where, if anywhere, this might lead.

She took a long, hot bath and washed her hair, before emerging from the bathroom feeling like a new woman after what had been a stressful day. As a treat, she decided to go along to Giovanni's restaurant, even though it was still raining heavily. She didn't have an umbrella, so she stretched her lightweight waterproof over her newly washed hair and made a run for it. The restaurant was packed, as the garden tables were out of commission due to the rain. Giovanni gave her a cheery greeting as she came in and she tried her best to shake herself dry.

'Good evening. Here, let me take your jacket.'

'Good evening, Giovanni. You're busy tonight by the look of it.'

'It's the rain but, don't worry, I'll find you a space. Just yourself?' She nodded. 'Then, if you don't mind sharing, I'll put you with Father Gregorio.' Seeing the expression on her face, his mouth curled into a grin. 'He's our local priest but, don't worry, I promise you he's good company. I'm sure he'll be only too happy to have such a beautiful dinner companion.' He pointed across the room to a table where an elderly cleric was sitting, clad in sober black robes. 'Is that all right with you?'

Alice would have preferred a table on her own but almost anything was better than going back out into the rain, which had suddenly increased in strength to the extent that it sounded like a waterfall on the other side of the French windows. She followed Giovanni across to the old priest's table and saw his face light up as he heard of her predicament. He immediately waved towards the seat opposite him and gave her a warm welcome.

'Good evening, *Signorina*. What an unexpected pleasure to have a dinner companion.' He extended a gnarled old hand across the table towards her. He spoke in a smooth musical tone and Alice was delighted to understand everything without any of the problems she sometimes encountered with the local Tuscan accent. He didn't sound like a local and his enunciation was perfect. Of course, he was a priest and used to public speaking, after all.

'Good evening, Father, thank you so much for letting me join you. I hope I'm not disturbing you.' She studied him surreptitiously. He was probably in his late seventies, maybe even older, and he was completely bald; the light reflecting on his shiny pate reminded her of the halos that medieval painters loved to give to the saints and deities in their paintings. He had a gentle face, and his brown eyes were still bright and perceptive.

'Congratulations on your Italian. I'm afraid my command of your language is next to zero. And what brings you here on an awful night like tonight?' He stopped and corrected himself. 'What am I saying? We've all been praying for this much-needed rain, and far be it from me to pour scorn on the Lord's bounty.'

Alice repressed a smile. Listening to his melodious voice and his choice of vocabulary made her feel as though she had stepped back in time and she found herself reflecting upon the endless succession of priests whose shoes he was now filling. She wasn't a religious person, but she loved the idea that he was the latest in an unbroken line quite probably stretching back to the Middle Ages. She didn't mention Conrad or her acting background, but told him that she was here on holiday because she loved Tuscany. He nodded sagely.

'It's a wonderful area and I feel truly blessed to live in this village, which has been my life for over fifty years now. But you're here on your own? Is that out of choice?'

Alice shook her head. 'Not exactly. My boyfriend dropped out at the last minute but now that I'm here on my own, I'm quite happy.'

At that moment Giovanni arrived with a steaming dish of pasta, liberally laced with a rich meaty sauce, and deposited a heap onto Father Gregorio's plate with a few skilful scoops of a spoon and fork held in his other hand. He then turned towards Alice to take her order. 'And what can I bring you? Some *pappardelle alla lepre* as well?'

Alice had never been too keen on eating rabbit, and *lepre* was a hare, so she shook her head. 'I think something light as a starter and then maybe some meat or fish? I'm hungry, but not really hungry enough for pasta. What do you suggest?'

At his suggestion she decided on a simple tomato, mozzarella and basil salad, followed by grilled calamari. She also ordered a bottle of Chianti Classico, determined to offer some to the friendly priest who, she noticed, only had a little quarter-litre carafe of anonymous red wine in front of him. It seemed like the least she could do after he had allowed her to share his table.

As Giovanni returned with the bottle and opened it, she looked across at Father Gregorio. 'I wonder if you'd be kind enough to help me with my wine, Father. I certainly don't want to drink a whole bottle by myself, so maybe you wouldn't mind...?'

He smiled back at her. 'If all my parishioners asked for that sort of help, I would be a happy priest – although it might add a bit too much spice to my sermons.'

They chatted throughout the meal and she genuinely enjoyed his company. She soon found herself talking about the events of the day – without naming names – and he quickly picked up on her internal confusion.

'So, you say this woman whose life you saved was in fact your worst enemy?'

'I don't really have anything as radical as a worst enemy, but from a work point of view, she could be really difficult.'

'And it bothers you that you saved her life?'

'No, it's not that it bothers me – in fact, I'm pleased I was able to help another human being. I'm just saying it's a strange twist of fate that it had to be her.'

'Life has a habit of doing that. So, you don't regret what you did?'

'Not for a moment. Some things are more important than work.'

'Absolutely. I commend you on a good deed. If more people did more such selfless acts, the world would be a better place. May I ask what work you do?'

Alice decided to leave out any reference to her earlier career, so she told him about her studies in art history and her specialisation in the art of the Renaissance. As she did so, she saw real interest on his face and, to her surprise, he raised his eyes to the heavens and kissed his fingers.

'Truly the Lord works in mysterious ways.' There was awe in his voice. He looked back at her again. 'You see, I have a problem.'

To her fascination, he then went on to tell her what had recently happened in the village church. During renovations of a damp wall, the decorators had happened upon an ancient fresco partially concealed beneath a layer of flaking whitewash. Why it had been covered and by whom remained a mystery. Father Gregorio's problem was that he knew what needed to be done next, but his poor parish just didn't have the financial means to do it.

'With just my bare hands, I've been able to wipe off much of the old whitewash and it's clear to me that the fresco beneath is old, possibly very old. What I need is an expert who can verify if what we have is a treasure or just the doodling of a bored painter a hundred years ago.'

Alice smiled at him across the table. 'I'm sure there are lots of experts better qualified than I am, but if you'd like me to take a look at it, Father Gregorio, I'd be delighted.'

'You would? That would be simply splendid. Thank you so much.'

They arranged to meet at the church next morning at ten and, as he stood up to leave, he clasped her hand in both of his and murmured what might have been a blessing. 'Thank you once more. Your kindness knows no bounds. Now, I wish you good night.'

'Good night, Father, and thank you for letting me share your table. It's been a pleasure.'

—

She received another pleasurable surprise as she was getting ready for bed. Her phone started ringing and, as it was a number she didn't recognise, she answered cautiously.

'*Pronto.*'

'Alice, hi – it's me, Matt.'

'Matt, hi, it's great to hear from you.' And it was. 'How was dinner?'

They chatted for almost half an hour. She discovered that his meetings had gone well, although by the end of the conversation she was still no closer to finding out what he did for a living. Dinner in the swanky restaurant had been fabulous, Rome was as spectacular as ever and his grandmother was in fine form once more. In return, she told him about the events of the day, from what had happened to Zoë – once again without naming names and without revealing her own Hollywood connections – to dining with Father Gregorio and news of the fresco. It was only at the very end of the conversation that he delivered the bad news.

'I know you and I made plans for dinner on Friday, but I'm afraid I'm going to have to stay on for an extra couple of days. There's a thing coming up on Saturday with another dinner that night, but I should be home on Sunday. Maybe we could meet up that evening?'

Doing her best to ignore the sudden wave of disappointment that she wasn't, after all, going to see him sooner, she assured him that she understood, and they arranged to meet up on Sunday evening for drinks at her place and then go to the restaurant for dinner together. As she put the phone down, she gave a little sigh. It was almost as if some malignant force was keeping them apart. It was frustrating to say the least.

Chapter 24

When she woke up next morning, she found a message on her phone and it came from an unwelcome source.

> Hi Alice. Am on my way back to Europe after making the biggest mistake of my life. I need to speak to you, to apologise for my behaviour, and I can meet you anywhere. Are you still in Tuscany? Just say the word.
> David x

The thing that annoyed her most of all was that little *x*. She lay in bed, staring at her phone for some minutes, before deciding upon the right response. After the way he had behaved, and since getting to know Matt better, she knew that her days with David were irrevocably over, so she decided to be brutally frank.

> Don't waste your time, David. You made your choice and you have to live with the consequences. I'll be back in Bristol in ten days and I expect to find all your stuff cleared out of the flat by the time I get there. Enjoy the rest of your life. Alice

At ten o'clock she went across to the church and pushed the heavy old wooden door open. She found herself inside a classical Romanesque church, with the usual simple interior and the trademark rounded window arches. Although she wasn't an expert in architectural styles, she felt sure this indicated that the little church had been built as long ago as the eleventh or twelfth centuries. Father Gregorio must have heard the door creak and he came down the aisle to greet her.

'Good morning, good morning. Thank you so much for coming.'

'Good morning, Father. I'm looking forward to seeing your discovery.'

Father Gregorio led her to a little side chapel, barely more than an alcove, and pointed to the back wall. Alice immediately spotted the fresco and went over to examine it. As he had told her, he had managed to rub away much of the flaking whitewash, exposing a faded, but still quite distinguishable, painting underneath. As she studied it, she caught her breath. There was no mistaking what she could see. It was a remarkably well-painted depiction of Noah and the ark, but what leapt out at her was the unnaturally large flag flying from the main mast. Even after the passage of so many centuries, it was clear to see it was a deep red colour with a diagonal blue stripe. She screwed up her eyes and leant closer. Were those little golden flecks on the stripe wasps? Could it be?

She took her time, deliberately stifling her enthusiasm until she had photographed it from all angles, and measured its height and width. Finally, she straightened up and turned back towards the priest, who was standing there, looking hopeful.

'It's beautiful, Father Gregorio. I love it. I'm pretty confident it's ancient – maybe even medieval, but certainly many centuries old. If you like, I can get in touch with a good friend who works at the Uffizi. I'm sure she or one of her colleagues would be happy to come down and take a look at it for you.'

He beamed back at her. 'That would be wonderful. You would be doing me a great favour.'

Then, as they slowly walked back towards the door, he said something totally unexpected. 'I wonder if I could ask one more favour of you? Would you mind letting me take your photo? When I tell my niece that I've had Polly in my church, she'll be amazed – and it might be prudent to have proof, in case she thinks I'm going senile.'

'Polly? You recognised me?' Truly, the reach of *Pals* – even five years after – was extraordinary if even a septuagenarian priest in the backwoods of Tuscany had recognised her. There was almost a look of embarrassment on his face, as he replied.

'My tastes in television are all-embracing. I watch all sorts, from game shows to football matches, murder mysteries to nature documentaries. I also have a particularly soft spot for romantic comedy – please don't ask me to explain or justify this; I fear it would take far too long. Suffice it to say that you're in the presence of one of your greatest fans.'

Alice was genuinely flabbergasted and she happily posed alongside him for some selfies, first with his phone and then with hers. As she finally left the church, she felt remarkably cheerful. Sometimes, being recognised as Polly the flirt could have its upside.

The first thing she did upon arriving back home was to send an email to Teresa at the Uffizi, outlining what she had just seen at the church and attaching a couple of photos of the fresco. She asked if she or one of her colleagues might be able to come down and take a look

247

at it for Father Gregorio and she hoped the answer would be yes.

That afternoon, her phone rang and she recognised the number of Conrad's daughter, Tracey.

'Hi, Tracey, I was going to ring. What's the news on Zoë?'

'Hi, Alice, she's home. We've just brought her back now, and she and my father would love it if you could come up to the villa around six for a drink. They both want to say thank you.'

'She already thanked me but, of course, I'd be delighted.'

By the time Alice walked up to the villa, last night's rain had already evaporated from the road surface, but the tracks through the vineyards and olive groves still looked pretty muddy so – keeping a wary eye open for paparazzi – she carried on to the main entrance and pressed the bell. Seconds later the gates swung open and she made her way up the gravel drive to the big house. After all the rain, the air was crystal clear and she could see right across to the distant Apennines. Matt's tower on its promontory stood out crisply against the blue of the sky, and she felt a shiver of pleasurable anticipation at the thought that she would be with him again before too long.

At the villa everybody was out on the terrace, and she was welcomed with hugs and kisses from all sides as the family members came up to thank her for what she had done.

Shrugging off the thanks, she felt she had to set the record straight. 'All I did was what anybody would have done. It's just lucky I was there and it all worked out so well in the end. Paolo did all the important stuff.'

'I'll never forget what you did, Alice.' Zoë came up to her and enveloped her in a warm hug. Alice was delighted to see her moving normally and looking far better than the last time she had set eyes on her in her hospital bed. As Zoë released her grip, she gave Alice a warm, genuine smile – for just about the first time in her life – and kissed her on the cheeks. 'Truly, thank you.'

It was a most enjoyable evening, although Alice still couldn't quite get her head round the change in demeanour from her former nemesis. She told them all about her visit to the church and the unexpectedly familiar flag in the fresco, and she saw a sparkle in Conrad's eyes.

'Amazing. Listen, Alice, would you do something for me? Would you go see the priest? Tell him I'd be happy to sponsor whatever investigations or restoration works need to be undertaken. Tell him to send any invoices to Paolo here at the villa. It would be my privilege.'

Alice was delighted and she knew Father Gregorio would be over the moon. She promised to pass on the message and she thanked Conrad on his behalf. He waved away her thanks and went on to indicate that his generosity didn't stop there.

'Zoë and I've been talking, and we have a proposition for you. How would you like to come and join us at *Pals Forever* for a few guest appearances? It would be great to have you with us. I quite understand and applaud your decision to head off in a different direction with your career, but hopefully you could fit in a few appearances on the new show. Pretty much as many as you like, whenever you like, to suit your commitments.'

Inevitably, Alice's eyes turned to Zoë and she was heartened by what she saw. Zoë looked genuinely happy – and it didn't seem in the least bit forced.

'I'd really like it if you would, Alice. It would be like old times.'

Alice wondered which old times – the first few years of *Pals*, when they all had so much fun, or the last couple of much more stressful years? Still, she told herself, while this remarkable new era of peace and tranquillity lasted, it would be churlish to turn down this second chance – and the money would come in very handy.

'That sounds wonderful. Thank you so much. I must admit it would be really good to work with the old gang again. There are so many people over in the studios that I haven't seen for five years.'

'Great, I'll get my people to get in touch with your agent.' Conrad clapped his hands together and waved across to Paolo, who was hovering by the French windows. 'Paolo, this calls for champagne, please.'

The rest of the evening sped by and Alice finally left the villa feeling remarkably happy. Somehow, the idea of doing a few cameos on the new show had real appeal. Of course, she reminded herself, this would mean that a full-time art history job – whether in an auction house, university or wherever – would probably be out of the question, at least for the first year or so, as she would obviously need to be able to take weeks off every now and then to fly over to LA. And then there was the matter of Fliss's movie, which could further complicate matters – but in a good way. She felt a little pang of regret that her new career path was going to have to be put on hold, at least for a while, but still, going back to *Pals* was suddenly a far more enticing prospect – particularly if Zoë really had undergone some sort of lasting metamorphosis. That, of course, remained to be seen.

Chapter 25

On Saturday morning Alice received an email from Teresa, saying that she and her husband would be delighted to come down next Wednesday and take a look at the fresco. Alice replied straightaway and invited them both to lunch at Giovanni's that day as her treat, to say thank you. After her run, she went over to the church and was pleased to find Father Gregorio there, pottering about with some hymn books. She related what Teresa had said about next Wednesday and invited him to join them for lunch, and he accepted most willingly. She then went on to break the news of Conrad's generous offer to cover any expenses he might incur with the restoration effort. The old priest was terribly grateful and she even saw little tears in the corners of his eyes. By the time Alice left the church, she was feeling quite emotional herself.

She drove to Florence after lunch and spent a happy couple of hours wandering through the historic streets and along the banks of the river. She even climbed up to Piazzale Michelangelo, from where she had a panoramic view across the roofs of this most magical of cities. It was another clear, cloudless day and last night's rain had washed away the familiar pall of pollution from over the city. As a result, she could see for miles, right across to Fiesole and the dark green bulk of the Apennines behind it in the distance. She leant on the stone balustrade and let her mind, as well as her eyes, roam.

Her rental of the little house would come to an end in exactly one week and, as things were at present, she would then be flying back to Britain. With her university studies finished and David out of the picture, there was no need for her to stay in Bristol, so maybe she should think about selling her flat there. But what then? A few guest appearances on the new series of *Pals Forever* would occupy her for a few weeks now and then, probably just in its first year of existence, and necessitate some commuting to and from the US, but that was hardly a real job. How would she fill the rest of her time? Of course, there was the possibility of a part in the new movie with Fliss but that, too, would only occupy her for a few months next year, after which she would once more be unemployed – although no doubt a good deal better off. Maybe she should concentrate on finding herself a full-time position in the world of art history and turn her back on showbiz altogether – as had been her intention until receiving Conrad's email last month. And the full-time job would determine where she lived, so maybe it would be wiser to hang onto her flat in Bristol for now. So many questions…

Which brought her onto the question of Matt.

What if their relationship continued to develop and became something serious? From the very first moment she had set eyes on him, she had been completely infatuated by him and, as far as she was concerned, she could see it going the distance. However, she still wondered whether he was holding something back – and if so, why – and just exactly who he was and what he did. She still barely knew him and, with only six more days left before having to leave the little house, there was a limit to how far down the line they could get.

His life was clearly firmly rooted here in Tuscany now, with his vineyard, his olives, his dog and his escape from whatever had been causing him so much grief before moving here. He had told her that he had a little place in London so no doubt if she returned to work in the UK, they would be able to meet up now and then over there or she could come to Italy to see him from time to time. But she had experience of the collapse of too many other people's long-distance relationships to harbour any realistic hopes of it succeeding for her. If it turned out he was equally serious about her, should she consider applying for art history jobs here in Tuscany? Might it be worth asking Teresa or Claudio if they knew of anything? Even more questions...

She met up with Antonia at five, as arranged, and was delighted to see her again. After exchanging pleasantries, Antonia launched straight into the main reason for this meeting: she wanted to offer her a job. Alice sat up and listened with rapt attention as Antonia went on to outline what she had in mind.

'It was that afternoon we spent together here at the Uffizi that gave me the idea. You're so knowledgeable about art, and you have a very natural and spontaneous way of speaking about it. At the same time, you're also such a recognisable and relatable figure that I'm convinced you'll be able to inspire a whole new audience with your love of art. What we're thinking of is an initial six-part series on Italian art followed by a number of others anywhere in the world – you tell us where – if this first series has the success we hope for. You write it, you present it and I know it'll be a hit.' She looked across at Alice. 'What do you think?'

What did she think? It sounded amazing and Alice hastened to tell Antonia so. Suddenly, a whole new career path was opening up, which would allow her to have the best of both worlds – a job involving her beloved history of art and a continuation of her life in front of the camera. And this time she would be able to choose her own wardrobe and, hopefully, avoid the kind of unwelcome publicity Polly the flirt had brought. Plus, she thought excitedly, with this sort of job it didn't matter where she was based. She could stay in Bristol, go to London or, indeed, even settle in Tuscany. She felt a wave of optimism bubbling up inside.

Antonia, encouraged by her positive reaction, went on to talk about the nuts and bolts of their offer. Filming would start as soon as this autumn or winter, whenever Alice had got it planned and written, and it would be up to her to decide where she wanted to go. All her expenses would be covered and her pay generous, with a bonus linked to the success or otherwise of the series. Whatever happened, it soon emerged that Alice would easily earn considerably more for just these first six episodes than the auction house had offered for a full year. It sounded perfect, but she felt she had to tell Antonia about the offer of guest appearances she had had from Conrad. To her surprise, this didn't come as news to Antonia.

'I know, Alice, and I'm delighted you've said yes.'

'You know about that? So, you and Conrad are still talking?'

Antonia grinned. 'Not only talking, but also working together. He's one of the partners in this new company.

In fact, he and Silas are meeting us for drinks a bit later on.'

They met in the slick cocktail bar on the top floor of the hotel near the station where Antonia and Silas, the third partner in the new company, were staying. Their table was by the window and they looked straight out over the old church of Santa Maria Novella, with its intricate marble façade. Conrad gave her a big grin when he saw her and apologised for not having said anything to her before, as the lawyers had been finalising all the intricacies of the contract. Alice spent an enjoyable hour with them and, although they invited her to stay for dinner, she declined – partly because she was sure they would have things to discuss privately and partly because she wanted to get home before dark. There was no question, however, that she came away confident that they were going to make a success of this new venture.

As she walked back to her car, she felt really happy with the way things were working out. The combination of this job and the guest appearances for *Pals Forever* meant she should have enough income to allow her to live anywhere and she could spend as long with Matt as she liked, assuming he felt the same way about her – which, of course, was still to be established with any certainty.

She got home as night was falling and she had just let herself into her little house, and was pouring herself a large glass of wine, when there was a knock at the door. This was the first time she had had a visitor, and she was surprised and even a bit apprehensive. For a moment, her heart leapt at the thought that it might be Matt making an early return, but her hopes were immediately dashed as she opened the door. Standing on her doorstep was a very unwelcome face.

'David?' She actually felt her jaw drop.

'Surprise! I had to see you. How're you doing, Alice?' He held out his arms towards her and took a step forward, a hopeful smile on his face. As he did so, her befuddled brain kicked into gear and she held up a steadying hand to block the way.

'Not so fast. How did you know where to find me?'

'The lady at the bar told me. Millie said you'd taken a place here in the village, so I came to look for you. I've been hanging around for a couple of hours now. I just spotted you getting out of your little Fiat.'

'Why are you here, David? Didn't I make myself clear enough?'

'Well, yes, but I knew I had to see you. I thought if we could talk, I could explain why I acted the way I did and, hopefully, you could think about forgiving me.' She could see he was turning on the charm and giving her his most endearing, little lost puppy look. 'It was a shameful thing to do and I'm so, so sorry. I wasn't thinking straight. I was just thinking of myself.'

Alice stood there, feeling completely stumped for a moment. She knew it was all over between him and her, but he had flown halfway across the world to see her after all. Should she let him in or tough it out? She took a deep breath and decided to stand her ground. After all, her decision was already taken and nothing was going to change that.

'David, let me make it perfectly clear so there can be no confusion. You went off and dumped me for your own selfish reasons and there's no way on God's earth that I want anything more to do with you. Is that clear enough?' She gave him the fiercest look she could muster.

'Well, yes, but...'

'No buts, David. It's over, finished, *finito*. Got it?' She saw what looked like resignation finally start to appear on his face. 'If it makes you feel any better, I was having doubts about us anyway, and that's what these few weeks in Tuscany were designed to sort out. Well, thanks to you, that got resolved sooner rather than later. So, we're done. Now do you get it?'

'But surely you don't mean that...' His voice tailed off helplessly, but she was running out of patience.

'I do, believe me, I do. So please just go and enjoy the rest of your life. But it won't be with me. Goodbye, David.' And with that, she closed the door in his face, resisting the urge to slam it. She rested her back against the door and did her best to bring her breathing under control, hoping that he had finally got the message and was out of her life for good.

Chapter 26

At five o'clock on Sunday afternoon she ran herself a long, luxurious bath and, as she lay in the water, she knew that she was really looking forward to seeing Matt again. During the hours she had spent walking with him on Tuesday, she had felt him relax more and more in her company, and the handful of kisses they had shared – although interrupted – had been sublime. She wondered how long it would be before he decided to let her in on the secret of why he had been feeling harassed on social media. What on earth could have caused this? Also, how on earth had a former journalist managed to amass the considerable sum of money needed to buy a medieval tower in Tuscany?

She spent the best part of an hour in the bath, washed her hair yet again and slipped into her new underwear. It then took her a further fifteen minutes of trying different clothes to feel satisfied she had chosen a dress that was a suitable mix of alluring and relaxed – although by this time she was feeling anything but relaxed. Yes, she admitted in a moment of self-awareness, she was behaving more like a schoolgirl than an adult.

He and the dog arrived at six, and she almost threw herself into his arms. As she did so, there could be no disguising the thrill that shot throughout her body. If she wanted proof that she had fallen for him, this was it – but she didn't need proof. She pressed herself against him and screwed her head up so she could speak to him.

'Matt! You can't imagine how happy I am to see you.'

He kissed her warmly while the dog stood up on his hind legs and tried to join in. Finally, Matt pushed the door shut behind him and beamed at her.

'That makes two of us.' He glanced down at the dog. 'Make that three.'

She poured two glasses of wine and then sat hand in hand with him in the little garden, as the Labrador stretched out at their feet. She could feel anticipation growing inside her as to what was going to happen next. They were sitting side by side on the bench underneath the branches of the walnut tree and, more as a displacement activity than anything else, she told him all about the discovery of the fresco in the church. For now, she avoided mentioning the exciting job offers she had just received from Conrad and then Antonia. There would be time for that once he and she finally started trading secrets. As it was, it transpired that he knew a thing or two about Conrad.

'You know the Hollywood people in Villa delle Vespe, don't you? Well, I get the feeling the paparazzi have got them in their sights.'

After Fliss's departure, Alice thought the photographers would have left, but maybe they had come back, harbouring hopes that she might still be there. For now, she affected a nonchalant air.

'I haven't been up there for a while. I hadn't noticed.'

'On the way down this evening I saw two guys lurking about by the villa gates. I thought they were up to no good and there was just something about them. Then I spotted the cameras and I bet that's what they are.' She saw him shudder. 'God, I hate those guys.'

'You know them?'

'Not these particular ones, but just paparazzi in general. Most of them are the scum of the earth, without a vestige of a conscience or scruples.'

'How come you feel so strongly about paparazzi?' She saw him hesitate and then those same familiar shutters came down.

'As a journalist, I used to have to deal with them and it made my skin creep to see them get rich on the back of other people's misery.'

Somehow she got the feeling there was more to it than this but, as ever, she didn't press him – not least as she still hadn't told him about her own background in *Pals*. She instantly stopped thinking about paparazzi, however, as she felt his hand land on her shoulder and gently turn her towards him.

'Alice...' His voice was low.

He leant forward and kissed her on the lips, at first softly and then with more passion. Her eyes closed and when she found the strength to open them again, his face was barely a few inches from hers, his eyes staring deep into hers.

'That feels so good.' His tone was almost reverent and she nuzzled against him.

'That, Mr Livingstone, was very nice indeed.'

They kissed again and there could be no doubt about it. This was without question the best kiss of her life and she almost fell off the bench, such was her state of abandon in his arms. While the dog snoozed at their feet, she let herself melt against Matt, cradled in his embrace. She lost track of the passage of time and when she finally heard his voice, it was like waking from a dream. Somehow, to her surprise, it was almost dark.

'We'd better make a move if we're going to the restaurant.'

She nodded languidly. If the truth be told, food wasn't high on her agenda at the moment, but she stood up and took a few deep breaths to regain her composure.

With Guinness trotting contentedly alongside them, they walked round to the restaurant and were shown to a table in the far corner of the garden, where the dog settled obediently at their feet. It was a lovely meal, although the details of what they ate soon blurred inside her head, which was still processing the wave of emotion that had swept over her back there in her garden. His touch had been gentle, his manner tender, and somehow this had only heightened the upsurge of desire in her. She had a feeling tonight was going to be a good night, a very good night.

However, things didn't quite work out as she was hoping.

As she was just finishing her dessert of fresh strawberries and meringue ice cream, she looked up and noticed two men coming into the restaurant. Both were carrying holdalls and she wondered idly if they were tourists, even though they weren't looking particularly happy, although that might have been down to the weather. As the waiter showed them to a free table on the other side of the garden, Matt looked up and followed the direction of her eyes. As he saw the two men, his reaction was unexpected in the extreme. To Alice's amazement, he dropped his head towards the table, covering the side of his face with one arm and overturning his little espresso cup – fortunately now empty – in the process. He screwed himself round, so the back of his head was towards the two new arrivals, shot a furtive glance up towards Alice and she heard him speak in an urgent whisper.

'It's them. I don't think they've seen me yet, but we need to get out, quick.'

'Them? Who?' She followed his example and kept her voice low, but she couldn't get her head round why he was reacting like this. Did he know them? Were they bad men? A sudden horrible thought came to her. Was he maybe involved in some sort of criminal affair? After all, he had amassed a hell of a lot of money. Her initial bemusement began to turn into something far more sinister. Who were these two men and, for that matter, just exactly who was Matthew Livingstone?

His reply went some way towards reassuring her that she wasn't in the company of a mafioso, but did little to explain what on earth had sparked off this reaction.

'It's the two paparazzi from outside the villa. I recognise them from earlier. I don't think they've seen me yet, but it's only a matter of time.' He looked up again and she read real concern in his eyes. 'Is there a back door to this place?'

'Um, I don't know. I don't think so.'

Alice's bewilderment intensified. Why had he said the paparazzi hadn't recognised *him*? Surely, she was the only celebrity at this table. Just who on earth was he? She took another look across the garden and saw the two men deeply involved in studying the blackboard with the menu on it, which the waiter was holding up for them. One thing was for sure: she had no desire to be recognised and photographed either – irrespective of why Matt appeared to be freaking out – so she made a quick decision.

'They're busy looking at the menu. If we want to get out, now's the moment. Come on!'

She got to her feet and made her way through the tables towards the bar, deliberately resisting the temptation to take to her heels and run. Behind her she heard footsteps as Matt followed on her heels with Guinness bringing up the rear. To her considerable relief, they managed to get past the paparazzi without being observed. They positioned themselves at the far end of the bar by the till and waited for Giovanni. As the friendly restaurateur slid the bill across the counter, and she dropped a hundred-euro banknote on top of it, he gave her a knowing wink.

'Paparazzi – I can smell them a mile off.' He tapped the side of his nose with a finger. 'Don't worry, Polly, they didn't see you.'

Alice smiled back at him, genuinely surprised that he was familiar with her alter-ego from five years ago. She had eaten here a few times now but this was the first time he had ever even hinted that he recognised her. Of course, maybe Father Gregorio had told him but, either way, he was an excellent, discreet host. As he took the banknote and produced the change and receipt, Alice glanced across at Matt, who was still hunched down, with his shoulders towards the room. Fortunately, he didn't seem to have registered that Giovanni had used the name Polly. He was still looking furtive and her bewilderment returned. Just who was her dinner companion and what did he have to fear from those two men?

Moments later they were outside in the street and she heard Matt let out a heartfelt sigh of relief.

'Wow, that was a close call.'

They walked back to her house in silence, both lost in their own thoughts. When they got there, to her surprise, he hesitated at the door.

'I think I'd better go, Alice. I'm sorry.' She saw his eyes glint in the orange glow of the streetlight. 'This is the reason I don't go out much. I'm really sorry.'

'You're sorry... but why, Matt? What have you got to be sorry for? And why were you so freaked by those men?'

'They're paparazzi and I've had it up to here with paparazzi.' She heard him sigh again. 'I was hoping to get to know you a whole lot better before I told you my dirty little secret. I'm sorry.'

He leant forward, pecked her on the cheek and turned on his heel. As he and his dog headed back along the street to the piazza, she stood and watched them go, a confused mixture of sensations rising up inside her. The overriding one was mystification. She just couldn't get her head around what had just happened. Along with it came annoyance, frustration and maybe even a little bit of fear. What exactly had he meant by his 'dirty little secret'?

Chapter 27

Inevitably, she didn't sleep well that night. She lay awake for quite some time, turning over and over in her head what had happened, his reaction and what he had said. What was clear was that he had a real terror of being exposed by the paparazzi, which meant that he had to be famous – or infamous – for some reason. Sometime in the middle of the night she even got out of bed and tried googling the name Matthew or Matt Livingstone, but without success. Although frustrating to find nothing, the fact that she didn't discover his name on a 'most wanted' list was heartening.

She returned to bed and lay there, staring up into the dark, turning over scenario after scenario in her head that might explain his weird behaviour. The most obvious one was that the name was an alias. Maybe he had adopted a false identity when he moved to Italy. What made this less likely was the invasiveness of Italian bureaucracy. In order to open a bank account and buy the tower, he would have had to prove his identity numerous times so, unless he had a range of counterfeit documents, it seemed unlikely. Besides, why would he change his name? It pointed towards him having a dubious background of some sort.

Given his obvious wealth and his relative youth, could he be involved in organised crime, maybe even a drug baron? Had his business in Rome last week been criminal business? Mind you, she reminded herself, paparazzi normally confined their attentions to celebrities rather than gangsters, for obvious reasons. Angry celebrities normally only sue, while gangsters kill. But why on earth would a normal, honest man choose to conceal his true identity? Somebody with nothing to hide would hardly do such a thing – unless he were in a witness protection scheme or similar. It was baffling.

She finally drifted off to sleep, but when she woke next morning, it was with that same feeling of bewilderment, plus considerable regret. It had all been going so well last night, up to the moment when the paparazzi arrived, and she knew she had been looking forward immensely to getting him back to her house. Now that had all been blown out of the water and she still didn't know why. She also didn't know where that left their fledgling relationship. She considered sending him an email to see how he was feeling, but somehow she felt it would be better to give him a bit of time and space. The fact of the matter was that the strange events of last night had dented her trust in him. She still didn't really know much about him, but she had believed everything he had told her up to now. Could it be there was a far less palatable Matt Livingstone hidden beneath the handsome exterior?

She didn't feel like a run so she went over to the bar for a chat and a cappuccino. Rita was most apologetic for revealing Alice's address to David. She had remembered seeing the two of them together earlier in the month and it hadn't occurred to her to query why he didn't know her whereabouts. Alice told her not to worry and explained that she had sent him off with a flea in his ear.

While she was there, her phone bleeped and she saw she had a message from none other than Felicity.

> Hi Alice. Just arrived back in LA. It was great to meet you at last and we must stay in touch. I've already passed on your name and the signs are good. I reckon they'll go for it. I do so look forward to working with you. Fliss x

This was brilliant news and Alice sent her a quick reply, thanking her and echoing the hope of working with her. This, coupled with the guest appearances and her very own art series, made it almost certain that she had a great future ahead of her.

Back at her house, she found an email from Matt and she clicked on it eagerly. She would have preferred a phone call, so she could speak to him directly, but she sensed he was trying to give himself time to explain – but he didn't. The message contained a long and profound apology for ruining her evening – which he said he had been enjoying immensely – but there was no explanation of what he had meant by his 'dirty little secret'. It did, however, contain an invitation to dinner with him in the tower that evening. She took her time before replying but, whatever her doubts and reservations, she knew she wanted to see him again so she sent him a friendly reply saying she would be there – not least in the hope of finding out just what on earth was going on.

That afternoon was still extremely hot, so she went for a short walk around the village, ending up at the bar again around four o'clock for an ice cream. As she waited for Rita to finish scooping up her portion of white chocolate and lemon ice cream, her eyes alighted upon a well-thumbed copy of today's paper, lying open on a nearby table. A photo on the right-hand page suddenly caught her attention. It was a picture of none other than Felicity at the foot of the Spanish Steps, in Rome. What was really weird, however, was that she was arm-in-arm with a man – and not just any man. He had obviously just realised that they were about to be photographed and was in the process of turning his head away from the camera, but Alice recognised him instantly all the same. To her amazement, she saw that the man was none other than Matt. The megastar was gazing at him with affection and the headline above it read: *Felicity Winter and Her Mystery Man in Rome*. The article went on to produce a handful of fanciful suggestions as to the *mystery man's* identity, but none even came close.

Alice just stood there, stunned. How on earth could it be that these two knew each other? Had they somehow met while Fliss had been at Conrad's villa? Why hadn't Fliss said anything to her about him? Of course, Fliss had no way of knowing she had even met Matt, let alone had a massive crush on him, but seeing them together was such a colossal coincidence that Alice struggled to get her head round it. Assuming the photo was genuine, could it really be that Matt had fallen under the thrall of the Hollywood star just as David had done with Layla? Alice took her ice cream to a table and sat down, trying her best to think logically. She knew only too well how the media could twist, misconstrue and invent stories. A single photo of two people arm-in-arm proved nothing. Fliss was a touchy-feely sort of person, and gripping somebody's arm was eminently normal behaviour for her. Somehow these two had met up and had been photographed together. It wasn't as if they had been caught in bed together, after all.

But how on earth had they come to be there – and just who was Matthew Livingstone? The seed of mistrust planted in her head now began to blossom and she came close to sending him an email, telling him she couldn't come to dinner with him after all. In the end, natural curiosity got the better of her and she decided to go, just to find out what the hell was going on.

She drove up to the tower that evening in a state of considerable agitation. Her head was still filled with the image of him arm-in-arm with Felicity and, to make matters worse, another thought had suddenly occurred to her: if Matt really was from a criminal background, he might have darker plans for her. Had she seen things she shouldn't have seen at the restaurant last night? Might this invitation be a means of luring her to a tragic death, maybe falling off the top of the tower? She very nearly slapped her own face. What on earth was wrong with her? Of course he wasn't a homicidal maniac! And of course she had nothing to fear from him. As for his connection with Fliss, she would ask him and he would tell her, and that would be that. This was just an invitation to dinner, and maybe more, although she knew in her heart that there was no way she was going to take things to the next level until he had explained in detail just who he was and what on earth was going on.

He must have been on the lookout, as the gates swung open before she had to ring the bell. She drove through and up the drive, parked alongside the old Land Rover and climbed out. It was comforting to find herself greeted by the rapturous Labrador, who jumped all over her as she emerged from the car. Behind Guinness was his master, looking decidedly... sheepish. Alice took this as a good sign. Of the many adjectives that could be used to describe a brutal criminal or a drug baron, she was pretty confident that sheepish wouldn't have made the cut. He appeared more interested in studying his feet than looking towards her, so she marched up to him, but stopped short of kissing him. He had a lot of explaining to do first. She did her best to keep things light – for now.

'Hi, Matt. You look miles away. Remember me? I'm the girl you invited for dinner.'

He raised his head and she saw a little smile spread across his face as he looked her straight in the eye.

'I owe you an explanation.'

'I rather think you do. At least one.'

Together, they went in and climbed the stone staircase to the top. It was all looking a lot tidier this time and she commented on it. In reply, he managed a hint of a grin.

'Just don't open any doors. I've been picking stuff up and slinging it into odd rooms to hide it. Now, first things first, I think we both need a drink. I've got some good champagne in the fridge.'

'There's no need for champagne. We just need to talk.'

He shook his head. 'In fact, there *is* a need for champagne. I've just had some very good news. I'll tell you all about it in a minute.'

He went over to the kitchen, produced a bottle of champagne from the fridge, opened it and filled two glasses. By this time the dog had stretched out at Alice's feet and was rolling about on his back, grunting happily to himself while she scratched his tummy with her toe. As she took her drink from his master, she pointed down at Guinness, keen to break the taut silence that had descended upon them.

'He may not help with the housework, but he's a lovely dog.'

'Like I said, he's my best buddy. The great thing about dogs is that they accept you the way you are. They aren't judgemental.'

'And people are? Towards you?'

He didn't answer. He just clinked his glass against hers and then sat down on the other side of the dog. He took a mouthful of wine and she could see him brace himself. She also took a sip and sat back, waiting to hear what he had to say for himself.

'Like I just told you, Alice, I owe you an explanation. Once again, I'm really sorry for ruining last night, which was going so well. The thing is, I haven't been completely honest with you.' He stopped and corrected himself. 'No, that's not right. Everything I've told you about me has been true, I promise, but I just didn't tell you the whole story.'

This was patently self-evident, but she just nodded and waited for him to carry on. She wasn't going to make it easy for him.

'You see, when I told you I was trying to write a book, that was true, but the thing is, it wouldn't be my first book. I've already written one.'

He hesitated and Alice wondered where he might be going with this. She saw him take a deep breath.

'I wrote the first one under a pen name, not my real name. The book's called *The Playboy and His Women*. You've maybe heard of it.'

Alice was glad she was sitting down. Of all the different scenarios she had been exploring in her head over the past twenty-four hours, this certainly wasn't one of them. He wasn't a gangster. He wasn't in witness protection. He wasn't some sort of crazy attention-seeker with delusions of celebrity. He was in fact the highly successful writer of one of the most controversial books of the twenty-first century, the book that critics had called 'a declaration of war upon the concept of love.' She found herself gawping at him in amazement.

'You are M. T. Landseer?' She could hear the incredulity in her voice. 'You're the guy they call the destroyer of romance, the anti-Cupid?'

He nodded soberly and hung his head. 'Guilty as charged, I'm afraid. M. T. Landseer shares my initials, but it's a made-up name.'

Alice took another, bigger, sip of champagne and let her mind consider the implications of this confession. Here she was, sitting opposite the man with whom she would have been only too happy to jump into bed as recently as the previous night, only to discover that his intentions – as so eloquently described in his book – were almost certainly just selfish sexual gratification. She took another sip of wine but barely tasted it, an overwhelming feeling of disappointment settling upon her.

'I see.'

'You know the book?'

'I've just finished reading it.'

'Ah…' He picked up the champagne bottle and reached over to top up her glass. She could see this was probably just to give him time to choose his words, and she took heart from the nervous expression on his face. He set the bottle back down again and took another deep breath. 'That book isn't me.'

'I thought you said you'd written it?'

'Oh, I wrote it all right, but it doesn't reflect the way I really think.' He took a mouthful of champagne before continuing. 'I told you I was a journalist, and I was. I first hatched the idea when I saw the amazing success of *Fifty Shades*. It occurred to me that millions of people around the world are prepared to pay good money to read about sex and not much else, so I set out to give them just that. It took me a surprisingly short time to write it, less than three months. I was pretty pleased with myself, particularly when the first literary agent I showed it to signed me up there and then.'

She saw him take another sip of champagne. 'It was only after publication that I finally began to realise the enormity of what I'd done. Little old ladies were posting online and saying things about me that would make your hair curl. The social media accounts I set up for M. T. Landseer were soon submerged beneath a tsunami of hatred. The book was plastered all over the tabloids and, although miraculously nobody ever managed to find out my real name, I was genuinely in fear for my life for a while. That's why I freaked out last night – I thought they'd finally got onto me. As the vitriol in the British tabloids increased, I decided to cut and run. I swore off social media, stopped watching TV, came over here, bought myself a fortress and a Labrador, and became a farmer. I escaped to Tuscany.'

'So you're saying you don't share your hero, Justin's, attitude towards women?'

He shook his head vigorously. 'Not at all. It was a con, a hoax, a way of hopefully getting rich quick without a thought for the deeper ramifications and consequences of what I'd created. I was unbelievably naïve. Looking back on it now, I can't understand how I couldn't have thought it through. I suppose I didn't really believe for a moment it would actually catch on and, even in my wildest dreams, I certainly didn't imagine it selling millions all round the world.' He had been staring down, as if addressing his comments to the Labrador, but now he raised his eyes and looked up, directly at her. 'Please believe me, Alice. You, of all people, need to believe me.'

'Why me in particular?'

'That's easy.' Although he needed another sip of wine before he said it. 'I think I've fallen in love with you.'

'You've what?' She also sought refuge in alcohol before continuing. 'You know you're crazy, don't you? We only met a couple of weeks ago. You hardly know anything about me.' Her head was spinning with thoughts at odds with her words. Crazy he might be, but there was no disguising the fact that she had also been entertaining similarly crazy strong feelings about this man she had only just met. Shaking her head to clear it, she let her conscience prick her. 'In fact, if it makes you feel better, I haven't told you the whole truth either.'

'You haven't...?'

He looked so bamboozled that she found herself beginning to feel sorry for him. She told him about *Pals Across the Pond* and her alter ego, Polly. She told him why she had been staying at the villa and how close she had come to signing up for the new series. As she revealed her true identity, she read amazement in his eyes – coupled with realisation.

'I *knew* I'd seen you before. How could I be so stupid?' He caught her eye. 'Mind you, from what I've just told you, I'm sure you can understand that I really *am* that stupid. All this time I've been thinking of you and picturing you in my head, but without making the connection.' He picked up the bottle. 'More champagne?'

'Absolutely.' As the wine hissed and fizzed into her glass, she decided to take the bull by the horns and ask the next big question. 'So how come you know Felicity

Winter?' He swung round in surprise and she explained. 'I just spotted a photo of the two of you together in the paper at the bar. It looked as though you were having fun.'

He gave a snort of annoyance. 'I saw the same photo. Bloody paparazzi! At least they were far more interested in her and they didn't manage to identify me. But anyway, she's part of the reason I'm celebrating.'

For a second, Alice's heart sank. Surely he wasn't about to announce his engagement to Fliss or anything so drastic. Seeing the confusion on her face, he was quick to clarify.

'I've just heard from my agent that they've finally signed the contract to turn the book into a movie. I signed on the dotted line over a month ago and I've been on tenterhooks ever since, but now it's set in stone. And, even better, this week when I was in Rome, I met the big stars who are going to be in it. In fact, I went out for dinner with Felicity and the director. She's a very nice lady.'

It took Alice a few moments to digest the fact that there was, after all, a logical and innocent explanation for his appearance alongside Fliss, and she felt a wave of relief. 'She is indeed. Did she tell you that she and I were drinking coffee together only a few mornings ago? She was staying at the villa very recently. That's who the paparazzi have been hoping to catch a glimpse of.'

'You know her too?' The expression on his face was a picture – probably not dissimilar to the expression on her face when he had revealed he was the author of the book.

'Yup, and I might even be acting alongside her in a movie next year.'

–

The dinner he prepared was perfect. He apologised for it being cold, but on such a hot, sticky night, she was more than happy to eat wonderful freshly carved ham, aromatic orange-fleshed melon, little mushroom vol-au-vents, bruschetta and a fine mixed salad. As they ate, they chatted and he told her more about his meteoric rise from middle-of-the-road journalist to multi-millionaire. For her part, she told him all about her years in Hollywood and the recent negotiations at the villa that had resulted in her decision to withdraw from the new project, only to say yes to a few guest appearances as a result of the events involving Zoë. It was good to talk freely – now that they had both revealed their respective secrets – and the more they talked, the more her conviction started to strengthen again that he was a good guy and not out of the same mould as his unscrupulous protagonist, Justin.

At the end of the meal, they went up onto the open roof where the hint of a breeze made the temperature more bearable. They leant against the hefty stone wall that ringed the top of the tower and looked out into the shadows of the Tuscan night. He pointed out little clusters of light here and there in the distance that were houses, villas and villages. It wasn't completely silent. Down below them, the shouts of children from the floodlit pool showed that Conrad's granddaughters were being allowed to stay up late. Alice could see a couple of adults there, too, but at this distance it was impossible to recognise who they were. This reminded her about the job that Antonia had just offered her and she told him all about that as well. He sounded enthusiastic and she quizzed him about his own future projects.

'By the way, last time I was here you were telling me you were struggling to get started on your next book. Is that true?'

'Like I said, everything I've told you has been true and, unfortunately for me, I really have the worst case of writer's block since Snoopy sat down and wrote, "It was a dark and stormy night."'

'What sort of thing are you planning on writing? You mentioned humour, I think, didn't you?'

'To be honest, that's at the root of the problem. My agent and publishers are pushing me to go for the same sort of thing again – you know, outrageous, offensive and controversial. Me, personally, I've learnt my lesson. I don't need the money now and I'd like to write something far less contentious. Living here in Tuscany, I've even been thinking about a historical novel. You're the historian, maybe you can come up with some suggestions. I'd be eternally grateful.'

An idea did come to mind. 'How about Amerigo Vespucci? After all, your home appears to be intimately connected with him. You could draw on the handful of hard facts that are known about him and about Columbus, and produce a dramatised version with the two of them competing for the big prize – although I'm not sure if they even ever met in real life. Certainly, it would be a good way of popularising a story that's shrouded in mystery and I'd be happy to give you a hand with researching the historical facts.'

His reaction was instantaneous. He turned towards her, caught her face between his palms and kissed her with real feeling. Finally, he drew back and she saw the moonlight reflecting in his eyes. 'Alice, that's brilliant, really brilliant! That should go down a bomb with the American market and my agent will love it. You've made me a happy man.'

Alice could think of a few more ways she could make him – and herself – even happier but, for now, she said nothing. Instead, she kissed him back and then buried her head against his chest, just savouring the fact that there were no secrets left between them. Hopefully.

'I'm glad you approve. I'll see what else I can dig up but maybe you could even write a romantic scene with Amerigo and the love of his life standing up here, in this exact same place. People like a bit of romance.'

'Don't we all?' His voice was soft and gentle.

She reached up again so she could kiss him long and lovingly on the lips. She felt him respond and his arms tighten around her, only for him then to straighten up and take a step back.

'And do you think you can forgive me for writing that damn book?'

'Only if you can forgive me for not telling you about my dodgy past on the TV.'

'That's good, it's a deal.' But then, instead of taking her in his arms, he glanced down at the dog by his side. 'I think it's time I took Guinness for his evening walk.'

A feeling of disappointment returned to Alice, but for a very different reason this time. She could tell he was hesitating before taking things further and she couldn't understand why. They had both now aired the truth about their past and she had come to terms with what he had referred to as his 'dirty little secret'. Surely, he could see that she wanted things to progress, but short of dragging him off to the nearest bedroom, she didn't know what else to do. Still, she followed him back down the stairs behind the dog, who had run on ahead, tail wagging in anticipation. She felt a pang of regret as they passed the bedroom doors on their way down, but she put on a brave face. When they got outside, Matt caught hold of her hand and turned towards her.

'If you'd like to walk a bit, the moonlight should be bright enough for us to see the way. We could go across to my vineyard, if you like, and you can see how I've been spending my time.'

There was no doubt whatsoever in Alice's mind that she could think of a far better way for them to spend their time, but evidently he didn't feel the same way. She wondered if he didn't want to, or maybe he didn't feel strongly enough about her, or even if something or somebody else was holding him back. Whatever it was, it was disappointing and highly frustrating. Still, she walked with him along the white gravel track, the outline of the bushes and trees around them becoming ever clearer as her night vision improved, until they reached the unmistakable sight of an unexpectedly large field of vines stretching off down the hillside.

'This is it, the place where I've spent the last couple of years on and off. In the light of day the view's spectacular, all the way along the valley.' She could hear that he was searching for words and she decided to help him – and herself – out.

'Matt, now that I've shown you mine and you've shown me yours, can I ask you something?'

'Anything.'

'Is everything all right?'

'Everything's great now.' He sounded surprised. 'Why do you ask?'

She decided that honesty was the best policy. 'Well, I've just been wondering why it's taken you so long.'

'So long to do what?'

'To decide whether you like me or not. I haven't been in any doubt for weeks now.'

He stretched out one arm and hugged her to him. When he started speaking, his voice was full of emotion. 'For the record, I've known the way I feel about you since that first time I saw you by the broken fence. The delay's been tough, but I needed you to know that I'm not like Justin in the book. You mean far too much to me for there to be any doubts in your mind.' He leant down and kissed her softly on the top of the head. 'This isn't just a fling. I'm in it for the long haul, Alice, if you'll have me.'

She reached up towards him with her arms and her lips. 'I'll have you, Matt. Oh yes, I'll have you.'

Epilogue

'And this year's Emmy for Outstanding Documentary Series goes to...'

Up on the stage, the glamorous presenter took her time opening the envelope, deliberately heightening the tension. Alice glanced around the table and gave Antonia an encouraging wink. She felt Matt's hand catch hold of hers under the table and squeeze.

'... *Wonders of the Renaissance*.'

Alice felt a surge of delight. They had done it! This year there was no need to fake a smile as she beamed at Antonia and saw her beam back.

'You did it, Alice, you did it!' Antonia had to shout to make her voice heard over the applause and she couldn't have sounded happier. 'Go on, up you go.'

Alice turned to Matt, threw her arms around his neck and kissed him. He grinned at her and echoed what Antonia had said. 'I knew you could do it. Off you go. They're waiting.'

Alice rose to her feet and went round to hug Antonia. '*We* did it, Antonia. I couldn't have done it without you. You made it happen.'

Alice straightened up and gazed around at the sea of faces, all looking in her direction, and felt a rush of pride. As she weaved her way between the tables towards the stage, people called out her name, shouted congratulations and reached out to shake her hand or high-five her.

Up on the stage, she took the award from the presenter, gave her a grateful kiss on the cheek and stepped up to the mike.

'Thank you, thank you so much.' The applause subsided. 'I'm so very grateful to the Academy and to all the viewers out there for choosing *Wonders* for this award. I'm delighted to accept it on behalf of the whole team, led so ably by Antonia.' She pointed down towards her and blew a kiss. 'There are so many people to thank.'

She had rehearsed the names in her head time and time again, just in case the series would be chosen for the award and she was pleased to see the pleasure on the faces of her colleagues as they were mentioned. Once she had given credit where it was due, she allowed herself a few more personal comments.

'As some of you may know, embarking upon this series was the culmination of five hard years of study for me and it involved a major change of direction in my life. I owe a lot to Zoë and all my friends at *Pals Across the Pond* for helping me to cut my teeth in the wonderful world of television. As for *Wonders*, my fervent hope is that this series and the subsequent ones will introduce more and more people to a subject that has become so dear to me.' She brandished the golden statuette in the air. 'Thank you once again.'

Amid more applause, she made her way back to her table and went round hugging everybody, before returning to Matt's side and kissing him again. As she did so, she felt a tap on her shoulder and turned to see Fliss standing there, looking predictably stunning in a pale blue silk dress that fitted her like a glove. She, too, was beaming.

'Brilliant, Alice. Really well done and richly deserved. I've watched all the episodes and I was so impressed.' She kissed Alice warmly. 'I'm looking forward so much to working with you when shooting of our movie starts next month.'

As she went off, her place was taken by Millie, who had more important things on her mind.

'Hi Al, massive congrats and all that. Now then, let's see the ring.' After her mother, Millie had been the first person Alice had called with the big news.

Alice grinned and brandished her left hand. 'Before you say it, I told Matt I didn't want a damn great rock.'

'Wow, Al, it's gorgeous.' While Millie took her hand and studied the ring, Matt leant across and confessed. 'As I know nothing about engagement rings, I just asked them for the oldest one they had.'

Alice gave him an affectionate peck on the cheek. 'What girl wouldn't love a ring that started its life five hundred years ago?' She kissed him again, this time for longer. 'Or a man who started his life thirty-seven years ago. I do so love you, Matt.'

He reached out and rested his palm against her cheek. 'And I love you too, Dr Alice Butler. Want to know something? I love you for the way you look, the way you act and the way you always try to do the right thing but, above all, I love you for your brain.' And he kissed her again. As she emerged from his embrace, Alice glanced up at Millie and grinned triumphantly.

'What did I tell you?'

Millie grinned back at her. 'Hang on to him, Al, this one's a keeper.'

Alice looked back tenderly at Matt, her heart threatening to burst.

'Nobody needs to tell me – I know.'

He smiled back at her. 'Forever?'

'Forever.'

Acknowledgements

With warmest thanks to my editor, Emily Bedford, and all the team at Canelo.